THE LADY, THE CHEF, & THE BUTLER

THE RABBIT HOLE SERIES

BRITTANY CULLEN

Printed in the United States of America.

First Edition: July 2023

For more information visit https://www.brittanycullen.com

Book Design by Brittany Cullen

Cover Design by Brittany Cullen

Edited by CordeliaGrey Oriana Allen

ISBN – Paperback: 979-8-9886546-1-2

ISBN – Ebook: 979-8-9886546-0-5

Thank you so much for picking up my book!
I would like to formally invite you to become a
Rabbit Hole e-club member.

Members will receive access to an exclusive chapter,
a continuation of this story.
Lily's first... SPOILER ALERT.
Well, I guess I can't tell you quite yet.

If you have yet to experience the pleasures that await you
at Castle Callahan, or are wondering what
"The Rabbit Hole" is, please, read on.
Trust me, you're gonna love it.

CONTENT GUIDANCE: This book contains graphic sexual content and language. Mention of forced sexual activity, violence, and witchcraft. Extra spice included for your pleasure: side characters from the LGBTQ+ community, Vampires, Fae, and Witches OH MY!

CONTENTS

NOW HIRING

Place of Employment:
Castle Callahan

Positions Available:
Home Chef & Caretaker

Start Date:
Immediately

**Living Expenses
and Competitive Pay Provided**

CLICK HERE TO APPLY NOW

Chapter I

The Interview

Doug

Tuesday, February 8th

The iron-wrought gates squeal open, signaling the beginning of our adventure. Iron and stone arch up and spread out to either side of us. A matching wall, boarding an enormous property. I creep the car forward past the gates, heading into the forest. The trees gleam like white glass.

Inside our car, the air stales in our apprehension. I crack the window as James adjusts his shirt collar. Cold air rolls in, soothing my heated skin. It does nothing to calm our nerves. This interview has us both sweating, and it hasn't even started yet.

As we drive, I think back over the last few days. From our phone interview to the office trip that followed. The entire process had definitely hyped up today in weird and awesome ways. We still have yet to meet the mysterious lady setting all of this up. I hope it's not too awkward, I would have preferred to get the dreaded introductions out of the way sooner. We might not be so stressed out if we had.

I glance briefly at James, trying not to laugh at the memory. When we went to the office, I had the honor of watching yet another man hit on him. He even begged me for James' number on the way out. The poor man will be heartbroken when he finds out he's already taken. With how often he gets hit on, you would think he could get his own dates, but nooo, I have to do it for him.

I take a deep breath, attempting to calm my racing mind. The stress of everything mixes with the winter wind- cold and vibrant. Today is our paid-interview test run. This will be the weirdest interview James and I have ever had.

James smacks my arm, getting my attention. "Look at that."

I stop the car and tilt my head toward what he is pointing at. Just over the tree line, something trots gracefully across the forest floor. Beautiful white fur covers the creature, helping it to blend among the iced-over trees. "What do you think it is?"

"No idea." James shrugs as the animal fades from view. "It wasn't close enough. But it was beautiful."

"Yeah, it was." I get the car moving again, elated. This day keeps getting more and more adventurous.

We continue down the dirt trail for what feels like an eternity. As we draw closer to the destination, the opportunity becomes increasingly more vivid. Like we're transitioning from an imagined fantasy into a very cool reality.

The sun streams brightly through the clouds, illuminating a large clearing. A picture-perfect brown and gray castle looms over us and my breath catches in my throat at the sight. Wow... This is amazing.

My heart pounds in my chest. "Are you sure we aren't dreaming?"

"If this is a dream, I don't want to wake up." James strains against the seat belt to get a better view.

"Me either. This place is stunning." My gaze darts around, trying to take in everything I see at once. The castle is at least three stories high, with arching windows and intricate patterns carved into the stone.

We approach the front of the house, where a small wooden bridge leads to the front doorway. Underneath lay a thin trench covered in a layer of ice.

"She has a moat! How cool is that?"

I smile at James, his jovial tone echoing my thoughts. I park the car just past the bridge and take a deep breath. My legs are shaking with a mixture of excitement and fear. "You ready?"

"No..." James stares straight ahead, apprehensive. "You?"

"Of course not."

"I feel like an adventurer in a video game."

"Except we aren't storming the castle." I gesture broadly in front of us. "We're just here to be the NPCs that cook and clean."

"Yeah, but if we get the job..." James turns to me, his eyes filled with excitement. "We get to live in a castle."

I shake my head and chuckle at his childishness. I turn the car off and step out. Anxiety fades into adrenaline. It pumps through my veins, spurring me forward. The trunk opens with a soft pop. James and I grab bags full of groceries and other items she requested us to bring.

I pat my front breast pocket for the tenth time that morning to make sure I still have the visa card her office gave us to pay for all this. James tilts his head from side to side and a soft cracking sound causes his shoulders to relax.

"All right, Sir Douglas." James dawns a British accent and stands in a dignified knight's pose, holding a spatula. "I have my trusted spatula of smiting. Are you ready to brave this new adventure?"

"Yes, Sir James." I match his tone and stand in a stoic position, holding a dustmop. "I shall fight by your side with my dustmop of doooom and together we shall defend this castle."

"Huzzah! We must protect Queen Callahan from the wicked witch of the forest, whose beasts prowl in the night."

"I can assure you, oh brave knights, that no queen lives in this castle." A soft feminine voice rings out behind us. I inhale sharply, the frigid air coating my lungs. As the color drains from James' face, I hold my breath and turn around. A woman stands on the bridge, her green eyes gleaming. "Maybe she moved to another castle?"

My body loosens up at the sound of her laughter, admiring the video game reference. I raise my eyebrow at the mysterious beauty before me. This must be Ms. Lily Callahan herself.

She looks better in person, but that is to be expected; A posed photo could never truly capture the beauty I see before me. The wind howls past, and I'm drawn to her legs where her long hair is dancing and twirling behind her knees.

I take a step forward and her laughter slows, allowing me to respond. "I apologize for the misunderstanding, Ms. Callahan. We are not here for Princess Peach."

"I'm glad to hear it," she says seriously. "I'm told she is a very demanding and selfish princess."

"As have I." James steps beside me, finding his courage.

"Seeing as I am no queen and in need of no knights, do you still wish to proceed with your new adventure?" She tucks her hands behind her back and smiles sweetly.

"Yes." "Of course." James and I say, our voices overlapping.

"Great..." Lily smirks and turns around. "Cuz it's dangerous to go alone."

James and I grin at each other. We follow her and when she opens the front door, a robotic voice announces, `"Front door open."` She closes the door behind us, and the robotic voice says, `"Front door closed."`

Well, that's annoying.

"I'm sorry about NASS," she says as she taps in a code on the security pad. "She's a clinging security system that loves attention."

"Is that right?" I ask, trying to make sense of her statement.

Right on cue, NASS speaks again. `"Thank you, Lily, for pressing my buttons."` Lily covers her face as it finishes. `"You know how to turn me on."`

"UGHH... Alex programmed The Necessary Annoying Security System to say five different things when I arm it and, of course, it had to choose the most erotic one today." She hangs up her coat.

"Seems so," I say.

"Sounds like this Alex fellow is quite the prankster," James says.

"Oh no, she is a sweetheart." Lily fluffs her hair. "My sister Layla is the prankster. She made her wife do this, knowing full well that I do not know how to change it."

Her hair flows straight down behind her, reaching the tops of her calves. It's a beautiful shade of red. My hand twitches as I force myself to stay put, fighting a longing to reach out. I have never seen hair so long.

The sun shines through the foyer and I gaze at the woman before me as she turns to us. Her green eyes light up in the sunlight and the rays highlight her figure. A tight-fitting purple sweater curves over her breasts as the black leggings attempt to trim down her wide hips. Her face, still pink from the cold, shows no sign of makeup. I don't blink as I realize she isn't wearing jewelry or fancy clothes.

"I'm sure it can't be that difficult to change," James says.

"Honestly, I've never bothered trying." She looks James over. "Since controlling the beasts that prowl in the night is a much better security system. Wouldn't you say, Sir James?" Lily's light giggle fills the foyer.

James stiffly nods. "Yes, much better."

"Since we got the awkward part out of the way first, I'd like to properly introduce myself. I'm Lily Callahan, but please call me Lily."

"I'm James Huntsmen." James outstretches his free hand, and they shake. "It's a pleasure to meet you, Lily."

"I'm Doug Beaufort." Her warm hand embraces mine with a firm grip. Our eyes lock. A jolting sensation spreads across my body, filling me with excitement. "It's a pleasure to make your acquaintance, Lily."

"The pleasures all mine." Lily steps back. "If you would be so kind as to follow me to the kitchen, we can start your interview."

She turns around and heads down the hall. We follow, eagerly. Her hair sways behind her, hypnotizing me. This short little beauty is unquestionably not a queen. Enchantress is more like it.

CHAPTER 2

PLAYING POOL

LILY

MONDAY, MAY 16TH

The leather couch is soft against my legs as I sit down. I am careful not to spill my go-to 'today sucked' dessert, as I place my feet under me and relax into the end of the couch. The smell of chocolate calms my nerves, and their enthusiasm fills me with vigor.

I smile at the sight of Doug and James passionately working at the other end of the couch, adding extra details to their game. Muscles flex under the fabric of James' tight shirt in an animated gesture to describe a creature. Doug cranes his neck over a sketchpad, his hand dancing lightly across the paper.

The TV screen shows an image of the game they are creating. It portrays a large open forest area, with a cliff wall scaling the backdrop. Purple moss grows up the cliffside and under the foliage of the forest. The scene is enchanting.

Games have come such a long way since I played them in high school. I swear I can feel the chill of the wind on my skin as the animated breeze blows through the leaves on the screen. The smell of the trees swirling around, like I am standing in the forest behind the castle.

The last three months with Doug and James have been exciting. Their focus, drive, and enthusiasm are contagious.

They have done more for me than I ever expected them to, learning to do things around the house that I never asked of them. I love having them around to liven up my home, and I love that they still make time to design this game. They pour their hearts into everything they do.

James shift in his seat to face forward. His face beams with joy as his eyes glance at both me and the TV. Goosebumps dance along my arm and my stomach tingles.

Why can't Dylan look at me like that? I sigh. Why can't he make me feel as incredible as they do?

James and Doug outdo him even in simple matters, like holding open doors and the occasional compliment. Even cooking for me on my birthday. They surprised me with an extravagant mouthwatering lobster dinner and abundant laughter.

Dylan can be just as sweet. But he's boring and puts little effort into our dates. I should have known I'd go home disappointed and frustrated.

I bet James and Doug don't leave their women unsatisfied.

My body warms, and my legs stiffen beneath me as I scoop out the last of my dessert. Chocolate dances across my tongue and I close my eyes. I leave the spoon in my mouth, savoring the flavor as long as I can.

I wonder what it would be like to be taken care of. To have James' muscular arms wrap around me as his soft goatee brushes my skin. To have my body soften against Doug's tall, slender frame as his gentle hands flow across my skin. Just like they glide across his sketchbook, so soft he's barely touching me.

The envisioned fantasy travels warmly down to my clit, tingling as my stomach flutters with anticipation. I want their eyes to fill with desire as I bare my naked flesh to them. I want to know the shape of their arousal.

Soft fabric slides against my palm where I caress my thigh. A shiver races up my spine.

No... Stop it...

I squeeze my thigh and inhale deeply.

You can't have them. You're just frustrated and horny. That's all.

"Ok Lily, what you think?" Doug asks, startling me out of my daydream.

Their bright eyes beam eagerly at me, willing me to get lost in them. I quickly shift my focus to the drawing that Doug holds out, slowly removing the spoon from my mouth. I take the sketchbook from him. My eyes skew as I stare at the page and its strange tentacle creature.

"What color is this octopus..." I tilt my head. "...monkey, creature gonna be?"

"We were thinking gray limbs, dark purple fur, and glowing orange eyes." James points at the TV. "So he can blend into the background."

I move the sketch in line with the screen and imagine this boss monster coming to life. "Oh... this is the one you were talking about popping out the cliff. Right?"

James' eyes shine. "Yeah."

"I'm surprised you remember. We haven't talked about this boss in weeks," Doug says.

"Eh," I shrug and hand him back his sketchbook. "I think it's a beautiful abomination of nature."

"You have such a way with words, Lady Lily," James says in his knightly accent.

I squint my eyes at him. "My sister is not here. You don't need to call me that."

"The princess demanded it, so we must, my lady," Doug insists playfully.

I roll my eyes. "Just because she is pregnant doesn't mean you have to do everything she says."

"And risk her wrath?" James says.

"Nope, don't think so!" Doug says, both of them shaking their heads dramatically from side to side.

A sliver of a smile lifts my left cheek as I flutter my lashes. I sigh as I stand up. "Will it bother you if I play pool while you work?" I take weighted steps toward the pool table at the other end of the room. "I need a challenging distraction."

"I take it your date didn't go so well?" James asks.

"It was boring and a waste of my time, as usual," I say, my mouth becoming dry.

"Oh, that bad?" Doug asks as I hear them shifting around.

"Yeah, I'm getting fed up with this whole dating thing." I squat at the front of the pool table and prep the game as they walk toward me.

"I bet," James says. "That's what, five dates in three months and you still can't find someone you can connect with?"

"Unfortunately."

"You want me to make you The Virgin Castle Special?" Doug asks.

"Yes, please." I beam, remembering the first time he urged me to try this drink.

A cocktail he created just for me when he found out I don't like to indulge in alcohol around people. I bend over the table to move the balls into place. Now that I think about it, neither of them has given me shit about that; like everyone else I meet does. James walks to the wall by the bar and grabs our cue sticks.

"You know you don't have to play with me..."

"What if we want to play with you?" James asks.

"Then I wouldn't say no." As I spin around, I flip a chunk of my hair to the side and watch Doug pour three drinks. "I believe it's your turn to start tonight, Doug."

Doug's eyes flash to me. "Not after the night you've had. You should go first."

"Aww... That's sweet of you, but I think you'll regret giving me this advantage."

"Would you like me to be on your team tonight?" James steps beside me and hands me my cue stick.

"No, you guys can tag-team tonight." I take the cue stick and his face lights up as he takes a step back from me. I point between the three of us. "Me, then Doug, then you sound good?"

"Works for me," Doug says.

James nods in agreement and motions for me to start. I bend my body to align with the table and prop the stick on my left hand. My auburn hair shifts and falls to the side, skimming the floor. I tease the stick back and forth, gliding the wood through my fingers to test the strength of my strike. Doug's muffled footsteps approach from behind me as I ram the stick into the white ball.

A loud crack resonates throughout the room. I slowly straighten as the balls smoothly flow across the table. Glass clanks against wood as Doug sets two of the drinks down on the bar table. He turns toward me, offering me the third. I purposely glide my fingers between his as I take the glass, delighting in the simple pleasure of his skin against mine.

The flavors of pineapple, strawberry, and peach dance over my tongue and down my throat. I slowly lick the remaining drops on my upper lip and tip my head back. "Thank you."

Doug's lips peak into his cheeks, accentuating his jawline. "You are most welcome."

"You're up." James hands Doug a cue stick.

He walks around the table, passing by an obviously easy shot, in favor of a harder one. I point my finger at him. "Don't you dare take it easy on me tonight!" Doug's deep blue eyes glint in the light, a smirk appearing on his clean-shaven face. My chest grows warm. I twist to James, pointing. "Got it?"

"As you wish." James bows his head. I lean against the bar chair, resting my cue stick between my legs.

Doug moves to the corner of the table and takes his turn, missing. He stands, giving me a look that makes my stomach flutter. "He leave you that frustrated?"

"Of course." I brush my hair behind my ear.

James squats down, holding the edge of the table as he finds a shot. "Another two-minute man?" James' hand flexes into a fist, twice.

I tilt my head as I note his tell. Why is he angry?

"Oh, no." I wave my hand. "Not at all..." I snicker and James' body relaxes. "This time... I was lucky enough to get a whole three minutes."

"Explains why you made it back in under two hours," Doug says.

My stomach churns at the blunt truth. James' cue strikes and the white ball roams the table. My shoulders slump and

I sigh. I feel like I have weights attached to my feet as I walk away from them to take my turn.

"Honestly, I don't know why I even bother anymore," I say as the blue-striped ball falls into the corner pocket. "I'm cursed. I should just get over it and move on."

"How are you cursed?" James' hazelnut eyes gaze at me with concern.

"I... um." Crap, I didn't mean to say that. A heavyweight presses in on my chest. I walk to the short end of the table and transfix my attention on the cue ball, avoiding their joint gaze. "It's a long story."

"Is it a story you wish to share?" Doug asks, while I take my next shot.

I fixate on the balls gliding across the felt. I don't know. Is it? Should I tell them an elf cursed me? I mean, they seem open-minded enough, but... My nails dig into my palm as I clutch onto the stick and sigh. I'm not ready yet. "Let's just say after so many times of being yelled at, it's easy to believe that it truly is your fault that they can't last."

"They yell at you for their incompetence?" Doug's tone deepens as he bites out each word, drawing my attention. They act like statues. Their eyes are as cold as stone. The anger that radiates from them is strangely comforting and protective. One foot quickly overtakes the other as I move without thinking.

I place my hands on their chests, hoping to calm them. My head tips back slightly to smile at James. "Not physically yell. It's more of a resentful unspoken implication. But it still hurts all the same."

I tip my head back farther to look at Doug. Suddenly realizing how close I am to them as my breasts brush across James' ribs and Doug's stomach. Their bodies relax under my touch. Their eyes gleam down at me, filling me with a desire to hold them. I force my hands away from their chests.

James' eyes follow me with purpose, grabbing my attention. "You don't deserve to be treated like that."

"You're sweet to think that. But you don't know what it's like."

"Actually, we do." Doug moves away from us to take his turn. "Just not for the same reasons."

"Really?"

"Yeah, we get treated like shit, too."

"I take it your girls are still giving you crap for pursuing your dreams?"

"Yeah. They don't like the fact that we aren't pursuing a 'real career.'" James' fingers motion air quotations.

"Like real men are supposed to." Doug mocks, missing. James moves around the table, preparing.

"That's stupid. How is what you're doing not pursuing an actual career?"

Doug's back straightens as his voice deepens. "Cuz being game designers won't make you money."

James' voice lightens. "It's a waste of your time."

They sound like parrots, repeating words they'd heard a thousand times before. It makes me even more impressed with their diligence.

"Let me guess…" Heat radiates through my veins. "They want you to work a boring, plain vanilla nine-to-five job, so they can stay at home raising the kids?"

"Pretty much," Doug says as James misses his shot.

"Well, that's stupid. That's not who you guys are! I don't understand how your girlfriends didn't realize that sooner."

"What do you mean?" James asks while my gaze roams the table.

"I know I haven't known you that long, but even in this short time, I can see that you don't fit into the cookie-cutter chauvinistic male mold. I don't get why so many women are drawn to such one-note assholes. But I guess if that's what gets them wet, then by all means." The cue ball jumps as the stick strikes it too hard.

"Sounds personal," James says.

"I take it you've met a few?" Doug takes his turn.

I grab my drink. "More than a few. They don't have any real interests. No goals. And they absolutely hate the fact that I make more money than them. They are nothing like you guys. They are so sleazy. It makes my skin crawl." My body shivers in disgust as Doug aims his stick at the ball. "It doesn't get me wet and isn't what I'm looking for."

The cold glass touches my lips, soothing the warmth that spreads through me at the sight of Doug's smile. James' hand grazes my elbow as he walks closely behind me, his hand trails across my hair. My body tingles at his touch.

James grabs his drink. "I've met guys like that. I find them annoying."

"Women can be like that too." Doug moves to the table and picks up his cocktail. "They just hide it better."

"Yeah, I had a girlfriend like that," I say. "We went out all the time. But as soon as she found Mr. Right, she changed. Unless you had kids, she wouldn't associate with you. I thought we were best friends. She didn't even invite me to the wedding."

"That's bullshit," James says.

"Yeah, but it explained a lot about her behavior and taught me how to read people better. I learned when to stay on guard and how to trust my instincts. Especially with the men I deal with at work. I had to learn how to move subtly away from them when they got a little too close for comfort. That's why I took so long to give you both passcodes to the house."

"That only took two weeks," Doug says, skeptical. "We gained your trust that quickly?"

"Yeah." I tuck my hair behind my ear as my stomach tightens. "Honestly, you guys are the first men I've ever given a key code to."

"Seriously?" "Really?" Doug and James' say, their voices overlapping one another. They lean against the pool table.

"Yeah... I mean, think about it. While you've been here, have you ever seen another man enter this house? Besides Grandpa, of course."

"Well, no." James strokes his goatee. "But we figured you just didn't bring guys home because it would be awkward with us here and all. You know?"

"Yes, but no... I've never..." I twirl my finger around a lock of my hair. "Umm..." Not able to face them, I focus between them. "I've never had another man in my bed before." My cheeks warm as their gaze studies me, considering this. I go on. "When we went over the rules, the one about not bringing lovers into my house, did you think it only applied to you?"

Doug shrugs. "Seeing as we never planned on doing that in the first place, we never thought about it that way."

"Honestly, I shouldn't be surprised by that. Your respect is the reason I'm ready to let you both into my bed."

They stare at me, frozen, as my eyes widen. My hands fly to cover my mouth and hit my nose. Fire blazes across my skin. My vision blurs at the implication of the words that just spilled out of my mouth.

"Room! Bedroom!" I mutter behind my hands while peering at their chests. My heartbeat pounds so loud in my ears that it threatens to drown out their voices.

"Don't worry," Doug says. "We know a proper lady would never say something so crass..." A sultriness spreads across his face. "Intentionally."

"We are but your lowly servants, Lady Lily." James places his arm across his chest and bows. "We know you didn't mean it like that."

Conflicting emotions ravage my senses. My face burns from embarrassment. The smell of cedar and citrus flows in through my fingers. Their scent tormenting me, drawing out the lust between my legs. The problem is, I do mean it. But of course, I can't tell them that. My stomach swirls and I place my hand on it, trying to ease the twinge of longing that threatens to burst free.

They rush the two steps toward me. James places his hand on my upper arm. "Lily, are you ok?"

"I'm sorry. We didn't mean to upset you." Doug caresses my hair behind my back.

Their touch sends a jolt of pleasure to my clit that straightens my spine. Their concerned eyes ground me to reality, and I realize I haven't spoken. I have to say something. I probably look like I'm about to cry or vomit.

"You are not lowly servants!" I place my hands at my sides and glare at them to mask my true yearning. "Never say that in LADY LILY'S presence again. Am I understood?"

"Yes, ma'am." They say in unison, removing their hands from me.

I sweep my eyes over each of them and hope my gaze is sweet. "Now, as I was trying to say. I think I'm ready to let you guys come into my room to clean."

"Are you sure? It's your safe space," James says as their bodies relax.

"Yeah." I grab my cue stick and they follow its movement between my legs. "I've been thinking about it for a while now and I've honestly put it off long enough. I trust you both."

Their smiles reinforce my longing, building that low heat again.

"Ok, we'll take it nice and slow," Doug says.

"If you change your mind, you tell us immediately," James says. "We promise not to take it personally and will leave without hesitation."

"Thank you, you guys are too sweet." I playfully brush up against their bodies as I step between them.

The sensation from their touch lingers on my skin as I walk to the other side of the table. My fingertips trail behind me along the smooth wood. Their scent follows me across the table, teasing me. I slowly bend, exposing my cleavage to them, and steady the cue stick in my hands. My lips lift provocatively as I smoothly guide a ball into a side pocket.

Without moving from my exposed position, I peer up at them. "And suave as hell, don't think I didn't notice."

Their faces become noticeably pinker. James raises an eyebrow and smirks. "You know it was my turn, right?"

"Oh, was it? I'm sorry." I bat my eyelashes and take my next shot.

"You don't seem all that sorry," Doug says as I pocket another ball.

I sway my hips and walk back around the table toward them. I fix my hair to the side and bend my body again, right next to them. This time, exposing my other curves.

"No, I guess I'm not." I take my turn. The impulse to tease them distracts me and I miss. "It's your fault, though."

"How so?" "Is that right?" James and Doug ask at the same time.

I gently flick my hair behind me. "It's what you both get for making a girl feel special."

"You deserve it!" Doug says.

James nods in agreement. "You're amazing, kind, and a very generous woman."

"Well, since you let me have two. I guess it would only be generous of me to let you both finish." I motion to the table as I lean my back against a stool.

"That is very generous indeed." James deepens his voice. "My Lady."

My stomach flutters as he walks away. I transfix my gaze on his flexing back muscles. I glide my hand over my forearm. Do they flirt with every woman they know this way? I know I shouldn't, but I truly enjoy the attention they give me. It's too bad that I'm their boss and that we are seeing other people. I guess I should be happy just fantasizing about—

"I saw that." Doug pulls me from my thoughts. His gaze sweeps over me. I squirm under his intense eyes as he prowls closer. My breath catches in my lungs, unable to escape. "What? You think I wouldn't notice? That was suave of you too... My Lady."

My heart pounds as the balls clash on the table. Their smiles ambush me. I grasp the cue stick tighter. I am like prey, about to be devoured. My chest relaxes a tiny bit as he turns away from me. Doug jerks his head to the side and James' expression changes to one of mischief.

James steps around Doug to stand in front of me, his hazel eyes glowing. Electricity scatters across my skin as his eyes lock on mine. I long for his touch. Please tell me I make them feel the same way. This can't just be a one-sided experience.

"You know how to make a man feel special, Lily. It makes my knees weak." James' sultry voice seeps from his lips, pushing my thoughts further into a place I don't want to escape from.

My gaze drops to his legs. Why do you have to be wearing pants today? I want to see those thick thighs. I bite my lip and tilt my head to the side, exposing my neck. Slowly, taking in his muscular form. "I'll take the compliment. I didn't think it was possible to make those tree trunks weak."

Doug huffs out a playful laugh as James twists away from me. Doug points at James. "See James, even Lily has noticed how good your legs look."

"Of course, I have. It's impossible not to. You exercise for four plus hours a day."

Doug takes a shot, pocketing a ball.

Why did he go? It's still James' turn.

James' foot fidgets with the floor. "I don't exercise that long."

"Yes, you do!" Doug and I say at the same time.

James points at me. "You're up."

I squint my eyes at him and then at Doug. I point my finger at the table. "No, it's not. You haven't finished."

"No. You took two turns." Doug's finger motions between us. "And we took two."

"Nooo... I took all three of my shots. So, you each get one more crack at it."

"That doesn't seem fair to me," James says.

"Is that so?" My eyes defiantly gaze at James and then at Doug. "Do you also think it unfair?"

"Yes."

"I see... However, I specifically remember telling you I wanted a challenge and asking you both not to take it easy on me." I place my hand on my chest. "And I know you are men of your word." I pout my lips, bat my eyelashes, and tilt my head to the side. "You wouldn't leave a lady unsatisfied, would you?"

My innocence shines playfully at them, hiding beneath the double-sided question. The corner of James' mouth twitches as Doug runs his fingers through his hair. I quietly giggle and continue to tease them. "Well, you either get one more shot each or... I could call the Princess and tell her you broke your promise?"

"Oh, no. Please don't." James flails his hand in dramatic protest.

"There's no need to disturb the Princess." Doug cautiously steps around the table toward me.

"That doesn't sound very sincere." I grab my phone out of my pocket.

"James!" Doug playfully pretends to scold James and points at him. "Hurry up and go. You're the one that promised we wouldn't take it easy on her."

"I'm sorry." James' arm outstretches toward me. "But you know I can't say no to a pretty lady."

Doug groans and places his hand on his forehead. "Oh, I'm well aware."

"That sounds like a juicy story. Do tell." I put my phone on the table; ready to listen to another one of their adventures.

I try to push my heated affection aside, knowing they won't go anywhere. This is fun and a much-needed confidence boost, but I know I'm not their type. They have picture-perfect girls waiting for them. Why would they want me? Even the men I have been with don't want to keep me after they see me naked.

Doug's sassy tone mocks James, and I realize I wasn't listening like I intended. I straighten my back and smile, giving them my full attention. Enjoying the moments I have like this with them is enough.

Chapter 3

Cookies & A Hot Tub

James

Saturday, June 4ᵗʰ

The smell of freshly baked cookies bombards me as I step inside the house. I inhale the sweet scent of peanut butter and my stomach growls.

Guess I didn't have enough to eat before drinking after all. Either that or I'm addicted to her baked goods. Both. Definitely both.

Doug rushes past me to the security panel on the wall. He mumbles as his hand balls up into a fist. What's he so worked up ab—

NASS! She didn't announce that we opened the door!

"Is she home?" I pull out my phone with a shaky hand and open the security app.

"Her purse is here, so she's home. But she didn't set the alarm." Doug peers over my shoulder and helps me search for her on the camera feeds. "There." Doug points at the pool. "She's in the hot tub."

I exhale my relief. "I thought I was having a heart attack."

Doug sighs, relaxing. "I guess that's one way to get rid of a buzz."

"I'm going to have a cookie." I make my way to the kitchen. "Want one?"

"Yeah. It's unusual for her to have all the lights off."

"She's been baking again. Maybe she's upset?"

"Then let's go cheer her up."

...

Sugary peanut butter melts in my mouth. I lick the tips of my fingers, rescuing every crumb left behind as we descend the stairs. Doug and I make our way through the dimly lit basement, past the bar to the connected changing room that leads to the pool.

I've been dying to use the pool all spring, but we have been so busy these last few weeks that we kept putting it off. I am excited about the chance to jump in. Maybe I can convince Doug to swim again. Like he used to in high school.

"You know, this will be the first time we see her in a suit," Doug says.

"Well, shit." I pull my shirt over my head. "Guess that means you'll have to behave yourself." I wink at him. "Especially if she's still a raging ball of furry."

Doug side-eyes me. "You like it too."

"What can I say... I like a fiery woman." I slide a basket out of the cabinet to place my clothes in. "This will be the first time she's seen us half-naked, too."

Doug pauses in the middle of removing his pants. "Fuck, this is going to be harder than I thought."

I choke out a chuckle. "In more ways than one."

Doug smirks. "Why, Claire, leave your scrawny ass hanging?"

I grumble. "Possibly." We finish getting undressed and his expression shifts back to the somber one he had on the drive home. I should say something to get him to talk. "Not to be a dick, but could you put a smile on? We're supposed to be cheering Lily up and your resting bitch face may scare her off."

Doug sighs and pulls up his swim trunks. "Yeah, I know."

"You ready to talk about it?" I tie the strings on my own, awaiting his response.

Doug rests his forehead on the wall. "I think Kelly is seeing someone else."

"Oh…" Shit… him too. Fuck, we sure know how to pick them. I let out a frustrated sigh. "Did she call you by someone else's name?"

"No." Doug's eyes snap open and fix on me. "Did Claire?"

"No, but she might as well have. She won't look me in the eye. She never says my name anymore." I lean my back up against the wall. "What makes you think Kelly's cheating?"

Doug runs his fingers through his hair. "She doesn't move the same. Asked me to do things she told me were a hard no before." He pauses, sighing. "She wouldn't let me bite her so I could finish."

"That's bullshit…" My stomach drops with realization. "I guess this just confirms the joke we made about turning into fuck buddies a few months back."

We stare at the floor and stand in silence for a moment.

"All right, that's enough sulking." Doug pushes my shoulder. "Let's go cheer up the fair maiden."

The changing room doors clank closed as we walk onto the patio toward Lily. The glow of candles wraps around the edge of the pool, illuminating her. She looks like she is sleeping.

"Hey Lily, do you mind if we join you?" I ask.

She startles and stifles a scream with her hands, quickly lowering herself into the water. "Didn't anyone teach you not to sneak up on a lady?" She scolds us. I smile, enjoying her adorable, fiery tone.

"I'm sorry," Doug says. "We didn't mean to scare you. We assumed you heard us come in."

Lily bunches her hair in front of herself. "No, I didn't."

She crosses her arms as I step into the hot tub. Flickering candlelight warms the space, accentuating her features. Her skin bathed in a deep blush, her hair catching copper tones in the light. It's alluring and romantic.

My gaze drifts to the water, to the view that must lie below its surface, but it is dark and unyielding to what my eyes are pleading for. I take a seat across from Lily. The heat soothes me, and I lift my lips sweetly. She smiles back and relaxes her arms.

Doug sits down next to me and points behind Lily. "Did you finish your book?"

Behind her rests a book next to a wineglass. She's drinking? That's a first. She must be extremely upset.

Lily sighs. "Unfortunately, a lot sooner than expected. So, I didn't relax as much as I was hoping to."

"Why didn't you grab another?" I ask.

"I was just about to, but then some jerks gave me a heart attack." She glares daggers at us, and I try not to laugh at her cute scowl.

"You started it." Doug points his finger at her. "We were worried sick about you."

Lily raises her eyebrow. "Why?"

"You didn't set the alarm, and the door was unlocked," I say.

"So, we panicked."

Lily's face softens as she touches her cheek and guides her wet hair behind her ear. Her fingernails drag across her collarbone and disappear under the water. "I'm sorry, I didn't realize." My eyes stay transfixed on her chest. "I must have been more pissed than I thought."

"Another disappointing night?" Doug asks.

"Yep." She reaches for her drink but stops midway. The frown I hate adorns her face.

Doug stands up, reaches for her drink, and hands it to her. "It's ok, we promise to behave."

"I take it you've had a few yourselves?"

"Yeah." I hold up three fingers. "We had three apiece."

Lily peers into the water, her eyes going vacant. "Do you want to talk about it?" Doug asks.

"No." Her hands sway just below the surface, rippling the water. "How were your dates? I can't help but notice you came home early too?"

I clench my jaw. "They were fine."

Her lips lift deviously as she places her glass down. "Did they satisfy you?"

"Why?" Doug asks, evading the question.

"What do you mean, why?" Her gaze shifts between us both. "You always want to know if I've been taken care of. Then get upset when you find out that I haven't. So, why can't I ask the same?"

Doug and I stiffen up as she leans closer to us. The line between her breasts parting just above the water, her hair curving around them.

"I... Um..." My gaze darts from her glowing green eyes to her chest. Doug is stiff as a board. Does she seriously not know how sexy she is right now?

"You guys are too cute when you're flustered." Lily giggles and sits back. "It's ok, I get it. You don't want to tell me you're being sexually satisfied or share all the ways you're satisfying other women when I'm having such problems. I'm grateful you care, but it's kind of unfair."

"How is it unfair?" Doug asks.

"It's unfair because you get angry at these men for not satisfying me, and then shield me from your stories by leaving out the fun sections just to spare my feelings. What if I want to be envious?"

"Why would you want to experience such a horrible emotion?" I ask, and Lily glides across the water to us.

"Simple..." Lily places her head in between ours and my eyes fixate on the arch of her back. "I want proof. To know that not every man is the same. That getting in and out isn't the only goal." Lily places her hand on my chest, another on Doug's, and my breath catches in my throat.

Her honeyed voice seducing me. "I want to hear you get excited about an experience I should be enjoying. To know that what I am asking of a man is not fantasy. I want to know what it is like to be wanted." Lily's gaze falls to the water, her voice softening sadly. "To not be treated like I'm a disgusting means to an end."

Lily trails her hands down our chests and over our legs. "There's so much I haven't experienced. So please... can you tell me what it's like?"

Speechless. My brain swirls in a hurricane of thoughts. Blood rushes from one brain to another as my heart pounds in my chest. She is tantalizing; I want to reach out and touch her. But she is so sad- I think I'd break her if I did.

"Lily?" Doug's stern tone draws our focus. "What do you mean by a disgusting means to an end?"

Anger courses through me, her statement finally dawning on me. How could any man think she is disgusting?

"Of course, that would be the only part you hear." Lily pushes off my knee and sits back. "You are way too sweet."

"Sweet?" Doug elbows me and relaxes his body. I follow suit. "Fine! Have it your way." He motions with his finger. "Stand up and take your suit off."

I match Doug's tone, catching on. "We'll show you what it means to feel wanted."

She sits there, her body rigid as her eyes dart between us. Her hand goes to her mouth as her eyes light up. Her throat rings out a beautiful melody I love to hear.

"Lily, I said stand! Don't keep us waiting." Doug motions for her to stand once again. "We'll give you what you want."

Her laughter stops abruptly. She frowns and lowers her gaze to stare at the water. "It's ok, you don't have to pretend you're interested in me."

"Who says we're pretending?" I ask.

"I know you're pretending. I'm not your guy's body type."

"And how do you know that?" Doug asks.

"I've seen your women." Lily over emphasizes her hourglass figure, as if she was fat. "They don't have my shape."

Is that how she sees herself?

"People can be attracted to more than one body type," I say, and her eyes dart between us.

"I guess. But it doesn't mean I'm wrong. If I was, you would have noticed already."

My eyes follow her hands down and it clicks. The way she is holding her chest... The way she has held her chest every time she has moved. Shit, she hasn't been wearing anything this whole time.

"We noticed." I deliver the lie smoothly. "It's called being a gentleman. Now, would you please stand up and let us give you what you asked for?"

She pauses for a moment, thinking it over before responding. "Fine." Her defiant eyes glaring at us. "But on one condition."

"And what would that be?" Doug asks.

"Promise me you won't treat me any differently." Lily's head drops solemnly, turning to the side. Her hand moves up her arm to her shoulder. She stares down at her body, her eyes showing no signs of her usual confidence. "Especially when you find all of this... to be disgusting."

What in the ever-living fuck have these men done to her? How could she ever think that? I place my hand over hers, grabbing her attention. "We would never find you to be disgusting."

Doug nods in agreement. "We promise we won't look at you any differently."

Lily takes a deep breath and slowly stands. With her arm firmly pressed across her chest, the underside of her boob readies to escape. She closes her eyes as she fully exposes her stomach to us.

Blood red scared skin stands out brightly. Etching a harsh line that extends at a slant from her belly button down her right side, under her belly's pooch, and across her upper thigh. My eyes divert to between her legs. Even though the water covers her, the beginning of her bush pokes out.

How dare men find her disgusting!

Her lips quiver. She's closed her eyes in... Fear? Shame? Doug grabs my wrist, pulling my view to him as he lifts my arm. I nod and we place our hands on her stomach. She gasps from our touch and her eyes flash open. Doug trails his fingertips gently over her scar. A glimmer of a tear escapes the corner of her eye.

Has no one ever caressed her stomach before? Touched her tenderly in these beautiful places?

"You are so beautiful, My Lady." My hand smoothly glides up her stomach. I want to caress her breasts so badly. Reach around and pull her into our embrace.

A small smile hints at the corner of her lips as she leans into our touch. "You promised me you'd behave yourselves."

"We are," Doug says. "But reminding My Lady that she is beautiful is more important."

Lily presses her lips together and hums. I stop moving and force myself to stay seated or risk the impulse of taking her right here and now. Doug removes his hand, and I reluctantly follow suit as we sit back.

"What happened?" I ask.

Lily sighs as she turns away from us and grabs a bathing suit I definitely hadn't noticed before. "There is a reason I don't let men that have been drinking touch me."

"I'm sorry," Doug says while she gets dressed.

"You have nothing to apologize for. I am not ashamed of my scar. I got it protecting Layla when she was eleven."

She pulls up a high-waisted suit bottom and I raise my eyebrow. "Then why do you cover it up?"

"I am hiding my fat, that's why." Her voice sounds defiant as she pulls on her top.

"If it bothers you that much, my offer to be your trainer still stands."

"No, I don't think so. I prefer living. Thank you very much." She titters. I catch Doug covering his mouth as his shoulders shake, failing badly to suppress his laughter. I squint my eyes at their jesting. "Plus, I just joined a dance class."

"Lily," Doug says, his tone stiffening. "Can I ask you something?"

"Yes." Lily wraps her hair around her arm twice and sits.

"If you're not ashamed of your scar, then why did you act that way?"

"Oh…" Her gaze falls to the water. "I'm used to men treating me differently than you did."

My heart twangs with a longing to erase her experiences. "We all have scars. It's just unfortunate that someone as kindhearted as you has hers on the outside. Whereas ours are on the inside." I motion to Doug and me.

Lily's eyes soften. "What scars do you have?"

Continuing our intimate moment, Doug and I talk with Lily about our pasts. What it was like for me growing up in foster care and how it was a stark contrast to living with Doug's family my senior year. Doug lived a very sheltered life in a gated community, with suffocating, loving, career-focused helicopter parents.

We open up to each other in ways that I never have before. Ways I have never done with any woman. It's like a deep exhale after holding my breath, a relief. Having someone other than Doug to listen to me and understand what it was like to grow up alone. Lily lost her parents as a teen; She understands what that is like. She shares more about those years with us, and it helps me picture her better.

I'd forgotten that she had a hard life, too. The connection she has to this forest preserve she bought, the focused way she maintains it, makes more sense now. It's sentimental to her in more ways than she'll let on.

I wish I could hold her. Smell her peach hair. Brush her soft skin under my palm again.

I close my eyes and take a deep breath.

Don't start that here. No more boners. You have to at least wait till you get to your room.

…

We make our way to the changing room and Lily stops just outside the door to smile at us.

"Thank you both for this lovely night..." Lily leans closer, pronouncing her cleavage. "James, how about we think of this as an early birthday present for you, and then next week I'll treat you two to dinner?"

"Thank you, My Lady," I say, drawing out the words the way she likes, getting her eyes to sparkle the way we like. "You are very generous, and we'd love to join you for dinner."

Doug and I bow to her. Lily glows brightly as she spins and shuts her changing room door.

CHAPTER 4

BBQ IN THE GARDEN

LILY

SUNDAY, JUNE 19TH

The blue sky is painted with perfect white clouds. Rays of sunshine gleam through them. The sound of dramatic, gothic music that James' recorded for their game fills the garden. It's perfect for their game, but a stark contrast to the beauty of this day. The smell of charcoal and smoke drifts in the air. James tends the grill, his back muscles flexing.

I rub my finger over my bottom lip and leave it nestled in the corner of my mouth. I want to place my hands on the tops of his shoulders and trace patterns along every curve. Press my fingers into his shoulder blades as he thrusts into me. Trap his hips in between my thighs and rock into him.

The soft padded sound of sandals on stone approaches me from behind, and I glide my wet finger down my chin. Stroking my fingertips across my neck to massage my shoulder, I wait. The anticipation of taking in Doug's figure, knowing he is only wearing jeans, consumes me.

I hold my breath as the footsteps continue their path toward me, pressing my hand deeper into my shoulder muscle as he walks past. His toned back muscles disappear into his waistline. These jeans are too forgiving for his figure. I sigh. I wish he had worn my favorite ones. The ones that show off his physique.

I imagine gliding my hand over his smooth skin. Hooking my fingertips into that waistline. Have his arm under my arched back, lifting me so I can wrap my legs around his waist, letting him drive into me.

Doug sets plates on the stone counter. "It smells great!"

A warm breeze washes over me, drifting me away. I turn my head to the garden clearing and close my eyes.

Trees encircle me. Trapping me. An enchanting moss floor tickles my toes. Eerie, seductive music echoes in the night. The moon's presence dances along my naked flesh. Their beastly eyes leer at me. I shiver with lust. My stomach twists. My heart rate quickens.

I am prey, unable to run from my predators.

I don't want to run from them. I'm ready to be devoured.

Doug's subdued touch reaches my body. His warm breath blazes down my neck. He spins me around and lifts me into his arms. I wrap myself around his body and meet his lips. James' rough and calloused hands press deep into my skin, gliding down my back.

A carnal desire tears through me, swallowing me whole. Doug squeezes my ass, holding me against him. James' hands flow smoothly over my stomach and up to my breasts. His firm grip massaging them. Their kisses tantalize me.

James grips my ribs, and slowly Doug slides into me. I tilt my head back and release a primal moan. I stare into the night sky and see more stars than there are. James' tip presses between my cheeks and I scream into the night.

Stop! You can't.

My head screams at me as I cover my mouth and grab my thigh. I stare at my feet and dig my nails into my leg, trying to ground myself. Bringing my senses back to reality. The pain covers up the lust building up between my thighs. I force myself to breathe.

Breath in, 1... 2... 3... 4... 5...

Breath out, 1... 2... 3... 4... 5...

Why do you keep letting this happen, Lily? You are going to drive yourself crazy. You can't have them. Calm down.

Breath in... Breath out...

Please don't notice me. I don't like it when you see me this dizzy and nauseous from longing. I don't want to lie to you both again. Not that you believe my lies. You probably think I'm pregnant.

Breath in... Breath out...

Stay calm, you got—

"Lily?" James' voice echoes in my ears.

Damn it. Why are they always so attentive?

I open my eyes and remove my hand from my mouth. Their beautiful, caring eyes gleam at me from across the stone counter. My lust surges again, overpowering the pain in waves. I squeeze my legs together, forcing the desire to open myself up to them desperately away.

"Are you nauseous again?" Doug asks.

"I think I waited too long to eat." My finger points toward them and the grill. "I'll be better once I get that in my mouth." Blood pumps into my cheeks so fast it burns. I smack my hand too hard over my mouth that my teeth clank together.

"Well, you heard the Lady." Doug elbows James and jerks his head in my direction. "You can't keep her waiting any longer."

"No, I guess not."

The joyous sound of their laughter helps me relax. Doug walks toward me, his face softening as he approaches.

Doug grabs my water bottle from the table. "Do you need your ginger?"

I shyly nod. "Please and thank you." He nods and walks away.

Perhaps I should tell them the truth. *Hey James... Doug... I have to tell you something. I lied. It's not stress causing my nausea. You see... I keep having these daydreams. I want you two to fuck me so hard that I won't be able to stand for a week.*

Yeah... very smooth. That's a great idea, Lily! Cuz that would go over so... well. They'll probably just laugh and think you're joking.

Should I call Layla? Maybe she would know what to do. I groan. But knowing my sister, if she found out I'd been fantasizing about being with them, nothing would stop her from trying to hook us up.

And you know she will do it in the most embarrassing way possible too.

What am I going to do? I can't go on like this. I have to figure something out.

I hide my pain and push my lust aside as they finish prepping dinner.

...

Roasted chicken, potatoes, and my new favorite side of spicy caramelized onions decorate the plate in front of me. Doug and James join me at the patio table, and I begin my routine of complementing the cook.

I enjoy the meal while we engage in small talk.

Doug finishes telling me about the impromptu vacation his parents, Denise and Fred, are taking for Father's Day. They are in New York City for some convention he doesn't remember the name of. His brother Paul, and Paul's boyfriend Dusty, are being tested while their parents are away.

They are handling the family's country club for the next two weeks. If all goes well, they will take over the family business. James chimes in with a quip about how Doug and Paul are enjoying the weekend away from their father's puns, pranks, and ridiculous antics.

The conversation dies down pretty quickly, and my mind wanders into curiosity. Why haven't we talked about last night? Are they avoiding it? Guess I'll get it started then. "How was your birthday party, James?"

"It was great. Our friends had a blast," Doug says.

"Thanks again for letting us use the game room." James shines a wide, toothy grin.

"Of course, that's what it's there for. You're welcome to have your friends over more often." I focus my gaze on James. "You don't have to use your birthday as an excuse."

"You got home early. You could have joined us," James says.

"Oh, no..." I shake my head. "I didn't want to intrude."

"You wouldn't be an intrusion." Doug points his forked potato at me. "Honestly, you'd fit right in."

"That's sweet of you, but I highly doubt you want to hang out with your boss on your night off."

"If we didn't want you there, we wouldn't have invited you." James takes a bite of his chicken.

How do I tell them I wanted to come but that I'm too scared to meet everyone? Especially the women they're having sex with. Well, maybe seeing that they are taken will help me stop daydreaming. "I might make an appearance next time if you insist."

Doug's blue eyes shine in the sun. "Great."

"Did your girlfriends join you?" The words tumble out, following my thoughts, and I instantly regret asking. My stomach swirls with anxiety.

"No!" they grit out in unison and stare daggers at their plates. James' nostrils flare as Doug clenches his jaw.

"Oh, I'm sorry. I didn't mean to upset you," I say, a bit shocked by their response.

"It's ok." Doug's shoulders slump. "We're just tired of being dicked around."

"What do you mean?"

James sits back. "They always say they are busy when we ask them to hang out with our friends."

"They only want to hang out when we're alone. It's like they don't want to be seen with us." Doug's solemn tone sparks something in me. My body swells with heat. That's bullshit. No wonder they are down. They must feel like they are being used. Like they are nothing more than sex toys. I know the feeling.

"So, when we invited them to come last night, they... well..." James sighs and Doug tears his gaze from his plate. His eyes giving encouragement for James to go on. "Claire told me she doesn't want to see the place where I lost my self-respect."

Doug's jaw twitches. "And she was the nice one about it."

"That was nice?" I turn my fork in my hand, grasping at it like I'm going to stab a bitch. How could they treat them like this?

"Yeah." Doug places his hand on the back of his neck, avoiding my gaze. He opens his mouth and then closes it. James nudges him to go on. "Kelly told me I'm a sorry excuse for a man. That she doesn't want to be dominated by someone that's a submissive dog to another woman."

"Oh... OOOHHH." I relax my grip on the fork as I process his statement. "Yeah, that... Ah..." My chest lifts toward them as I lock my ankles together. "Wait..." My eyes widen with realization. "So, she thinks I'm your Domme?"

"Yes." Doug's voice softly falters, eyes brushing over my chest. James shifts in his chair, and I catch his eyes hovering as well. I subtly peep at my bikini top to see my nipples tenting the fabric. I smirk, grabbing my knife to cut a piece of my chicken.

"Good," I say, my voice coated in sass. I take a calm bite. The smoky taste of the chicken melts in my mouth.

Doug's gaze studies me, processing my response. I challenge his gaze, keeping my composure as I swallow. His lip twitches. "How is that good?"

"Oh, it just means that I don't have to feel bad for hiking up my skirt to kick her in the cunt for hurting my pet."

James bursts out laughing. The rich sound makes it hard to keep up with my serious charade. Doug keeps his eyes locked on mine. His jaw slacks and his cheeks grow pink. I think this is the first time his composures slipped. He takes a deep breath and James quiets down.

"My dear Lady Lily..." Doug's voice deepens into a husky tone. "You would come to my rescue like that?" An alluring deviousness lifts his lips.

"I'll defend your honor any day, Sir Douglas." I move my arms to my sides to give them both a better view.

Is this my fault?

I frown at my food.

No.

My stomach churns.

Maybe? I mean, I knew that coming to work for me could cause friction in their relationship. But this. This is all—

"Lily?" Doug's demanding tone lifts my gaze. They are sitting up straight, no longer staring at my chest. "What's bothering you?"

"I'm fine, it's nothing..." I stop as Doug's features tighten. His stern gaze telling me I'm not weaseling my way out of this. I sigh. "I'm overthinking things is all, and I'm sorry."

Doug and James' faces soften. "Why are you sorry?" James asks.

I rake my fingers through my hair to calm myself as I keep my eyes focused on them. "It's just that I didn't think—" No, *Lily. Tell them the truth.* "I knew if you both came to work for me, it could impact your relationships. You were moving in with a single woman, after all. So, I'm sorry I didn't mean to ruin—"

"You had nothing to do with it." James' stern voice shocks me into silence. I think that's the first time he has ever taken that tone with me.

"We knew the risks, too. This isn't your fault." Doug swiftly sits back in his chair and huffs. "We're the ones that held on too long."

"We were having problems long before we came to work for you." James' eyes become vacant, his voice toneless. "We should have both known it wasn't going to work."

"How so?" I place my fork down and give them my full attention.

"I met Kelly in October of last year and I introduced James to her best friend, Claire, a week later at a Halloween party." Doug's fingers play with the condensation on his water glass. "It was great at first. But a week after the party, they started talking about holiday plans. Both the girls had so many plans."

Doug's tone deepens, anger seeping in. "Things we were just expected to do with their family, the parties their friends were having. They practically demanded we attend them all. Never even asked us or invited us… just expected. Because that's what you're supposed to do. And with the relationship being so new, it threw me off. Kelly got pissy when I told her no and tried to set boundaries."

"It was the same with Claire." James hunches over the table and rests on his forearms. "She was just as angry and irrational. Neither of them understood why we weren't ready to do the whole 'meet the family' shit yet."

James huffs. "But a few days later, they went back to acting like their normal sweet selves. I thought they were just hurt at first… that maybe they just got ahead of themselves. We convinced ourselves everything was fine and ignored every sign, trying to make things work."

"We thought it would improve after the holidays," Doug says as they take turns telling the story.

"But once the new year came around… they became distant." James fidgets with his fork, unable to keep eye contact. "They stopped wanting to hang out with our friends and theirs. They didn't even want to do anything publicly for Valentine's Day."

"We thought it might be because we started taking our game seriously. We were spending a lot more time learning the software, planning the plot, and all that stuff."

"Nobody, not even our friends, thought that we were actually going to pursue our dream. It's something that we have been talking about doing for ages, so I get why people didn't take us seriously at first."

Doug runs his fingers through his hair. "But the girls were worse. They didn't even try to show interest; thought we were all talk. We hoped that once things settled down, and they saw how serious we were, they would come around. But this week we just needed to end the charade."

"We've had enough of waiting and decided to give it one last shot." James pauses, fixating his gaze on his plate. "I invited them to my birthday party, hoping. Not only were they so, so busy, they couldn't make it. Claire…" James' jaw muscles firm into a ridged line. "She didn't even wish me a fucking Happy Birthday."

"Seriously?" I say, a bit too aggressively.

"Yeah, it pissed me off. She couldn't even put in that bare minimum effort. When you…" James' eyes drift to mine. "You baked me a whole ass cake AND took us out to dinner."

"Oh, well…" I play with my hair. "I can see why that would upset you."

They are so sad… I wonder if that's what I look like when I come home disappointed after my dates. Well, let's cheer them up.

I face my body toward James and straighten my shoulders, lifting my chest ever so slightly. James' eyes light up as I apply a sultry smile. "You want me to lace up my thigh highs and kick her in the ovaries for you, Sir James?"

James tenses up and doesn't blink as his hand moves under the table. "No, that's ok." His head gently shakes. "I don't want you to hurt yourself on my account."

"Hurt myself?" I place my hand on my chest. My arm lifts my breast as I do. "I highly doubt it. Oh, no… I'm more worried about ruining my leather outfit." I motion my hand over my body, knowing their creative and vivid imagination will fill in the picture.

They squirm in their seats, their lingering gaze tracing a line of electricity over my body. I carefully observe their every movement. Doug's hand clenches onto the armrest, his knuckles white. James' head tilts away from me as if he is hiding, but his gaze is locked into the corner of his eyelids, peering through the table at my legs.

My sigh breaks the tension between us. "But seriously…" I brush my hair behind my ear as I gently tilt my head to the side and expose my neck, deeply enjoying their reactions.

"It sounds to me like they didn't care at all about you, and they are being completely selfish."

Doug sits up straight. "Why do you think they are selfish?"

"Well, any woman that doesn't support the one she loves only cares about what is in it for her. So, if they only care about serving their own needs and interests, that leaves no room for you to grow. A healthy relationship can't blossom without light, nurturing, and tilling of the weeds." Their eyes question me. "Sorry, my horrible gardening metaphor fell apart there, didn't it?"

"No..." James says with a smirk while nodding his head in agreement. "Not at all."

"Oh good," I say, returning his sarcasm. "I'll keep going then since I'm already knee deep in the dirt."

"Well, you do love being on your knees in the garden." Doug's body stiffens as his eyes bulge, obviously not meaning to say that out loud.

Is that what I look like when I embarrass myself? A smile peaks at the corner of my mouth. "No. I prefer being on all fours when caring for my garden." Doug's mouth twitches as James' eyes roam over me. A sweet laugh passes over my lips, calming them and I ask, "Can I continue now? I'm enjoying my gardening puns."

"Then, by all means." Doug motions for me to continue.

"We'd never want to get in the way of your enjoyment." James shines. "My Lady."

My legs tighten as a jolt of longing cascades through me at the sound of his elation. "What I'm trying to say in the weirdest roundabout way possible is that..." I peep through my lashes at them. "If they aren't willing to share the sun with you, they either don't understand or don't care about your interests. Or they simply refuse to have faith in your ability to succeed."

"Which is bullshit." My hands dramatically move as excitement rushes through me. "The energy you exude when you talk about your dream is exhilarating. The passion you have for your game is overwhelmingly infectious.

I mean, you guys convinced me in less than an hour that you are serious about this, and you have a solid plan. Which told me that regardless of any setbacks, you will fight tooth and nail for this. So, I wouldn't be surprised if they were more upset to no longer be the center of attention than by the fact that you are actually pursuing your dream."

James rubs his fingers over his forehead, considering my words. "That explains a lot about their behavior."

Doug stares at his plate, his eyes transfixed and unyielding. James' concern fills his eyes. I grab James' forearm, getting his attention. "I think I broke him."

James places the back of his hand on the other side of his lips. As if to whisper but doesn't. "Should we call it a night and put him to bed?"

"Ha, Ha." Doug mocks. "I can tuck myself into bed, thank you very much." Doug's eyes linger on me, and his mouth twitches. He recedes and takes a bite of his dinner.

I reluctantly pull my hand off James' arm and wait for Doug to catch my gentle gaze. "What's bothering you?"

Doug's eyes study me as he finishes chewing. "It's ok. I don't want to bite the hand that feeds."

"Oh..." I stare at my half-finished plate. He thinks he'll upset me. I take a bite of potato.

James nudges Doug, and he sighs. "I guess since I just stuck my foot in my mouth, it would be better to ask then, wouldn't it?" I curtly nod. He pauses, then goes for it. "Is that why you hired us?"

I swallow, and confusion wrinkles my forehead. "What do you mean?"

Doug sits up straight and his tone boldens- as if to give himself courage. "Did you hire us because of our dream?" Doug motions between James and himself. James leans in, anxiety straining his features. I put down my silverware and Doug goes on. "We were never qualified for this job. It surprised us to even get an interview. Let alone to be hired on the spot."

It seems like this is something they have wanted to know for quite some time.

"Well, you're right, you weren't qualified. At least, not on paper. But..." I gesture to stop Doug from interrupting me. "I interviewed you for two reasons.

One... I asked every applicant to tell me why they wanted the job. To tell me how it could improve their lives. Your letter intrigued me, and the honesty was refreshing. Two... You were the only ones that actually completed that request. Which told me that regardless of your qualifications, you could follow directions."

"Seriously?" James' posture straightens, his face etched in disbelief. "We were the only ones to write that letter?"

"Yep."

"I'm assuming that's why you gave us 'an unconventionally long, paid practical interview.'" Doug motions air quotes.

I nod. "Yes."

"Is that the reason you hired us?" James asks.

"No. That's how you got in the door. The reason I hired you is a bit more complicated." I take a sip of water as they patiently wait for me. "Do you remember the gentlemen I called during your interview?"

"Yeah." Doug raises his eyebrow. "Our landlord."

"Your grandpa..." James' eyes shift upwards "Walter? Right?"

"Yes, but he wasn't my grandpa when I first met him. He was the realtor that helped me sell my folks' place after they passed away. I was so intrigued by his work. I became attached to the idea of it all and asked him a million questions.

During this time, unbeknownst to me, I reignited the flame in his heart that reminded him why he got into this business. And... well... my grandmother ignited another type of fire in his..." I dart my eyes down to their legs. "Heart."

"So, what does that have to do with hiring us?" James asks.

"Everything! You guys got a fire in your belly." I point at them. "And all you need is a chance to shine and show the world what you can do. That passion inspired me. So, yes, I care that you guys do your job, but I care more about making sure that fire doesn't die.

Your confidence raged through my home like an unforgiving storm that told me nothing will stop you from obtaining your goal. So, I turned around and flung the doors wide open."

I turn my body toward the garden and motion to its landscape. "Showing you a garden, you could thrive in. A truly magical place that could keep your dreams alive." I pause, stopping myself before I say too much.

I smile secretly, hoping that the magic of this place rubs off on them. "Plus..." I shift in my seat. "The choice was... well... quite selfish, too."

"Selfish? How?" Doug asks.

"Honestly? I had become cold." I run my hand along my thigh, unable to hold their gazes. "My home was cold. My sun was fading. Looking back, I think I was in real danger of becoming stagnant."

I peer at them through my lashes. "I realized it when I saw the real James and Doug. When you relaxed and shook off the anxiety-inducing interview masks you both had on."

I tuck my hair behind my ear and shyly gaze at them. "It had been so long since I had seen anyone that passionate. I forgot what it felt like. So, this choice was selfish. I felt a hint of that fire when I first met you, and I didn't want that warmth to leave me."

James slumps back in his chair. "That was not the answer I was expecting."

Doug nods in agreement. "I find it ironic, cuz that's the same reason we took the job." I tilt my head and apply the gaze he gives me when he wants me to keep going. A faint smile lifts his cheek. "We thought you had the most brilliant flame we had ever seen. It was addictive, so we jumped at the chance to have the coolest boss."

"So, I guess that makes us selfish, too. Right, bro?" James says.

"Yeah, it does!" Doug says as their fists bump.

Excitement consumes me, running up between my legs. They relax in their chairs. My heart pounds as they ogle my red and blotchy chest. I want to get up and kiss them. It hurts so much not being able to touch them.

"Stop, you're gonna make me cry." I joke away the heartache. "Let's switch the subject."

"As you wish, My Lady." They say in unison, intensifying the heat radiating through me, threatening to send me back into that daydream fantasy again.

"Want to hear about the new creature design?" James' excitement seeps from his lips.

"Of course I do!" I lean forward, eager for the distraction, trading one heat for another.

Chapter 5

Brownies & What?

Lily

Friday, July 29th

The sky darkens, the sun glowing orange behind the clouds. Energetic music plays while I sit on the kitchen island and swing my feet. A beautiful glow shines through the window, bathing me in its light. The energy from the forest washes over me, surrounding me in its tender care.

I take a deep breath and let the setting sun take all my unease and frustration beyond the horizon with it. My gaze flows to the patio garden. Doug's apartment light is on. Good. I'm glad they are still working. I'll text them again when the brownies are done.

Or... you could put on the new lacey white lingerie outfit with heels you bought today and bring the brownies to them.

No, down girl.

Why not? You bought it just so they can see you in it.

Absolutely, under no circumstances, can I sexily walk to their place wearing nothing but lingerie!

Fine, then put a robe on too.

I groan. Am I this desperate that I'm now arguing with myself?

Yes. Yes, you are.

Damn it, why am I still acting like this?

Because you are horny and frustrated... and you know that no one else has or will compare to them.

I sigh. My hands roam over the cold counter as I lean back onto my elbows. I tilt my head and close my eyes.

A vision looms over me, their bright smiles filling me with longing. Warmth radiates from their bodies, heightening my arousal. I long to take care of them.

Rough hands explore my skin. A kiss graces my shoulder. James' soft facial hair sensually brushes up my neck with every kiss. He awakens something inside of me. Doug leans up against the counter across from me, beaming. One tender kiss on my lips is all James gives me.

It leaves me wanting... hungry... ready.

They beam at me and remove their shirts. I take in the view of their bodies, growing warm and wet from my center. I lift my shirt over my head and toss it to the floor. Propping my hands back on the counter, I let them admire my bare breasts. Doug licks his lips as James kisses my breast, his hands caressing.

My gaze locks with Doug's, and I moan. My fingertips trail across James' muscles as he enjoys playing with me. James wraps an arm around my waist, lifting my butt off the counter. Doug grabs my pants and tugs them.

They wear matching devious smiles.

Doug stops, leaving them to constrict my thighs closed. James runs his fingers through my hair, quickly finding what he is looking for. I cry out as his fingers make circles over my clit.

I want to let him into me.

Doug watches me struggle to open my legs, my pants offering me no mercy. My eyes beg him for help. He obliges, fully removing my fabric prison. I spread my legs wide, giving James the power to push his fingers into me.

I bare everything to Doug as James takes his time with me. His mouth on my breast, his fingers deep inside. I sing my pleasure out. Doug's excitement grows as the show pleases him.

As Doug unbuckles his belt, I tell him to stop and grab James' hand at the same time. I ambush them with a seductive smile, my eyes shining with lust at the thought of being filled. I remove James from me and slide off of the counter.

Naked and on my knees in front of Doug, I unbutton his pants and let his arousal escape. His eyes gleam at my touch. James leans on the counter next to us and I tell him to take his cock out.

I lick the tip of Doug and stare into his brilliant blue eyes. James' rock-hard shaft glides in my grasp. I tease and pleasure them. Doug's eyes beg me to swallow him whole, and making sure I have James' attention, I open my mouth wide, inviting all of Doug inside me.

The sensation of having them both subject to my mercy is exhilarating.

The oven timer rings loudly throughout the kitchen and the fantasy fades. I hop off the island and see the brownie pan still sitting on the burner.

Ok, this is ridiculous.

Did I seriously set the timer and not put the brownies in the oven? How?

I turn the timer off and try again.

You need a better distraction, something that will help you release all this pent-up energy. Or you're going to explode all over them. And not in a good way.

I turn the music up and climb on top of the kitchen island. I stand in this open space and imagine a dance floor below me. My bare feet glide along the cold, smooth marble, my body swaying to the beat.

Music takes control of my senses. My body relaxes. My endorphins pump through me. I drift into a trance I don't want to escape from. For when I do, reality will come rushing back to me, reminding me I can't have what I truly desire.

Chapter 6

Dancing in the Kitchen

James

Friday, July 29th

A swift beat pulses. From here, the music is faint but audible. I reach the bottom of the basement stairs as Doug closes the patio door. I turn to him and point up into the house. "Brace yourself."

"Brownies and loud music? Well, she's definitely angry about something."

"I guess we'll find out if it's her cute angry or gonna-stab-a-motherfucker angry." We prepare ourselves for the adventure that awaits us. We turn the corner and I freeze, taking in the sight. "Um, are you seeing what I'm seeing?"

Doug pauses next to me. "Do you see Lily dancing on top of the kitchen island?"

"Yes."

Doug nods stiffly. "Then yes."

"I don't think she's angry." I'm mesmerized by her curves and the way her motions flow into one another seamlessly. "She looks so happy."

"She's radiant." Doug takes a step toward her.

Lily's spellbinding emerald eyes gleam. Without skipping a beat, she reaches out. I follow Doug as her enchantment pulls us to her. In a moment of brief clarity, I peek past them to the timer.

Twenty minutes still? I thought they'd be closer to done by now.

We rest against the counter across from her, giving ourselves the best seat in the house. My hand aches with the urge to touch her. Doug grips the edge of the counter. I smirk, knowing that he wants to touch her, too.

Lily is enchanting. Her body glides gracefully with the music. I usually can't stand listening to this pop club crap. But the way she moves... Her beauty... It's captivating. One song blends into the next, and her hips echo the notes.

Doug and I push off the counter, readying to catch her when she swiftly gets too close to the edge. Hypnotized by her reassuring glance, we stop. A chill runs down my spine. My arm hairs stand on edge. My body burns to touch her. To take her.

Lily's hand trails up her chest and separates her breasts. Her other hand caresses her hip. The music's tempo quickens, and she sways with the beat. Her hands make sensual motions across her thigh as she takes her time to kneel.

My hand tightens around the counter and, unable to take my eyes off her, I hold back my urges. Agony grips my heart. The need to have her intensifies with every pulse of music and blood. Her wrists turn in circles as she gradually raises her hands. Fingers tangle in her hair, scrunching it up.

Fuck. This is the sexiest she's ever been. I never want to forget this.

She denies us her face, bracing herself on all fours to show off the side of her glorious figure. Her hair sprawls out on the island. Lily's beauty amplifies my senses, seducing every atom in my body.

I leer at her, taking in every curve she shows off. Her hips, her breasts, the arch of her back bowing deep... She tilts her head back and I lick my lips.

Lily's sensual movements turn her onto her back. Her hips rise and her shirt slides to her breasts, showing off her supple skin. My arm throbs, wishing it could slide under her, wrap around her, to pull the heat between her legs close to me. I resist my urges.

The song fades, and she sits on the edge of the counter. Another song finds its beat, and a sparkle catches in her eyes. Excitement radiates from her. Bare feet smack against the floor as she hops down, moving without a care in the world.

Willing myself to look away, I catch Doug smiling. He hasn't been this happy in a long time. His joy mirroring my own. Doug glances at me and I jerk my head toward Lily. He shakes his head.

"You sure we can't go to her?"

"No, not yet." Doug's posture relaxes against the counter. "Just enjoy the show."

"Just because you like a cock tease doesn't mean I want to deprive myself, too, you know."

Doug snorts. "Who are you trying to convince?"

"The time hasn't come." Our bodies stiffen at the sound of Lily's voice. It's unusually deep. "You can't touch me yet." Her emerald eyes glow, ensnaring me. "I just want you to watch. Please..." Her voice drips with honey. "Just look at me. Make me feel wanted again."

Lily steps backward toward the counter, her hips making sharp movements as she goes. Her back reaches the edge, and she grabs hold of it. Enthralled, my eyes catch on her legs as they spin her around to face the counter.

The smell of chocolate fills the kitchen. It entices the allure of her seduction. This is so hot. I didn't think she could get any sexier.

Doug elbows my arm, and I pull my focus away from Lily. He is holding his wrist. His hand spread out across his crotch. His gaze darts down. Quickly, I cover my erection. I turn my attention back to Lily, her hips shaking along to the music. Her happiness radiates, flowing to us. My chest ac hes.

Lily has captivated my heart.

...

The timer rings out loud over the music, shattering the anticipation in the air. Lily stills. I stare at her back and the oven rings again. As I take a step, her body shivers and she focuses on her objective.

Doug and I study her rigid movements. His brow wrinkles. Both of us confused by her behavior. Should I say something to her? The music stops, grabbing our attention.

Lily stares out the window and sighs. "I can't keep doing this."

"Can't keep doing what?" I ask.

Her shoulders rise as she spins around. "I umm..." She tucks her hair behind her ear. "I didn't mean to say that out loud." Lily's forced smile falls. She grabs the counter. Her chest crests as she holds her breath.

Did we mess up?

Doug moves first, walking toward her. She wraps her fist in her shirt. Lily closes her eyes as Doug and I get to the island. An exhale escapes her lungs.

"Lily, what's wrong?" Doug asks sweetly. Lily grips her fingertips into her thigh, her eyes darting between the two of us.

"You can talk to us. It's ok," I say to reassure her. Lily's eyes glisten. She opens her mouth to speak, but quickly presses her lips together.

"Lily! Talk to us." Doug bites at her.

Her hand balls up. She tilts her head and glares at Doug, radiating anger. "I'm so fucking frustrated, angry, irrational, and tired." Lily bursts with energy, her voice raised, and her hands gesture violently with every word. "I thought if I baked you brownies, I could relax and ease some of the tension.

But that didn't work. My anger was so overwhelming that I forgot to put the brownies in the oven. I don't want to go on my date tomorrow. I don't want to date anymore. Period.

I'm so sick of being sexually frustrated. And I don't think I'm asking too much. But apparently... my standards are too high and I'm not worthy of such a lofty ambition... As to have a stupid fucking orgasm! I want to curl up into a ball to cry and kick the shit out of our punching bag at the same time.

The brownies I made for you were supposed to be ready by the time you got here.

I'm mad at myself because my stubbornness won't let me tell Brian, 'No, I don't want to go on a second date with you.' Cuz if he asks why, I'll be the bad guy for telling him I'd rather spend time with two other men."

She points between me and Doug as she goes on, barely taking any time to breathe. "Two men that are ten times better than all the men I've seen these past five years combined.

Our first date wasn't the worst and Brian apologized for drinking, which was a first for me. Usually, they yell at me for being no fun.

I have a bad feeling about tomorrow. Something is going to go wrong because I'm being selfish again. I just want to belong somewhere. To prove to myself that I'm allowed to be truly happy around others.

I just needed an outlet and so I turned the music up and danced. My imagination took control, and I went into a trance.

Now I've hurt you both and I should apologize. Though I don't know how, because it wouldn't be genuine... it felt amazing. I enjoyed dancing for you. I am truly sorry. All I've ever wanted is to make you both so happy and I mess—"

"Lily! Look at us!" Lily and I jerk our heads at Doug, both startled by his outburst.

Lily's ragged breathing calms as Doug holds himself back. He wants to hold her as much as I do.

"You did nothing wrong. You didn't cross any lines." Doug's voice holds Lily captive. "You didn't hurt us. We are grown men, with our own free will. We could have left. Seeing you dance was beautiful. So, don't you dare apologize... Am I understood, My Lady?"

"Yes, Sir Douglas." Lily's mouth trembles. Light glints off the water in her eyes, pulling at my heartstrings.

"Why don't you sit down, and we'll serve the brownies," I offer, hoping to relieve the tension between us.

Lily nods and walks toward the table. I don't know what to say to them. Usually, I rely on Doug's skills in this area. He always knows what to say to calm someone down. Doug nods at me. We move throughout the kitchen, acting like it's just any other night.

We join Lily at the table. A faint smile lifts her cheeks. Warm chocolate melts my nerves. Doug's shoulders relax with his first bite. I enjoy another, savoring the delicious taste. My addiction to her baked goods fills me with guilty satisfaction.

I relax my grip on the fork and turn my gaze to Lily. Her brownie is untouched. She hasn't even lifted her fork. I study her face, unable to figure out how she is feeling.

Her attention shifts towards us after a moment. "Doug?"

"Yes, Lily?"

"Can you promise me I was only dancing, and that I didn't hurt either of you?"

"Yes. We promise," Doug says.

She turns her gaze upon me. I nod in agreement. "You didn't hurt us."

Lily's cheeks pinken as she fidgets with her hair. "So, did…" Her soft voice wavers. "Did you enjoy it?" She strokes her hair down across her breasts. Doug's hand twitches and his gaze drops. I fail to keep my eyes on her face.

My hands ache. I want to touch her. "If we say yes, will we get in trouble?"

Lily's innocence twinkles as she shakes her head. "No."

Without a second thought, Doug and I both blurt out. "YES!"

"We enjoyed watching you have fun." My voice springs with excitement. "You lit up the room. It was amazing."

"It's been a long time since I've danced like that." Lily trails her nails up and down her bicep. "I've never danced for anyone before."

"What do you mean?" Doug asks. "I thought you were in a dance class?"

"I am. But to me, that's exercising. Plus, it's different because I don't perform for anyone there."

"Is what you did tonight, what you do there?" I ask.

"Part of it, yes. But… This felt so free. Plus, when I'm there…" Lily eyes her breasts as she pulls her shirt out from her chest. "I rarely wear this much clothing. Nothing this loose-fitting, either."

Doug raises his eyebrow. "What kind of dance class are you taking?"

"Pole dancing," Lily says without hesitation.

Astonished, my eyes widen and my gaze floats over her. Images of her in heels dancing around a pole flash in my mind, adding another layer to her dance I never want to forget. "Is that why you got scared?"

"No… Embarrassed maybe."

"Can I ask why?" Doug asks, and Lily's eyes shift between us. She takes a deep breath and puts her hands under the table.

"Before my parents passed away, I wanted to be a dancer. But no one ever came to watch me. So, after a while, I developed a bad habit of imagining I was on a stage and had my own private audience." Lily's shoulders fall as she sighs. "I have quite the vivid imagination."

"We're sorry we watched you without your approval."

"No!" Lily points at Doug. "If I'm not allowed to apologize because…" Her finger taps the side of her mouth. "How did you put it? Oh, yeah." She stares Doug down. "Your grown-ass men that can make your own decisions. Then you can't apologize either."

Doug sucks in his cheek and smacks his lips upon release. "Those weren't my exact words."

A genuine laugh breaks out of Lily. The tension clouding the room dissipates as she relaxes. Her melody warms me, lifting my lips with joy.

"Do you think that maybe…" Lily's voice drips with honey. "I could dance for you both again sometime?"

"Absolutely," I say. "You can dance tomorrow night at the party we're having downstairs. The girls love to dance."

"Er..." Lily bites her finger. "I..."

"If you're worried about intruding, don't," Doug says. "Our friends really want to meet you and we think you'd fit right in."

Please say yes! We want you to meet them. We want them to meet you.

"Ok... I'll be there after my dinner with Brian tomorrow." Lily's lips barely lift into her cheeks.

Seriously! Why do you still want to see that asshole? He isn't worth your time.

I grind my teeth, my anger brewing. The vein in Doug's head pulses. He is biting back his own words. I sigh and inspect Lily's untouched plate. "Take your time. We'll be here all night."

"My stomach is still in knots." Lily stands up and grabs her plate. "I'm going to get in the hot tub and relax for the evening."

"Did you want company?" Doug asks.

Lily stops. "I..." She clings to the chair, her hand shaking. "I do, but... I think... I need... to be alone... till tomorrow night... I can't right now."

Unable to look at us, she walks away from the table. Doug stands up. "Lily?"

"Please. Don't ask again." Her voice cracks. "I'm scared I'll take my anger out on you. Please..." Her breath catches. "You can't be the ones I hurt."

"Why do you keep saying that?" The chair screeches as I stand abruptly. "You really think you could hurt us so easily?"

Lily spins around. Her face is emotionless. "Yes, I do." She points outside. "This new moon I will hurt a man. And the pain I cause will come back three-fold. I can't lose control. Not with you two.

So, please, we can't be together tonight. It's not time yet. Not today. Not like this." Her words are bold and certain. Those brilliant green eyes bare into us. Her back straightens. "You can't touch me till tomorrow night."

What is she talking about? She's not making any sense.

"Ok..." Doug's voice softens. "We are sorry we pushed. Go relax, we'll take care of the dishes."

I glare at Doug.

Ok? What do you mean ok? She's not ok. Why are we letting her go?

Lily sets her plate down on the counter, nods, and walks toward the hallway. I reach out, but Doug grabs my wrist and shakes his head as she leaves.

"She shouldn't be alone."

He lets go of my wrist. "Yeah, I know."

"This is bullshit." I grip Doug's shirt, taking my anger out on him. Frustrated that I can't help her. "Something is wrong. I want to fix it." I jab him in the chest. "We need to fix it." Doug grabs hold of my shoulder. His gaze holds me, calming me. "I don't understand why she is scared."

"She is a control freak, and she believes she lost control, or believes that she will."

"I don't like this."

"I don't either. Unfortunately, we have to do what she asks." Doug picks up the plates and we walk to the sink. "We need to respect her wishes. Be patient with her and not push her away."

"UGH... This sucks." We begin the mindless routine of handwashing the dishes. Images of her dance replay in my mind on a loop. "Lily gave me an idea for a new boss."

"Oh, yeah?" Doug asks, his voice inflecting interest.

"A dancing succubus that uses illusions to dodge attacks."

"That sounds amazing!" Doug pauses. His eyes sparkle. "We should place her in a garden surrounded by red lilies."

I hand him the next dish. "Are those the flowers Lily said were her favorite during our interview?"

"Yeah." Doug's eyes sparkle. "They are perfect."

"Her or the lilies?"

"Yes!" He sharply nods, a smirk plastered across his face.

"You think she'd get mad if we turned her into a succubus?"

"Doubtful." He shakes his head. "She gushes over them every time they show up when we watch anime."

"True..." I dry my hands while he takes care of the last dish.

"What if she levitates, too?" Doug suggests. "Make it look like she's gliding through the flowers."

"Yeah! Let's do it."

We head to the studio to get to work, inspired once again by our Lady Lily.

CHAPTER 7

LET'S DECORATE

LILY

SATURDAY, JULY 30TH

With an almost empty coffee mug in hand, I make my way down the hall. The distinct sound of someone rifling through a cabinet reaches my ears. I step into the kitchen to the sight of James and Doug standing in front of the baking cabinet; the doors spread wide open. They've sprawled an array of miscellaneous things all over the countertop.

Their backs are to me, and Doug's hands are deep inside a cabinet. James casually holds open a door, his finger tapping against the wood. Their biceps and muscles are in full glorious view as they study the contents before them.

James leans forward. "How about cupcakes?"

"I don't think that's enough." Doug shakes his head and shuffles a few boxes over. "It seems too simple for her tastes."

I make my way to the coffee maker. They stand in silence, staring at the cabinet, still unaware of my presence. I lean up against the counter and listen while I finish drinking.

James groans. "This should not be this hard. Why do women have to be so damn picky?"

"They are not picky. Women simply have standards." Doug's gaze travels over James, goading him. Though James is turned away from me, I can picture the annoyed look on his face from the way his back muscles tense up. The way his eyebrow twitches and his lips pucker. Doug taunts him further. "Your scrawny ass should be familiar with a woman's standards."

I smile, enjoying the endearing bickering.

"Yeah, well, this scrawny ass leg is gonna kick you square in the nuts so hard that you're gonna choke on your balls." James stares daggers at Doug, challenging his gaze.

I force back my laughter and take a sip from my mug.

Doug unlocks his gaze first, losing this round. "Why don't we just call that place that Lily likes?"

"Do you remember the name of it? Because I sure don't."

"Swirls and Pearls," I say, taking my opening to startle them.

James' hand clutches his chest. "Fuck Lily. Don't scare me like that."

I ready myself, reveling in the opportunity to use their own words against them- from when they scared me. "Sorry." I place my hand over my chest, feigning my apology. "I thought you heard me come in."

Doug crosses his arm and his lips pout. His eyes gleam with mischief, giving him away. "No, I didn't"

"Sorry, not sorry. Your obliviousness was too tempting." I gently titter. "Maybe next time I'll wear a bell."

James snorts. "Like that will help. You move like a cat."

Joy lifts my lips, brightening my features. I turn my back to them and take a few steps to the fridge, swaying my hips as I go. "So…" I grab the milk. "Who's the dessert for?"

"Bill finally proposed to Heather last night," Doug says. "So, we're going to celebrate tonight. AND James here thinks he should make dessert."

"Are you going to decorate?" I ask as I finish preparing a fresh cup of coffee.

"No?" James' voice questions. "Are we supposed to?"

"Depends." I take a sip and turn to them. "Do you want it to be just another night, with a bit of celebration? Or… do you want to make her feel special and truly honor their engagement?"

"The second, for sure," James says. "Heather would be ecstatic if the night was all about her."

"Then you should decorate."

"I wouldn't know where to start. Let alone what to get," Doug says. "This isn't exactly our area of expertise."

I raise my eyebrow. "You design stunning backdrops for your game every day. I don't believe this is beyond your capabilities."

"That's different." They say in defiant unison.

I roll my eyes at them. "How?"

"It's fiction, for one thing." Doug counts with his fingers. "A backdrop takes a minimum of three days to design. Plus, the weeks of planning beforehand."

"How are we supposed to do all that and apply it to real life in just one day? It's completely different." James' hand cuts a line through the air.

I smirk, getting an idea. I set my mug down. "Guess I'll show you how it's done!" I swing my hip around and motion for them to follow.

We climb the stairs to the storage room loft on the third floor. I walk to the back corner and face them. "If you would be so kind. I need these white boxes brought down to the basement, please." I grab a box and head toward the stairs. As I turn to face the stairwell, I catch them stacking the boxes. "One at a time, some items are fragile."

"The boxes aren't that big. They'll be fine in our big muscular arms," James says, flexing. Doug nods in agreement as they both give me a wide, toothy grin.

"Oh, I don't doubt that." I ogle their arms. "But..." I lower my gaze slowly to their legs. "I don't know... I'm worried about those poor little legs." My eyes dart up. They raise their eyebrows. "They are so fragile looking. I think you need an extra leg day."

"Bro..." Doug elbows James. "I think she just challenged you."

"No! I think she challenged you." James twists a leg out to the side, lifts his gym shorts, and flexes his calf muscle. "See... Mine are immaculate!"

"Ok, give it to me gently." Doug takes a mirrored step and turns his head away in an overly dramatic gesture as his hand covers his eyes. I giggle at the sight. "Do I need an extra leg day?"

"I'm sorry bro, but Lady Lily is right."

"Here Doug, you can take my box down too." I set the box down at the top of the stairs. "An extra trip is sure to bump those legs up to God-like status." I deepen my tone, trying to sound like James. "Oh, and don't forget to take your time. You can't rush perfection."

I reach the bottom of the loft stairs and hear Doug's voice. "Did you hear that? Now she is quoting you! She must reallllly like you. She might even give you a cookie!"

I turn around, waiting. Their jesting gets louder as they approach. I brush my fingers through my hair and fluff it to the side of my face. As they come into view, I peer up through my lashes at them. They stop. Their faces go blank with shock.

"I'll give MY cookie to whoever finishes first!" I tilt my head, acting innocent. Their eyes widen. I turn and descend the stairs to the kitchen. This time they don't follow.

...

Warm chocolate enchants my taste buds. I exaggerate a moan. I wish I could have dessert for breakfast every day. Hot coffee follows the next bite.

Oh my, this tastes so good together. Maybe I will try that new recipe I found for mocha brownies. I think they'd like that. Who am I kidding? I know they would!

"Hey," Doug says as they enter the kitchen. "I thought you said that the winner gets the treat?"

"And she did. I finished first!"

"Yeah, I guess you did." James tries to hide his smile as they both pretend to pout.

"We were looking forward to having your delicious warm cookie."

"I bet you were..." I flick my head toward the counter. "Your treats are in the toaster oven." They grin as they walk past me, and I patiently wait for them to notice their other surprise.

"Coffee too?" James' joy bounds in his voice.

I listen as they take a sip from the cups I prepared for them. "I hope I did it to your liking."

"Yeah, it's perfect," Doug says as they join me at the table.

"Thank you," James says.

"You're very welcome." I watch them take the first bite of their morning dessert. "So…" I begin. They stare at me with their mouths full of brownies. "Which one of you would like to explain how you both finished at the same time? Because… I'm sure… such outstanding gentlemen wouldn't cheat. Now, would they?"

Their cheeks turn pink as they swallow their food and shake their heads frantically at me.

"Nope," Doug says. "We would never cheat."

"Oh… Is that so?" I grab my coffee, waiting for them to expand on this.

"Yep!" James says. "We just took our time."

"Just like you asked." Doug's voice deepens. "Nice and slow."

I press my thighs together to stifle the flutter in my clit. "Then I guess I should thank you." I lift my mug toward them. "Cuz it's about damn time I got to finish first."

James shifts in his seat, staring at his brownie as he mutters. "It's not like it's hard."

"Speaking of something hard…" I pause, teasing them back. James and Doug glance at me silently, stiffening in their seats. I continue, amused. "You don't have to bake tonight. I placed an order at Swirls and Pearls. It will be here around five."

"You didn't have to do that. I would have made something," James says, relaxing a bit.

"Yeah, I know. That's why I placed the order."

Doug bursts out laughing. I cover my mouth at the sound, trying to resist.

"Ha. Ha. I get it. I can't bake."

"It's ok…" Doug pats James' arm and bats his eyelashes. "You're still one hell of a cook, sweetie."

Not able to hold it in any longer, laughter spills past my lips. I try to control my breathing, but snort instead. They jovially gleam at me.

"Seriously…" James says, as I settle. "Thank you."

I wave my hand. "You don't have to thank me."

"Yes, we do." Doug's voice firms, while his eyes remain gentle. They shine.

My hand clenches around my leg. I wish I could kiss them. Have their warmth under my fingertips. I crave their touch so badly it burns.

"Ok well, you can thank me by bringing my kitchen step ladder downstairs and then staying out of my way till I am done decorating." I stand with my plate and mug in hand. "Focus on what you are amazing at." My gaze catches James. "Make some delicious appetizers." My eyes travel to Doug. "And experiment with a new drink idea to go with it."

"We can do that," James says and Doug nods in agreement.

As I rinse my dish, I take a deep breath.

If I don't feel a connection with Brian tonight, I'm calling it quits. I need to focus on myself. Have some fun and see where it takes me.

I twist my hair in front of me as I pass them on my way out of the room.

"I'll bring the ladder down in a few," Doug says.

"No rush." I sway my hips. "You guys take your time and enjoy your treats. If you keep up the hard work, I might have to up my game on your rewards."

CHAPTER 8

MAKING FRIENDS

LILY

SATURDAY, JULY 30TH

The mirror reflects my pain. Red marks blaze angrily across pale flesh. The distinct shape of fingers... an imprinted hand wrapped around my forearm. My small hand fits inside the borders of the mark. Thankfully, it only hurts when I squeeze.

You know it will be purple by morning. You can't hide what Brian did to you for long.

I just need to hide it tonight. Only for one night. I just want to have fun... I don't want tonight to be about me and my drama. My eyes plead with my reflection, hoping I can fade into the background of this party.

Soft footsteps approach. I grab my black cardigan to cover myself as Doug steps into view. "Is the invitation to join you guys still open?" I ask, not giving Doug the chance to speak first.

"Absolutely. The girls are excited to meet you. But fair warning, Heather is going to be all over you. According to her..." Doug's voice whisks into a feminine tone. "Tonight is going to be the best. Lily is amazing. I can't wait to hug and kiss her and cry all at the same time."

"I appreciate the warning." I hide my pain behind a joy-filled look.

"I'm grabbing some more snacks, so I'll meet you down there in a few." Doug heads to the kitchen, my thoughts trailing after him. Please don't leave. I need you to hold me and tell me I'm safe.

Doug walks out of view, and I force myself to breathe.

Breath in... 1... 2... 3... 4... 5...

Breath out... 1... 2... 3... 4... 5...

I turn my attention back to the mirror.

I sigh and glide a hand over my braid. It's still good.

My eyes open wide. They aren't red.

You can do this.

I spin and force my feet to walk.

Joyous energy radiates from the basement. I inhale the energy deep into my lungs, inviting it to balm my wounded nerves. A genuine smile forms on my lips as I descend the stairs.

My eyes are drawn to James, sitting on a bar stool by the cue sticks. His gaze trails over my body, filling me with warmth. A tall thin girl with light blonde hair talking to him takes notice. She turns and the bride-to-be sash I left out lies elegantly across her slender frame.

"Yay! You're here!" Her decorative coin belt rattles against her bell-bottom jeans as Heather quickly makes her way over. Her long legs make it an easy feat. "Thank you so much. For all of this. Seriously! It's so beautiful."

"You're welcome, Hea—" Her hug interrupts me.

"Heather, let the woman breath." She lets go of me to glare at the bald man with a full beard. He is as tall as Heather and, somehow, even skinnier than Doug.

I catch a glance of James getting elbowed by a round man with unkempt facial hair. The man whispers to him and gestures toward me. James' shoulders stiffen.

Soft footsteps descend the stairs behind me, and I plant my feet, unwilling to move. I need him close to me, even for just a second. Doug's body connects with mine, his fingers trailing across the arch of my back as he passes slowly by. I relax, the brief touch subdues my pain. I keep him in my view as he sets down a tray of snacks.

"Introduce us, dude." The man that elbowed James insists.

"Ahh..." James flusters for a moment. His gaze meets mine and I give him a soft smile of encouragement. James sits up straight and gestures to the group. "Everyone, this is Lily... Lily, this is Bill, Heather's soon-to-be husband. Zach and Jane. Susan and Matt."

"It's nice to finally meet you all," I say to the group, mentally cataloging each face with a name. The man that whispered to James is Matt. And Bill is the bald one next to Heather, her fiancé.

"It's nice to meet you too." A honeyed voice floats over to me. I beam at Jane, admiring her floral maxi dress. She is cute and shorter than the rest of the group. Good, at least someone is close in height to me. I'm still the shortest one here, but at least I'm not entirely alone.

"We have heard a lot about you," Matt says.

I smirk. "Oh, I've heard plenty about you, too."

"I'm sure none of it good," Matt remarks, somehow finding pride in the statement. The room fills with laughter.

Doug's hand presses subtly into the middle of my back. A plate of mini sandwiches appears in front of me. "Considering the time, I'm assuming you haven't eaten." His warm breath blows over the tip of my ear and flutters down my neck. "If this isn't enough for you, let us know and we will reheat you something more satisfying."

I take the plated offering, resisting the urge to touch him. Doug's hand skims across my ribs as he steps around me. His blue eyes shine and my body warms as he says, "I'll make you the drink special for the night. Virgin. Just the way you like it."

I swoon from his lingering gaze. A hand gently grasps my shoulder, pulling my attention away. Heather gestures to the pool table. "We were about to start another game. Would you like to join us?"

"I'd love to! What are we playing?"

"Men vs the Women," Matt says.

"Minus the show-off twins over there." Zach puffs out his chest, pointing at James and Doug with a glare of jealousy.

Doug lifts his hands in surrender. "It's not our fault. We get a lot of practice in now."

"No..." James strokes his goatee and glares back at Zach. "He's just salty that he can't grow a beautiful goatee like me."

"You leave Zach's sexy soul patch out of it." Jane steps in close to Zach and nestles her small body around him. Zach grabs her round ass as she continues. "I like it just the way it is!"

A gentle puff of a laugh escapes my lips.

Susan steps into my view. I turn my attention to the wide-hipped woman as she joins the conversation, addressing me. "Anyway..." She swishes her freshly dyed, ocean-blue hair, its beauty briefly distracting me. "We're told you play well, and we could use the help. Plus, if we win, we get control of the stereo for the night."

My body relaxes at the sight of the girl's pleading faces. "That sounds like fun."

Susan, Heather, and Jane exclaim their joy. I catch James and Doug's mischievous smirks. They didn't tell them exactly how well I play, did they?

I hold James' eyes hostage, as I sway my hips. The walk to him seems longer than I know it should be. I set my plate down next to him. Placing my hand on his forearm, I lean over him to grab my cue stick. He leans in closer, his bicep flexing to hold me. My breast pining for contact.

I tilt my head toward his ear and whisper, "What level of difficulty should I play at tonight?"

James peeks past me, his eyes scanning them. "End them with a flawless victory." He responds coolly.

"Ooh…" I feign a wince and shift, brushing my breast against him. "Harsh… You sure?"

"They have been brutal on the girls. Fight for their honor and show them how it's done, My Lady."

I beam and turn around, letting my hips skim across James' thigh. "All right, ladies. Let's do this."

....

Heather, Susan, Jane, and I sway to the beat on a makeshift dance floor, celebrating our victory. We dance and talk. Their skin blushes from the drinks and the heat. It's been so long since I've had this much fun. I forgot what it felt like. A happy contentedness settles over me.

Masculine laughter booms over the music. I step off the dance floor to take a sip of my drink, masking my glance over at the pool table. James and Doug shine from across the room. The sight of them enjoying themselves so fully fills me with joy. It's nice to see this side of them.

My heart rate quickens as I process my emotions, realizing that they treat me like they treat their friends.

There isn't a boss-employee façade. Who they are around me is genuine.

The warmth of the room glistens on my skin. I set my drink down on the coffee table. Becoming too warm, I toss my cardigan onto the couch.

"Are you ok?" Jane's eyes overflow with concern as she zeroes in on my wound.

Crap... my hand covers it- too late. In the heat of the moment, I forgot to be careful. Heather and Susan stop chatting, taking notice as well. I uncover it. The handprint stands out against my pale blush skin. Its condition worse.

"It's nothing... I'm ok." My heartbeat goes into overdrive.

Heather steps closer. "What do you mean?" Her caring eyes will not let me turn away. "That's not nothing."

"I'm ok I promise." I tuck my arms behind my back to hide the mark from their gaze.

"What happened?" Susan asks.

Jane's gentle touch graces my shoulder. A tingling rushes to my fingers. Her jaw twitches. "It's ok," I say to Heather. "Let's get back to dancing. We don't need to ruin your night with my drama."

"Oh, please." Heather waves her hand in a dismissive gesture. "You could never."

Care settles in each of their eyes. Jane lets go of me and rubs her shoulder. I tilt my head, studying her. Why does she look like she's in pain?

"You can talk to us." Jane invites me to open up with a smile. I take a deep breath in surrender, steadying myself to tell the story.

Chairs screech across the floor, startling us. "What the FUCK did he do to you?" James' voice booms from across the room.

My mind races, fearing the worst. I spin around stiffly, afraid of what will be reflected in their eyes. Doug and

James push past their friends to get to me. My eyes widen, now realizing that moving my hands behind my back must have given the others a full view of the mark I'd been trying to hide.

My ears pound and muddle the surrounding noise. I've never seen that look in their eyes. I take a half step back as James snatches my hand quickly, yet carefully. His touch gently examining it.

"Did he hurt you anywhere else?" Doug's fingers brush against my neck, moving my braid. Their caressing touch is tender. It's familiar. I close my eyes and remember the night in the hot tub when they did this to my stomach. My body warms. I could melt in their hands.

"Step away from her!" Heather yells and my eyes fling open. "Can't you see she's scared?"

They let go of me and step back. "I'm sorry Lady Lily." "I'm sorry My Lady." James and Doug say over each other.

Scared? I'm not scared. Quite the opposite, in fact. My gaze scans the room as my flustered thoughts consume me. I try to process all the feelings and expressions before me.

Jane's sweet voice drifts to me, waking me. "You don't have to tell us what happened if you don't want to."

As I turn to Jane, I notice the genuine concern written on their faces. Despite having just met, they truly care. I take a deep breath and lean against the couch. "Well, long story short. My date didn't end well."

"Yeah, no, shit," Matt says, and the group turns to him, glaring. He puts his hands up in surrender.

"Just ignore him," Susan says, and Matt nods enthusiastically in agreement. I silently chuckle at the spirited dynamic between them.

"So, what happened?" Heather says.

I keep my eyes focused on the girls. It will be easier for me to talk to them. The irritation in my voice peaks as I begin. "Honestly, the moment we took our seats, I could tell he wasn't thrilled to be there. All he did was complain. First, it was the beer selection, then the menu was shit. He treated the waitress like garbage AND kept whining about how we should go to a bar to get better food and beer."

"I thought you went to The Rose Garden?" Bill asks.

I sigh. "We did."

"Wait..." Zach crosses his arms. "So, instead of the best steakhouse in town, he wanted to go to a bar?"

I nod. "Yeah. He just wanted to watch some game, even though I know he was already watching it on his phone."

"What an asshole," Heather says.

"Yeah, that's some bullshit. Especially for a first date," Susan says.

"Second," I mumble, not enjoying correcting her.

"I don't care if it was date thirty or a damn grocery trip." Matt's anger drips from his voice, his outburst surprising me. "You give your woman quality time, no matter the occasion."

The implications of his words hit me like a ton of bricks. Their expressions telling me they agree. That's how it's supposed to go. That's what I've never experienced. My eyes well up with tears.

A soothing sensation flows through me as Jane's arm grazes mine. "What happened next?"

"When Ella came back to take our order, I told her to put this on my tab and that we would be out of her hair soon. He got excited. Until I told him off and wished him luck at the bar. I stormed off, not caring about all the attention I drew to us. I had reached the lobby when he caught up with me. He grabbed my arm and yanked me toward him."

The sound of growling makes me pause. I wasn't the only one to hear it. Everyone stares at James and Doug. James' hand is flexing at his side, pumping into a fist repeatedly.

Doug's fingers dig into the edge of the pool table, turning his knuckles white.

I turn my focus to Jane. As I do, I catch Zach smiling at them. I rest my arm across my body, holding onto my forearm for comfort.

Jane leans up against the couch and puts her arm around me. Her touch brings another cooling wave of comfort that courses through me. I study her curiously. This sensation is familiar. I wonder...

Her eyes flick to mine, noticing my unshed tears. Her sweet voice asks, "That's not all, is it?"

I steady my breath to continue. "Brian tried to drag me out the front door, demanding that I go home with him. I was livid. My hand was already numb from the force of his grip. He wouldn't let up and I... snapped... I told him I wasn't interested in being disappointed."

The girls put their hands to their mouths and gasp, understanding what I meant.

"I didn't mean to bait him further. I regretted insulting him when I saw his eyes. He raised his hand to strike me but caught the ire of the bartender instead. Frank took him down to the floor and kept him away from me so I could leave."

"What a loser," Susan says. "I mean, I have been on some rough dates with some real creeps. But yeah, that is bad."

"Yeah. Men can be such dicks!" Heather says.

Jane gives me a comforting smile and I manage to faintly lift my lips in response. She pulls me close; her hug lingering. She is so sweet and kind. I take a deep breath, tuning out the voices still discussing my drama. James and Doug haven't moved. I gather my courage and go to them.

I step in front of James and Doug. Their gazes remain transfixed on the floor, despite my presence. "I'll be ok," I reassure them and myself. "It will just bruise and be sore for a while. He didn't hurt me that badly. Thankfully." My feet shift nervously.

Come on, do something. Say something. Anything.

I take half a step back, not wanting the torture to continue. They reach out to me, their arms mirrored. I'm pulled deep into their embrace. My heart flutters. I wrap my arms around their waists and nestle my head in between them. Their hug is like being wrapped in a warm blanket.

A bittersweet mixture of concern and rage radiates off them. James' hand trembles against my back. I close my eyes and relax, curving my body into theirs. Doug shifts and presses me closer to him. They make me feel safe. I hold back the urge to kiss them, knowing I should be content with this.

"Ooh..." The sound of the men's teasing melody surrounds us. James and Doug's arms tense around me.

"Stop that," Susan says. Her voice echoes that of a mother scolding her children.

James and Doug's hands glide to my waist. Their grips tighten as they glare past me at the sound of the teasing.

"Come on, Lily," Heather says. "Let's go to the hot tub and let the boys play with their balls and sticks alone."

I shift, trying to move. Their grip not letting up. They don't want me to go, and I don't want to leave. My lips press together, stifling the whimper from what I'm about to do. I guide my hands up their sides to lie on their chests. I straighten up, giving a weak push, and they reluctantly release my hips.

"Yeah, that sounds great." I step away and walk to the back patio with the girls.

"Don't put your arm in the water," Doug says as Heather opens the patio doors.

"Keep it elevated," James says. "Rest it on the outside of the tub."

I stop and peer over my shoulder at them. They're going overboard again.

Doug's body snaps awake. "I'll get you an ice wrap."

"Yeah, good idea." James nods.

"HEY, mother hens." Susan pulls their attention. "Leave the poor girl alone."

James and Doug stop; their eyes immediately dropping. Doug grumbles under his breath as James' foot shuffles against the floor. Both upset over her comment. I huff out a quiet giggle, knowing their efforts would not be so easily dissuaded if the others weren't here with us.

"Fine," James says.

"But you should ice it tonight." Doug's eyes defiantly insist.

I tilt my head. "Ok, I promise."

...

The warmth of the water is soothing. The night air is calm. This is one of those nights that I would be out here with a book. Or walking in the forest. My gaze travels across Jane, Susan, and Heather. This is better. Listening to the girls happily talk about boys, dating, and how they met the men they are with is just what I needed.

"You're being awfully quiet Lily," Heather says. "Come on spill. What's the best date you've ever been on?"

I shrug. "I don't know."

"How do you not know?" Heather squints, her brow furrowing.

"I mean, I don't think I've been on any I can boast about." I shift in my seat, adjusting my arm along the edge of the hot tub. "Nothing like you guys have described. I've been on dinner and movie dates, and they were nice. We'd talk, and I would think there was some chemistry. But there was always something missing. I always ended up leaving their place unsatisfied."

"Have you only ever done 'dinner and a movie' dates?" Susan asks.

"No. When I was younger, we'd go dancing, roller skating, or to amusement parks." I groan. "But I don't like the idea that my high school dates were my best."

Jane sets down her drink. "I'm sorry hon."

"You have nothing to apologize for. It's my fault. I've never been serious about dating. My focus was caring for my sister and grandmother for so long. Plus, I was pursuing my career, then running this property. Dating just kind of got away from me. When I started again, I found out way too quickly that my successful career was a turnoff."

My voice deepens, heating. "They hated that I worked, and they hated that I put my family first. They wanted a fan girl to worship the ground they walked on because they had money. When they found out that wasn't me, they changed. They only cared about getting their dick sucked." Covering my mouth, I stare at them wide-eyed as my heart races. I can't believe I just said that.

Heather's wrist flicks. "Oh, tell me about it."

"I hate when men expect you to give oral, but they won't," Susan says, and I relax.

"Do they satisfy you guys?" I point at their men inside.

"Oh yeah, Matt loves giving oral." Susan places her hand on her chest. "And I love it because it's the only time he ever shuts up."

"Bill isn't that good at oral. But what he does with his dick... Ummm..." Heather quivers as she closes her eyes. "Bill is slow and gentle with me."

"Yeah, Matt, not so much. He likes it fast and rough."

"Zach likes to tie me up and play with me in public." Jane's blunt statement catches me off guard. Heather and Susan titter.

My eyelashes flutter. "Excuse me? He does what to you?"

Jane locks eyes with me. "Zach and I are into bondage and having sex in front of strangers."

"Is she serious?" I ask Heather and Susan.

"Yep," they say with another bout of giggles.

"Our little sweet Jane is quite the heathen," Heather says, and Jane brushes a strand of hair up into her bun, grinning. I peer down into the water and rub my hand over my leg.

"I'm sorry. I didn't mean to make you uncomfortable." Jane leans forward, putting her hand over mine.

I shake my head. "I'm not uncomfortable. It's just…" I grab my forearm. "Uh… Can I ask you guys a personal question?"

"Yeah," Heather says, they nod in agreement.

"…What's it like?"

"What's what like?" Susan asks.

I try to lift my gaze to them, but quickly drop it back to the water. "What's it like to be taken care of… you know… to be satisfied?"

"What do you mean by satisfied?" Heather asks.

"Well…" My face gets warmer. I mumble my question.

"Are you asking what it's like to have an orgasm?" Jane asks and I nod.

"WHAT!" Heather abruptly stands up. "YOU'VE NEVER HAD AN ORGASM?" I peek past her at the guys inside. They are no longer playing their game and are staring at us. "HOW HAVE YOU NEVER HAD AN ORGASM?"

"Heather, sit down!" Susan grabs her wrist. I quickly lower myself further beneath the surface of the water. "The last thing Lily needs right now is more gawking from the cavemen over there."

Heather glances over at the boys. "Shit, I'm sorry, Lily." She sits back down.

Susan sighs. "Yeah, just ignore her. She is like a puppy that can't control itself."

"Uh. No..." Heather folds her arms over her chest. "I am just a passionate person."

The girls laugh, but the tension in my constricted muscles doesn't dissipate.

I risk a peek back inside. James is scolding Matt. Doug is staring out at us. He points deliberately at me as he lifts his arm, then he points at his arm, then back at me. I roll my eyes as I raise my arm out of the water and rest it on the side. He shines a bright smile at me before returning to the game.

"So, seriously," Heather says in a softer voice. "You've never had a man give you an orgasm...?"

I shake my head.

"What about a woman?" Susan asks.

"My sister and her wife asked me the same thing." I pause, sighing. "If it wasn't for them, I wouldn't have known women could have orgasms."

"Really? I just can't imagine..." Heather looks up and to the side. "Like never, ever?"

"Never, ever." The girls stare at me in disbelief.

"Sorry if this is too personal..." Susan says. "But have you tried to masturbate?"

"Yes, I have... I just can't do it. I even saw a sex therapist for a while. She couldn't help, either."

"Why not?" Jane asks.

"Basically, I can't relax enough to let it happen. At this point, I have such a specific idea about it I'm mentally blocking myself from any other alternative." I peer inside the house at Doug and James. "I want my first time to be special... To be by a man's touch."

"No, wa—" Heather's voice becomes muffled. The water ripples, getting my attention. Susan and Jane's hands are placed over her mouth as she glares at them.

"Why don't we change the topic?" Susan asks.

"No more talk about stupid boys," Jane says. "How about we go back inside, grab another drink, and annoy the men with Heather's wedding ideas?"

Heather nods enthusiastically, and the girls remove their hands from her face.

Susan and Heather get out of the tub and as I go to leave, Jane grabs my wrist to stop me.

"We'll be right there," Jane says to them. "I want to talk to Lily."

"Ok," Heather says, and they walk off to the changing room. I smile at Jane and sit beside her.

Jane's gaze flicks down to my stomach. "Does your scar have anything to do with your mental block?"

I knew it! She is gifted. A rush of excitement waves over me. Maybe I finally have someone to talk to about this stuff. "No. My mental block isn't from the scar. An elf cursed me."

"Oh..." Her gaze transfixes under the water.

"So..." I say to ease away the awkward silence. "Can you sense the pain or see it?"

"Both." Jane stares at my arm, her eyes filling with concern. "But my sight is more than aura. I struggle with controlling it sometimes. And I'm sorry if I stepped over the line."

"Could you see what Brian did?"

Jane's eyes glow in the moonlight. "Yes, and I felt your pain when he dislocated your shoulder."

That explains her reaction when she touched me. My eyes widen. "Please don't tell them."

"Why not?" Her eyebrow raises.

I glance down and to the side as I rub my legs. "I don't want James and Doug to treat me like a victim."

"They won't do that, sweetheart." Jane lifts my chin. A sweetness graces her lips.

"You don't know that."

"I know James and Doug. And trust me, they will not view you any differently."

"Do they know what you are?" I blurt out, only realizing that was too blunt when Jane's body leans back from me. "I'm sorry... I didn't mean for that to sound so rude."

"It's all right. You surprised me is all. I've never had anyone ask me that. But yes. James and Doug are the only ones here that know about Zach."

"Oh... I didn't realize that Zach is fae touched as well."

Jane giggles. "Did you just call him fae touched?"

"Yes..." I fidget with my fingers.

"Oh, that is golden." Jane giggles and glances inside. "I can't wait to tell him."

"I take it he isn't fae touched like us?"

"I..." Jane tilts her head, her expression twists. "I'm not fae touched."

"Yes, you are." I motion with my hand, pointing up and down at her. "You were given a gift or you have fae lineage." Jane is still confused. I tilt my head. "Do you not know?"

"I'm not..." Jane peers past me, and I glance over. Zach, James, and Doug are huddling by the window, talking. My eyes shift around, searching. I can't find Matt and Bill anywhere. "I'm not special. Zach is."

"I don't know what Zach is. But you are special."

Jane opens her mouth, then pauses. Her gaze flicks inside again. "Zach's a vampire."

My head instantly snaps in Zach's direction. He waves at me, grinning. No way, I never would have guessed. I'm overjoyed at meeting my first vampire. "What kind?!"

"Just a plain vanilla one." Her lips deviously smirk at Zach. He squints his eyes at her. I chuckle at their playfulness.

The changing room doors clank shut, drawing my attention to Susan and Heather. "Hurry up, you two. I want to plan my wedding."

"Just a few more minutes," Jane calls to them. She turns back to the boys inside and if it wasn't for my ability, I would not have caught her say, "She's almost there."

Zach, James, and Doug leer at us. They heard her. But how?

Zach's gaze shifts to Heather and Susan. Out of the corner of my eye, I notice shadows gliding across the patio floor.

Bill and Matt tip-toe like cartoon villains behind the unsuspecting girls. They grab them. "BOO!"

Heather and Susan's screams harmonize.

"I'm going to kill you." Susan smacks Matt's arm, and he sticks his tongue out at her.

"You guys are going to pay for that," Heather says, as Bill and Matt run away. Glee rings out into the night as the girls chase after them.

Jane's lips move without speaking, grabbing my attention. I stop laughing and follow her gaze to Zach. He is staring at her while the boys roar beside him.

Is he a telepath? Maybe that's how James and Doug heard her. An idea pulls at the corners of my mind.

I lock my gaze on Zach as I slide behind Jane in the water, resting my chin on her shoulder. "Can I have permission to take your beautiful, sweet girl on a date?"

"*Depends on what you have in mind.*" Zach's voice sounds in my mind.

James and Doug's giddiness abruptly stops. Their eyes focus on us. Jane's giggle is sweet as she lifts my hand to touch her lips. My chest burns with desire. I glide my fingertips over Jane's face and down her neck. She leans into my tender caress.

A bolt of electricity flows through me, giving me a rush of confidence. Something I have not felt in years. "*I want to take her into the woods and show Jane how special she is.*"

James' lips move and his voice sounds in my head. "*Fuck, that's hot.*"

My... My... Zach is exceptionally powerful. To experience this depth of telepathy. To be connected to multiple lines of thoughts like this is astounding. My elation fills my features, wanting to test the bounds of his ability further.

I set clear intentions as I think the words, aiming for only him to hear me. "*That's one hell of a power, Zach.*" He winks. The others don't react, and I'm consumed by giddiness at the success of my experiment.

I speak aloud again, directing Zach to use his gift like before. "Oh, James, it's so hot." I playfully lick my lips. James and Doug stiffen up and their eyes widen.

"*Lily's touch is tantalizing.*" Jane exaggerates a sigh of pleasure. "*You don't know what you're missing.*" Her body relaxes into the curve of mine. James stares daggers at Zach.

"What?" Zach leans back from James. "*I didn't think you'd be a perv.*"

"*Yeah, you did,*" Doug says without removing his gaze from Jane and I. Zack smirks and puffs out his chest.

"*Is this what it feels like to be watched?*" I ask, caressing her collarbone. I skim my fingers across her chest. The three of them captivated.

"Yes." Jane's voice drips with honey.

Emotions swirl inside me. I experience things I never have before. They carry a contagious boldness with them. My gaze fixes on James and Doug. "*Do you like to watch?*"

James' lips press together and Doug's eyes light up, telling me without words.

"*Damn right, I do!*" Zach's voice carries loudly through my thoughts.

Jane subtly shakes her head, puffing out a sigh. James and Doug's attention snaps to Zach, but silence fills my mind. The three of them turn their gaze to the sky and press their hands together in prayer.

Zach's voice turns serious as he prays. "*Thank you, Artemisia, for blessing us this evening with this beautiful sight. Praise be on to you, oh Lady of the Moon.*"

I raise my eyebrow and tilt my head to the sky. The moon isn't visible tonight, but their playfulness charms me. I don't think I have ever heard a prayer quite like that to Goddess Artemisia. Jane's amusement is infectious, and I join in the chorus. James and Doug's eyes catch my attention. The space between my legs warms.

I twist Jane's head to face me. "*I think I see what you like about it.*" My fingers tease Jane's neck. She closes her eyes and hums, playing into our fun of toying with them. "*Thank you for giving me a new experience.*"

She smiles at my words and gets close to my lips. They hover over mine as her caressing touch flows over my skin. A blooming need spreads through me. Her touch is euphoric.

I turn my attention to the boys. Their delight radiates from them, spurring my boldness. "So, *what do you say, Zach? Can I whisk your woman away into the forest tomorrow and show her how special she is?*"

"*I don't know. The forest doesn't seem safe for two pretty ladies to be roaming around in all alone.*"

His playful tone lets me mimic him. "*Don't worry, I'm the wicked witch of the forest. None of my beasts will harm her.*" I tilt my head. "*Isn't that right, James?*"

James covers his face. *"You're going to hold this over my head for the rest of my life, aren't you?"*

"Yep."

Zach turns to James. *"That sounds like an embarrassing story. Do tell."*

"Stop ignoring me Zach or—"

"Or, what?" Zach peers over his shoulder at me.

I squint my eyes at him. *"Or... I will have my way with Jane right now."*

Zach's gleaming focuses on James and Doug. *"So, what's the story?"*

Jane and I titter. Doug's arms move as he talks. I no longer hear them in my head. I step out of the hot tub and offer my hand to Jane. "Come on, let's go get undressed."

In the changing room, I take off my suit when Jane asks, "What's so important about the forest?"

"I'd like you to meet Jade, the fae mother of this forest. I think she can help you learn to control your gift."

Jane's curiosity seeps into her voice. "You actually think I'm gifted?"

"Yes, I do." I glance at her and catch her staring at my breasts. "I have fae blood but am also fae touched. By Jade herself, in fact. I mean, she wasn't the only one. I've been touched by four others. Jade's elven mates, Liam and Greyson. You'd really like them. They..." I pause, caught off guard by her eyes.

Crap, I was rambling again. "Anyway, what I'm trying to say is that they can teach you how to control your gift. Just like they did for me. Trust me. It's more than just good intuition, Jane."

I hang my suit up on the drying line, completely comfortable. My lashes flutter as it dawns on me. I haven't felt this comfortable in my own skin in ages. Is it because of Jane? I glance over at her, admiring her beauty. Maybe? Or maybe it's because I'm so relaxed after spending time with new friends.

All the nerves I had at the beginning of the night are now gone. I've shared things I haven't talked about with anyone in ages. I wonder if I can tell James and Doug I'm gifted, too. That I'm—

A squeak gets my attention and I scan the room. Jane hangs her suit up. I put a finger to my lips and point at the door. We wrap ourselves in towels and I quickly fling the doors open. "Can I help you?"

Doug, James, and Zach comically step back, acting guilty. I silence my giggle, attempting to remain intimidating.

"Shame on you all." Jane bounces her finger at them, continuing the ruse to scold them. "Trying to catch a peek at us sweet, vulnerable ladies."

"Sorry, dear." Zach drops his head to his chest, feigning his innocence. "They made me do it."

"Oh, don't play coy with me, you troublemaker." Jane jabs her finger into his peck. His smirk lights up his face. He quickly picks her up into his arms and she wraps her legs around his waist.

"You caught me. I can't resist you when you are naked." Zach pinches her butt, and she lets out an adorable squeal.

I giggle at their cute display of affection. This entire night I've been enjoying observing these interactions. Watching the couples, seeing what it's like to have someone love you back. It's refreshing to view it up close with people that aren't my family.

James and Doug's gaze travel over them, lust glimmering in them. I push aside the knot brewing in my stomach.

"Zach, you're a bad influence on My Knights," I say, my honeyed tone drawing out the last two words. The four of them eye me as I pull my bun apart.

"Oh, yeah?" Zach asks.

"Mhmm..." I steady my gaze on James and Doug, curious if they are as fond of their titles as I am of mine. "My Knights are gentlemen."

I hold their eyes carefully, but the light doesn't let me know what I desire. Zach's laughter rings out.

James puffs out his chest. "See we're gentlemen."

"Perfect gentlemen," Doug says.

Zach sets Jane down, the towel exposing her ass as he does. His gaze locks with mine. "What kind of lies have they been telling you?"

"Hey..." James crosses his arms. "I take offense to that."

Doug stands straighter. "Yeah, we don't lie. Our actions speak for themselves."

My lips lift into my cheeks. I step into a walled-off part of the room, leaving the curtain open as I dress. They continue to bicker as I put my bra and underwear on.

"Please..." Zach's tone prods them. "I've met enough gentlemen in my lifetime to know that you two don't fit the picture."

"Oh, is that right?" I can hear through his tone how Doug is standing now, defensively. That cocky smirk shining on his face. The image makes my nerves dance under my skin.

"Well, I'll have you know..." James' tone deepens, filling with pride. Another image flashes in my mind, honing in on the way his muscles tense and pronounce. "We caught her naked before and kept our hands to ourselves."

I snort. "No, you didn't." I peek my head out, wanting my imagination to come to life. My stomach drops into an abyss, tearing my emotions out of my heart, sending me into a freefall. This isn't what I expected.

Jane's bare skin glimmers under the light. All eyes are on her. The way her perfect rosy complexion accentuates the shape of her ass. I can understand their attraction to her. It sobers me, reminding me why I set boundaries. Why I can't go any further than entertaining these fanciful thoughts.

James and Doug stand at attention, noticing me. I duck my head back into the stall. I squeeze my eyes shut. Of course, it wasn't me they were watching.

"Lily, it's not what it looks like." James' tone pleads with me.

"We can explain." The strain in Doug's voice shoots envy through my veins.

Explain? You have nothing to explain. I get it.

I scrutinize my body, it's flaws stabbing me. My mouth dries, my envy a spreading infection. It rages through my blood like a storm. It hurts, the visual confirmation that I'm not what they want. I shouldn't be surprised.

Strangely, I calm. It doesn't matter. I promised myself yesterday that this was going to be MY time. To find out what I like and want. I exhale, making room for my confidence to fill me again.

I grab my clothes and step out of the stall, ignoring their faces. I put my pants on. "You don't have to explain." The distinct sound of James' inhale- the one he makes before he speaks- hits my ear. "OR apologize for!" I snap before he says anything.

My leg lifts, propping up on the bench. I bend over it to fix the fabric that has bunched up around my calf. "It's ok..." My gaze rolls to Jane, her bra and thong now on. "I understand the appeal."

I step toward them and, keeping my focus on Jane. I glow with seduction. Hoping I'm showing them it's ok to pick up where we left off earlier. "I like the way Jane looks, too."

Jane reaches out to me, her fingertips trailing up my arm. "We like the way you look, too."

I huff, ignoring her comment. Instead, focusing on being touched like this, even if it goes nowhere. I caress Jane's cheek, tucking a loose strand of hair behind her ear. She leans into my touch, her eyes giving me what I crave. Our hands explore each other softly. We pay no mind to the others.

No one has ever taken the time to touch me like this. I think back. There was that short moment in the hot tub when James and Doug caressed my stomach. My emotions flush through my cheeks, and I step softly away from the warmth of Jane's fingers. I rapidly blink before the flush reaches my eyes.

"Damn," Zach says at the same time I stepped away, grabbing our attention. He peeks outside. "Just when it was getting good." He turns back to us. "We have to wrap it up. They are on their way back."

Of course, they are. Nothing ever lasts for me. I take a deep breath as I put my shirt on. I turn to James and Doug. "Is everyone still spending the night?"

"We told them they could, but I'm not sure," James says.

"We can ask them in a minute," Doug says.

I turn to Jane as she pulls her dress over her head. "Are you guys staying?"

"Yeah." Jane fluffs out her dress. "Why?"

I peer into her caramel eyes. "I was just curious if you would stay the afternoon as well?"

"We'd love to." Jane grabs my hand, and we walk between the boys back into the house.

CHAPTER 9

FUN IN THE SUN

JANE

SUNDAY, JULY 31ST

Lily reaches up to unhook the last piece of the banner from the wall; Pain from the movement spills out on her face. She is so stubborn, so independent. It makes me wonder how long she's had to play the role of caretaker. For herself and for others. I take the banner from her as she steps down the ladder.

"What kind of photography do you do?" Lily's voice jolts me from my thoughts, reminding me what we were talking about.

"I specialize in boudoir photos."

Lily's eyes shine in the sunlight. "That sounds like so much fun." We go back to the pool table to finish packing up the party decorations. "How did you meet Zach through work then?"

"He's my boss's accountant. She introduced us." A giggle escapes, slipping past my lips as a memory resurfaces. Lily's eyes question my random outburst. "Sorry..." I fight the laughter off and go on. "I was just remembering the first time he asked me out. The first time out of many."

Lily tilts her head. "What do you mean by many? Like in the movies when the guy follows the girl around begging for dates, till she finally gives in?"

My throat belts out joyously.

"Hey, *I was not that bad.*" Zach projects his thought desperately trying to defend himself. I glance out the patio window. He, James, and Doug are still playing volleyball in the pool.

I ignore him and continue talking with Lily. "It was just like that. He even pulled the..." I deepen my voice to mock him. "I need you to come to my office to explain this charge to me- bit."

"No way..." Lily beams, staring out the window at them. "That's hilarious."

Zach squints his eyes at me, ignoring the game. He snatches the ball out of the air without looking, successfully showing off his skills. James throws his hands up as Doug points at Zach. They bicker at him. I can't make out what they are saying, but I'm sure they are accusing him of using his gift to cheat. Lily's gleeful melody rings out like a beautiful bell chime.

"All right, you had your fun. She's impressed." I shoo him away. "Now no more interruptions."

"And keep your ears to yourself." Lily steps beside me. "You promised us alone time."

Zach bows his head at us before turning back to James and Doug.

"So anyway…" I tell Lily all about how Zach swept me off my feet and how I found out what he was. It's been so long since I've shared this story, I find myself being carried away by the details.

An icy shiver flows over me, and I turn toward Lily. She is curled up by the window, gazing out at them. I was so engrossed in my gabbing that I didn't realize her mood had dipped again. Her emotions have been a roller coaster all morning. At lunch, she was thoroughly turbulent.

From where I sit, I can see the dull sadness that has crept into her eyes. I lay my hand on her knee and her features brighten.

"I'm sorry, I got distracted," she says, as if out of habit.

Knowing she put a mask on, I gently push at her defenses. "What's wrong?" She fidgets with her fingers and checks outside. I hold her hand. "Sweetheart, it's ok. I promise you he isn't listening. You can talk to me."

"Nothing's wrong per se… I was just thinking about what you said. As James would say, it struck a chord."

"I didn't mean to upset you."

"You didn't upset me. I'm jealous." Lily blazes with passion. Her spirit lifts, and warmth fills her.

The sudden wave of happiness confuses me. I study her, trying to unravel the contradiction. "I don't follow."

"I've never experienced what you have. I've only ever seen or read about it." Lily peers outside again, and I follow her gaze. "Doug and James said they would tell me what it's like, but they never did. But hearing your story. It gives me hope. Proves that it's not just fantasy."

"What's not a fantasy?"

"This!" She motions between me and Zach. "You. Him. Just knowing that there are men out there who actually care about pleasing their woman makes me happy. How did Matt put it? They should be giving me their attention no matter what we're doing." She lets out a light-hearted chuckle. "He's right. I should have dates that are better than my grocery shopping trips with James and Doug."

"Well, he's not wrong. You deserve that too."

Lily twirls a strand of her hair around her finger. Her emotions tittering. "Can I ask you something?"

"Of course."

"Do you think they would get upset if I told them?"

I dampen the rush of excitement that flows through me at the idea. I mentally cross my fingers, hoping she wants to share her romantic feelings with them. My voice piques with interest. "Tell them about what?"

"Everything." She hunches over and sighs. "The dislocation. That I'm part Fae and have magical powers. I never gave them the full story behind my scar, either." She hesitates. "I'm scared to open up to them. I've never talked about my past or who I am with anyone that wasn't family."

I smile, yearning to ease her fears. "You have nothing to worry about. They are both very accepting. They're allies to the magical community, after all." I lift her chin, capturing her gaze. "They would love to know you better. That includes the parts that are hard to talk about."

I pause, giving her a moment to process. "Have they ever proven they can't handle something? Especially when it comes to you?"

Her eyes widen in shock. She shakes her head in dismissal of the idea. Her big green eyes betraying her, giving me the answer to my question. We share a comfortable moment of silence as I run my fingertips over her jawline. "You could always start with something fun. Ease your way into the hard stuff."

Her face lights up with an idea. "Do you think they would get mad if I played with them?"

"Ummm." I raise my eyebrow and press my lips together.

Her cheeks flush. "NO... That's not what I meant."

The heat from her desire burns, spreading to me. *Are you sure about that...?* "What did you mean, then?"

"I meant; can they take a joke? Like if I threw a bucket of water on their heads- kind of play." Lily's gaze travels outside. "Do you think they'd get upset?"

Excitement bubbles up inside of me, understanding her train of thought now. The prospect of getting back at them is delicious.

"Absolutely not." My voice squeaks. "If they did, I would never let them live it down. Considering all the times they have pranked me, and the others over the years... They have it coming. I'm so down."

...

We step out onto the patio in our swimsuits, and all eyes are on us. Their leering is apparent. The sudden attention plummets Lily's confidence. My mess up last night hit her hard. It devastated her to see me naked in front of them. She would never admit that, but I know what I felt. I should have realized sooner.

Ugh... I'm so stupid.

Though James and Doug's idiot statements didn't help either, that was the last thing she needed to hear.

We sit down on the edge of the pool to let our legs dangle. The cool water is refreshing in this heat wave. We've had no reprieve from the sun in over a week. Lily's anxiety exudes from her as she fidgets with her arm wrap. Her gaze trembles, unable to steady on James and Doug. The three of them swim to the side of the pool, grabbing their drinks.

"Would you ladies care to join us?" James asks, breaking the silence.

I wait for Lily to speak. My shoulders slump after a moment's pause and I say, "No, thank you. We are fine for now."

"*Is she ok?*" Zach silently asks as James and Doug study Lily.

"*No, she's scared to open up to them.*"

"*Is she finally going to tell them how she feels? Because the tension between them is suffocating.*" Zach lets out an exasperated sigh. "*I don't know how much more I can handle.*"

I match his sigh. "*Unfortunately, no.*" Lily leans in closer to me. I lay my hand on her thigh. "It's ok, go ahead."

"I don't know where to start." Her voice shakes.

"Start with Brian. That won't be too bad. Then you can play with them. Wink. Wink." I nudge her as Zach chokes on his beer.

Doug grabs Zach's arm. "You ok dude?"

Zach nods his head as he coughs into his elbow.

"Hey, Lily has something she wants to talk to you about." I motion with my eyes for Lily to go ahead. The boys give her their attention.

Lily holds onto her bicep, her arm resting under her breasts, lifting them. "So, I don't want you to get upset, because it's no big deal. It happens all the time. It's an old injury... But I know if I tell you, you're going to freak out," she says without taking a breath.

Her eyes stay transfixed on the rippling water. I rub her thigh, trying to get her to calm down as she practically repeats herself. "When I wanted to be a dancer, I injured myself and I mean it all worked out in the end for me, but..."

Her word vomit keeps going, she is talking in circles, and my touch isn't doing anything for her. James and Doug quickly swim over and place their hands on either side of her knees. She instantly calms and lifts her head to them, her voice trailing off. Their faces shine softly for her.

Zach wraps his arm behind me, and I pout at him. "*You have no idea how good they make her feel.*"

"*I can see it.*"

"*I don't know how she has lasted this long.*"

Lily's voice finally finds the courage to speak. "I didn't tell everyone the whole story last night."

A fiery bolt shoots up my arm. My gaze draws to Lily's knees. James and Doug's grasp has tightened slightly. I pull my hand away, unable to take the heat spreading through her. As Lily shifts in her seat, her legs open slightly. My stomach flips from her arousal.

"Go on," Doug says.

"When Brian grabbed me, he dislocated my shoulder."

"Damn it, Lily." James' protective anger rages. He steps closer to her, his hand gliding up her thigh as he does. "Why didn't you tell us?"

"We don't like it when you hide things from us." Doug steps closer, following James' lead.

Her legs open wider. "I wasn't hiding it. It's just not that big of a deal. It dislocates all the time."

Doug's eye twitches. "If it's no big deal, then why didn't you tell us?"

"Because I was worried you would treat me differently. Just like everyone else. I don't like it when people do that to me. I'm not a helpless victim!"

The need to comfort her shines in their eyes. "We know you're not," James says.

"We would never treat you that way because of somebody else's actions," Doug says. They ache to wash away her pain. Their desire is so strong, it breezes over me. It's contagious.

"We promise we will never look at you any differently." James' hand trails to her stomach.

"Remember." Doug's hand following, nestling in next to his.

A wave of emotions washes over the three of them. Those words igniting Lily's desire. *It's more than I can handle.* "AHH…" I scream into Zach's head. "Kiss *already.*"

"*Calm down.*"

I glare at Zach. "*If I was Lily and that worked up. I'd be tearing your clothes to shreds and bouncing on your cock so hard, you'd be worried I was gonna break it.*"

"*You that turned on?*"

I whimper in his head. "*James and Doug want her so badly. I don't understand how she thinks they don't want her.*"

"*I don't—*"

"See Zach," Lily says, interrupting our thoughts. "My Knights are gentlemen."

Zach's gaze bounces, taking the three of them in. "Looks to me like they are copping a feel."

Lily's chest instantly blotches as James and Doug remove their hands from her. Doug points at Zach. "We would never disrespect Lady Lily."

James puffs out his chest. "But you wouldn't know that since you're not a gentleman."

"Hey!" I splash James in the face with water. "He is plenty gentle."

"Not from what I've seen." James splashes back, but Zach shields me.

"I'm a gentleman. I defend my lady." He grins.

"One time doesn't count." Doug expertly kicks up the water, splashing Zach, Lily, and me.

Lily's laughter bursts out at their childish play. James and Doug turn their backs on us as the three of them shoot water at each other. Lily's eyes light up as she nudges me.

She flicks her fingers and the water splashes up, hitting them in the back. They spin to face us, and Lily raises her hands.

"Wasn't me!" She beams and twists her hands from side to side. "See all dry."

Zach chuckles, knowing full well that's a lie. Lily's magic flows, forming into something deviously beautiful. I hold in my elation, waiting for my revenge.

James taunts Zach. "Having your woman fight your battle for you."

"Not very gentlemen-like," Doug says.

They turn around and something catches their eye. Their heads tilt back, taking in the sight. Three swirling spheres of water floating in the air. Lily's finger flicks down, dropping the spheres over each of their heads with a magnificent splash.

Lily and I roar, overjoyed. Their reactions, priceless.

Zach tilts his head. "Really, Lily? Me too?"

James and Doug turn, staring wide-eyed at Lily. She wipes the happy tears from her eyes and resumes the show. She pinches her fingers above the water and pulls her hand upward gracefully. The water follows her movement. She brings the pocket of water to her mouth and blows, scattering it into bubbles that dance around James and Doug.

"This is so cool. You're a water bender!" James shouts as he throws his hands up, elated.

"You are amazing," Doug's soft awed tone barely audible over James' liveliness.

Lily tucks her fingers behind her ear out of habit, even though there is no hair to follow her command. The bubbles pop. "I'm not just a water bender."

James rushes through the water to her, his eyes bursting with energy. "What else can you do?"

"James," Doug grabs his arm.

"Sorry, Lily." James lowers his gaze.

"It's ok. I get it. I get giddy too when Mother teaches me something new."

"Mother?" Doug questions.

"Mother is a title. Her name is Jade, and she is the Dryad of this forest." She looks at James. "Jade and her two elven mates, Liam and Greyson, are to me what Doug's family is to you."

"We still have elves here?" Zach glides over, his curiosity piqued. "I thought they all left."

"They are the only two. The rest left when I was fifteen."

"So, this forest truly is magical?!" James tries to contain his excitement.

"Yes."

Doug motions his hand out toward the forest. "Is that why you have such a connection to this place?"

"It's more than that. I'm one of its protectors." Lily leans over the water, her cleavage perfectly on display. "James, the reason I tease you about calling me the wicked witch of the forest is because, well, that's what I am. I have fae blood flowing through my veins and there is so much more that I can do. I can..."

I inch my hand to her back, wanting to push her into them. They yearn to touch her. Just a little nudge would be all it would take to get those glorious, envy-inducing tits to fall on James' face.

"*Jane.*" Zach's stern voice rings in my head. "*Don't you dare! Lily is enjoying flustering them. Look at her eyes. They are the same as when she was touching you last night.*"

I twist my body and notice the glow in her eyes. Zach is right. "*Awe.*" I bat my eyelashes at him. "*Please?*"

"*Oh, don't give me those doe eyes. Let them figure this out on their own.*"

"*Fine.*" I huff and give Lily my attention, resisting the urge to intervene.

She points at a hanging plant behind us. Its foliage grows and unfurls in new leaves and vines, cascading down to the floor. "I can also talk to plants and animals."

"You're shittin' me!" James bounces with joy.

Doug can't contain his excitement anymore either. Lily beams. Her confidence drowns her anxiety and hesitance away. This is the beautiful confidence I saw when she wiped the floor with the boys, winning that game last night. They go on talking and I observe their every move. This is them. How they act when they are alone.

When James and Doug talked about her before, I didn't realize just how happy they were. But now it's as plain as day.

"*Come here.*" Zach takes me into the pool, resting my back against his body. "*You need to cool down.*"

"*Water won't be enough to cool me off.*" I reach behind me and gently capture him in my hand.

"No. No..." Zach grabs my wrist. "*You naughty girl. You're supposed to be listening to Lily and helping her come out of her shell.*"

"*Fucking them will help her come out of her shell.*" I snip at him.

Zach chuckles as Lily stands up and walks off. Her hips sway, hypnotizing me. James and Doug walk out of the pool, their gaze never wavering. Zach's member twitches in my hand, delighting me. I squeeze him, making him moan.

"*You like that ass too, don't you, baby?*" My palm rubs over him. He purrs for me. "*Do you want to see them together?*"

"*Mmmm... You're not playing fair. You want to watch them care for her too.*" I squeak as he picks me up and throws me over his shoulder. He smacks my ass. "*I'll give you what you want when we get home.*"

Zach catches up with them in a second. Just in time for me to hear Lily's voice. "You sure?"

"Yeah, of course, we have enough food," James says, puzzling me about what I missed.

"It's no big deal to add a few more plates," Doug says.

Lily's voice rises. "Jane, are you cool with meeting Jade and them tonight?"

I easily piece together the part of the conversation I missed and say, "Of course. We'd love to meet them."

Zach sets me down. The garden clearing surrounds us and Lily's smile shines in the sunlight. She keeps her eyes on me, and I note a hint of mischief there, mixing with the green. In the very next moment, the ground beneath me shifts and Zach swiftly steps away from me. I fall back softly onto the moss bed that sprung up from the earth.

My giddiness explodes this time. "Ohhhh Lily! It's like I'm on a cloud. It's so soft and fluffy!"

Lily's eyes captivate me as she joins me on the bed. She lifts her hand delicately, creating a flower canopy to shade us from the heat. "I'm glad you like it. You guys don't know how exciting this is for me. I've never shared my gifts with friends before."

...

The shade paints pretty patterns over our skin. We bask in the warmth of sunshine and each other's company. I sit comfortably between Lily's legs as she plays with my hair. The boys sit across from us in their custom-made moss lawn chairs.

The contagious joy of new beginnings energizes the group. Zach is just as giddy to show off his strength as Lily creates things for him to punch through. He doesn't get many chances like this. She is just as enthralled with him as we are with her.

My lashes flutter in amazement as Lily makes a phone call through a plant. She invites her adoptive parents, Jade, Liam, and Greyson over for dinner. A chipmunk crawls into my lap as Lily politely asks him if his friends can go find Snowball.

"Who's Snowball?" I ask.

"That's a surprise." Her eyes light up as she grins from ear to ear.

We swap stories, learning more about each other's worlds as the performance of abilities carries on.

Lily stops braiding my hair to place her hand over her throat. A cat's roar echoes out of her. James and Doug pose excitedly as she places her hands over their throats. She tells them to scream, and as they do, the sound transforms into the glory of squealing anime schoolgirls. I clench my side from the painful, tear-inducing joy that bounds from all of us.

The boys were so excited by the big things that I'm pretty sure they missed a bunch of the smaller details. Like how Lily placed a sound barrier around the garden patio, and Doug and James' apartments. And they definitely missed the explanation on her heightened hearing, a bloodline trait that both Lily and Layla share. I titter at the irony.

"There. All done." Lily places my braid over my shoulder. The intricate design she made is beautiful.

"Thank you." I run my fingers over it, my spirit glowing under her attentions. "It's stunning." I quickly turn over, getting on all fours to straddle her leg. "Ok, my turn."

Her cheeks turn beat red and I don't need Zach's ability to know what she's thinking. I nestle my body behind her and play with her hair, trailing patterns of lavish peace through the strands.

I get lost in my task, focusing on the details. Zach and her talk about the similarities between his clan's ability to shadow walk, and the tree step ability she is trying to learn, but most of it goes over my head.

They go on and on, talking circles around a bunch of things I don't understand. It's like they are talking in another language, all this magic stuff. I shake my head at the thought of learning any of it myself. They make it sound so easy, but I know it's not.

I peek around Lily, catching James and Doug as they lean back in their moss chairs, gazing at her. Their dreamy eyes tell me they aren't following the conversation either. The breeze brushes over my skin, carrying their intentions to me. Their longing burns just as brilliantly as Lily's.

I shift, getting their attention, and wiggle my eyebrows at them while jerking my head toward Lily. Their eyes widen, fixating on us as I stroke my fingertips over Lily's arm.

Lily leans back on my chest, her body melting into mine like it did last night. As she relaxes, her speech only grows more fluent. Her conversation with Zach never falters as she goes on about her gift of intuition- or foresight- as she calls it.

Her fingers trail circles over my leg. My mind drifts, trying to figure out why she leans into me so easily, why she enjoys my touch so much. It's almost like she's exploring her sexuality, but that's not what this is. She isn't into women; I can sense that much. So why?

I study James and Doug, trying to piece the puzzle together as they watch her. Their eyes follow my hands, each caress of her pale skin. My hand flows over her stomach and Lily's emotions skyrocket. Her eyes enchant me.

Something inside of her opens up, and I realize what this is. She's never experienced this. She's never felt love. The ache from earlier, the urge to wash away her pain that came from James and Doug, floods through me now from my own heart.

Lily places her hand over mine, stopping my caress. Her anxiety flares. Fear consumes her eyes. Her pain shoots up my arm.

"It's ok..." Lily's voice softens, her eyes dulling. "You can't take this pain away."

James and Doug quickly stand, stepping to her. "Lily, what's wrong?" James asks.

Lily sits up and scooches to the edge of the moss bed. "I want to tell you about..." Her voice falters as she lays her hand on her stomach. "This... It's just..." Her emotions waver. "It's difficult for me to talk about. My family and my therapist are the only ones I've ever told."

Doug lays his hand on her knee. "There is no need to rush."

"We can take it nice and slow." James grabs her thigh.

Excitement, confusion, fear, desire, and anger swirl like a hurricane of flavor inside of her. Sending my senses into overdrive. Lily looks sternly at James and then at Doug. "Can you promise me something?"

"Anything," James says.

"I want to share this with you. But I want something in return. When I'm done telling you my story in all its horrific details, you'll **explain**," Lily bites out the word, "this thing you've got going on with them."

James rubs the back of his neck as Doug hunches his back. I giggle as I scoot to her side, my feet dangling off the side.

Zach's eyes light up with excitement. "Oh, now that is a juicy and embarrassing tale."

"We met at the sex club I work at," I say, teasing the group with my tone.

She blinks rapidly. "Wait, I thought you were a photographer?"

"I am... at the club—"

"Hey, no spoilers," James says.

"Lily needs to finish first." Doug's voice is adamant. Lily rolls her eyes, hiding the spark that lit them up. The way their words affect her never ceases to amaze me.

"Go ahead," James says.

Lily shakes her head. "I'm not letting you weasel your way out of this like you did to me last time in the hot tub." She stares daggers at them. "You need to promise that you'll tell me."

"Ok, we promise," James says for them and Doug nods in agreement.

Lily stares Doug down. "Say it!"

I press my lips together, holding back my giddiness as Doug challenges her gaze. His lip twitches. "We promise."

Lily motions for them to sit. "It's awkward with you both so close, do you mind?" James and Doug nod and sit down. Even though they're not much further away, Lily relaxes. She keeps her eyes on them. "I got this scar, protecting my sister." She takes a deep breath. "From a drunk man that wanted to rape Leilani when she was eleven."

Fury from all three men floods over me in waves. My rage mixes in with theirs. It flows into a sort of protective bubble surrounding us, holding space for Lily to share her story.

Lily continues, telling us about her biological alcoholic parent's party. Putting Layla to bed and the bad feeling she got while drying off after her shower. How she found her father's friend standing over Layla's bed while she slept. What she had to do to get him away from her.

She explains everything. The pain he dealt her shocks me, spreading goosebumps. I catch the hidden suffering in between the lines of all the things she doesn't say.

She tells us about the fear she felt. How it was replaced by momentary relief when he was done using her body in only two minutes. How that relief turned into something else when a great rage built up inside of him. The disgust sewn into his face and words.

Something inside James and Doug snaps, their emotions spiking.

She tells us about how he let that rage fuel him in that moment, using it to choke her. Her attempt at kneeing him in the balls to keep him away from her. Then... the knife.

A soft pain runs along my stomach. I wince as the taste of bile floods my mouth.

"*You ok, sweetie?*" Zach silently asks me, his worried gaze travels over me.

"*I'm ok,*" I assure him and twist to see if Lily noticed my reaction. A sigh of relief passes my lips. She hasn't.

She has paused her story here. I study her face. Her gaze is steady, lingering on James and Doug. It's almost like she is searching, waiting for something to happen. She's confused and I don't understand; What outcome was she expecting?

I wait another moment before asking, "Did he take your virginity?"

The corner of her lip peaks into her cheek. "I've never been asked that before."

I match her smile, remembering my words from last night.

"No. Though my first experience was only a few days before that. The boy broke up with me a few days later when we returned to school. It embarrassed him to be seen with me."

James and Doug growl. Zach shoots a glare at them, and the vein in his neck bulges slightly. He turns to Lily. "Continue."

She squints her eyes at him. "What did you say?"

I hide my delight at her quick intuition. She has already learned his tell for when he is using his telepathy.

"Nothing. I just told them to calm their shit."

Lily turns to James and Doug. Her spirit lifting. "It's ok, the worst of the story is over. It's only funny from here on out." That brings a flavor of shock to their emotions.

"There is nothing funny about you being raped, Lily." Doug's face is stern and unyielding.

"I know... It's what comes next. Finding humor, and giving myself permission to laugh over this, has helped me heal."

"So, tell me how you bleeding out is funny." James dramatically gestures for her to proceed; exasperation and anger radiate from his eyes.

"Because the fucker had hemophobia... He fainted."

Zach is the first to laugh, and I quickly join in. James and Doug's composure slips into a smile, keeping their amusement at bay.

I gain control of myself. My curiosity wanting to know. "How much blood did you lose?"

"Why?" Her eyebrow lifts adorably. "Do you know a thing or two about blood loss?"

"Yeah, she does!" Zach flashes his fangs and dashes between my legs. "She enjoys losing it right here."

He tickles my inner thigh, and I fall back, giggling. Lily shifts in her seat, intrigued. Zach takes notice of Lily's gawking. He grins widely to show off his fangs from between my legs.

"Yeah, it shows," Doug says with sass. "Maybe you should slow down on your drinking."

"We know that belly isn't from beer, you glutton."

Zach spins around to face them. "Your just jealous."

I lean up on my elbows, enjoying the teasing. Doug and James shake their heads.

"Nope, I'm good," James says.

"No thanks, not interested," Doug says. "That's all you, bro." Zach and I both give him the same questioning eye. Doug leans his body back, raising his eyebrow. "What?"

"Well..." Zach points at him. "I figured your affinity for biting would leave you eager for the taste of blood."

Doug's anxiety flares as embarrassment consumes him. His eyes flash to Lily. "Again..." He stares daggers at Zach. "Not interested."

"Not everyone wants to be a vampire, Zach." James gives him the same 'what the fuck dude' look. "Now can we get back to Lily? She still needs to finish."

Lily blushes and lays her hand over her stomach. It flips with excitement. "I only lost a pint and a half." Her voice softens as she pushes her lust aside.

"How?" Zack's eyes glance down. "You had to of lost more than that."

"No. Thanks to Layla, I didn't." Lily tells us how her manic sister hilariously stuck pads to her wound to stop the bleeding. How she wrapped her up as best she could. I sit back up as Zach leans against the bed next to me. She tells us about stealing her parent's car to get Layla to safety and then getting to the hospital.

"I got patched up. Had him arrested. Went back to school, got dumped, and that same day I passed by this forest." She gestures to the trees beside us. "I went for a walk. Met a giant white-talking cat, who I named Snowball. She sent me on a quest, and another looong story later... I got these superpowers!"

Her eyes light up. The four of us on the edge of our seats waiting for more.

"Oh, come on!" I throw my hands up in frustration, knowing full well she is holding back on purpose. "You can't end a story like that. That's not fair."

"Unfortunately, that's not my story to tell." She smiles coyly. "When you meet Jade, if she wishes to tell you, then you'll hear it." Lily bends toward James and Doug, and their bodies stiffen. "I finished first, so now it's only fair that you go."

James scooches to the edge of his seat, his desire for her growing. "But, Lady Lily, you're not done."

"It would be unfair to leave you unsatisfied, My Lady." Doug gently rests his hand on her knee. She explodes with excitement at his touch.

I hold Zach's hand and fan myself. Lily moves the ugly braid I gave her and tilts her head, exposing her neck to them. "Then don't." Her sultry eyes spark lustful fireworks off inside them. "You promised to tell me what it's like."

Their elation for her makes my clit ache with its own yearning. Zach leans into my leg, his hard cock pressing into me. "*Fuck babe.*" His husky tone echoes in my head. "*I owe you an apology. This is intense. How can they—*"

"I want to know more about this sex club." Lily grabs my leg, getting my attention. "And all the delicious details of how you know this beauty so intimately." Her eyes make me swoon. Lily caresses my chin. "You won't leave me hanging? Right, Jane?"

"Don't worry Lily, if they don't take you there..." My fiery gaze sets its sights on Doug and James. "I will."

"Sweetie," Zach runs his fingertips along my arm. "Since you always get us going, why don't you start?"

"I work at a club called The Rabbit Hole." I turn my body to face her and lean back against Zach. "A year after they opened, I helped co-organize an invitation only event. I called Heather, and she helped design costumes for the night's festivities. So, of course, I invited her. But she couldn't make it, giving her invite to James and Doug."

"And that's when all the shenanigans started!" Zach booms with energy. "Jane mistook them for a couple and left them in a room filled with male strippers."

Lily hides her giggle under her hand.

"Don't laugh," Doug says.

James pokes her leg. "You did the same thing when you first met us, too."

"Seriously?" I grin from ear to ear.

"Yep." Lily unapologetically chortles.

Zach's fit of laughter rings out, earning him a glare from James. Doug sighs and drops his chin to his chest.

Lily interrupts. "So, is that it?"

"Not quite." James' eyes gleam with excitement. "Not wanting to embarrass Jane. Doug and I thought it was a good idea to go exploring."

"But we didn't realize how big the place was."

"And down the rabbit hole, we went."

"We found the female stripper room," Doug goes on, both of them taking turns to tell bits of the story. "Then we made our way to a bondage show lounge area."

"We didn't stay long, soon heading further down the hall. That's when we found a hidden entrance." Enthusiasm exudes from James. "So, being the brave knights we are, we headed down the stairs and made our way to another set of doors. The guards didn't stop us, so we just went right on into the basement."

Zach grunts and crosses his arms. "My dumbass clan mates thought that since they weren't drunk, they must not be human. Nor did they ask for their pass."

James sits up straight, beaming proudly. "They thought I was a shapeshifter because of these muscles." James flexes and Lily and I chuckle. Doug and Zach roll their eyes.

"That's when we found out we were in the wrong part of town." Doug continues.

Lily nestles into me, her feet cuddled under her. Her eyes stay glued to them as they describe the women and the things that were done to them. They weave the story seamlessly in and out of its turns, building a labyrinth of desire. Even I am mystified. I wrap my arm around Lily, enjoying the pull of her curiosity.

"Don't keep her waiting." I flick my wrist to shoo them along. "Get to the good part."

"The next performance was Zach and Jane," Doug announces dramatically. "Zach brought her up onto the stage and slowly revealed her naked body to us."

"He suspended her on a bar that hung from the ceiling and thrust his fingers into her."

Being this close to Lily, every sensation that courses through her travels to me. The way her nipples harden, her wet lips, and her stomach swirling with desire. Doug describes me cumming and my yearning heats between my legs. Both the description and the memory warming my body.

Zach's fingers brush my thigh. "*Your arousal smells so sweet. Mixed with hers, it's divine.*" His touch draws circles over my hip. "*You would love the taste of Lily.*" I bite my lip and moan for him. "*Can you feel how wet they make her?*"

"*Can you see how much they want her?*" I purr.

They replay our story in slow, sensual detail. Their eyes hungry, savoring each of Lily's subtle reactions. They describe the promise ceremony of Zach claiming me to become his life partner and sealing the deal with a bite.

Her clit tingles, sending a jolt of pleasure straight to mine. It's almost too much. The desire they have for Lily, the way they wish they could do this to her; It washes over me, enchanting me.

The way they narrate our lovemaking makes my eyes water. James and Doug stand, ending on the beautiful note of our big finish.

James' eyes comfort her as his thumb brushes over Lily's cheek. It hits me. Those aren't my tears.

"Why are you crying?" I ask Lily, but she doesn't turn to me.

She keeps her eyes on them. "That's what it's supposed to be like, isn't it?"

"Yes, My Lady," Doug says. "That is how a man is supposed to care for a woman."

Their yearning makes me want to weep. They want more than just sex. They want to care for her. Make her happy. Show her she deserves so much more.

Zach's hand reaches for Lily, and she flinches. James' hand immediately latches onto Zach's forearm, and Doug's anger explodes onto Zach. The three of them crowd each other, the sudden tension pulsing through the space.

"You do NOT have permission to touch her." Doug bites out at Zach.

My senses snap back together, realizing Lily can't breathe. "Oh, my." I intertwine her arm in mine. "This is getting exciting."

Lily exhales. Zach smirks, breaking the surface tension, and James lets go of him. They remain standing, their eyes darting between one another, still wary.

"I apologize, Lily." Zach places his arm across his heart and bows his head. "I was unaware of your rule. Please forgive my forwardness."

Lily's back straightens, her confidence shining in her voice. "It appears they defended my honor. So, you're forgiven."

Zach raises his eyebrow at our embrace. "I take it the rules only apply to men?"

"Why?" Lily leans forward, showing off her cleavage. "Is there something you want to see Jane and I do?"

Zach turns to James and Doug. "She's a feisty one, isn't she?"

"Yeah." "Yeah, she is!" Doug and James say, their voices overlapping one another.

"Actually..." Lily's confidence dances across my skin, making me shiver. "There is something I'd like to do."

A wickedness appears on her face as she kneels, leaning over me. The boy's heat radiates off each of them. Her tits dangle in front of me and even I have to hold back the urge to take her. This is torture... I gleam, thoroughly seduced by her... Now I get why they like it so much.

I soften my voice. "What would you like?"

"Can I come to The Rabbit Hole with you all?"

"The next open house for the underground isn't until January. But you can come to the public strip club side, and I'll introduce you to the owner, Tara."

"Does the strip club have VIP rooms?"

"Yes." My gaze drops to her breasts. "Why?"

She turns her gaze to James and Doug. "Would any of you be interested in watching me strip?"

A mix of surprise and delight warms their faces. I glow, soaking in the collective energy; it consumes Zach and me.

"*Baby...*" I whine. "*I will not last in time to make it home.*"

Zach's delight chimes in my head. He doesn't want to wait either.

Chapter 10

Just Watch

Doug

Thursday, August 11ᵗʰ

The full moon shines brightly through the patio garden. A warm breeze brushes over my skin, calming me. The natural ambiance of the night plays softly around us as James and I unwind. It's nice to just come out here and talk, without focusing on our game. I'm glad Lily suggested we do this, though I was hoping she would join us.

James' voice falters. I realize I wasn't paying attention to him. His gaze shifts, peering behind me. I crane my neck around. Lily is opening the long curtain, walking it to one end of her bedroom.

On this side of the castle, all the details of the architecture stand out. Beautiful carvings, and this floor-to-ceiling glass wall that shapes her room.

Lily gingerly trails her hand across the glass, making her way back to the center of the window. The bedroom lights perfectly illuminate her every curve. Her white lace robe contrasting with the deep green accents of her stage. Her hands rise above her head as her hips sway to a beat we cannot hear. That beautiful, long auburn hair flows behind her.

"We should look away," James says.

"Yeah... for sure..." I lift my chair, positioning myself for the perfect view. James sets his chair beside mine.

Gracefully, her body sways, pulling on our strings, enthralling.

My lip twitches. This was no mere suggestion. It was her directions that urged us to take the night off, sit in the garden, and recharge. She planned this. No wonder she was so excited.

I relax back into the chair, drinking her in. A flash of glitter catches my eye. "Our succubus is wearing heels."

"I thought she hated heels?"

"She does."

"Do you think she, umm..." James shifts in his seat and adjusts himself. "Does she want us to come up there?"

"Why?" I nudge his arm with my elbow. "You hard already?"

"I can't help it, she..." James sucks in a hard breath. "Fuck, just look at her."

"I am." A heavy sigh escapes my lungs as my nostrils flair. "I want to go up there and give her what she needs."

"You think she would let us?" James fidgets with the armrest. "It's been so hard to read her. But this... I mean, come on, it's just plain unfair."

"Yeah, it is." I let out a two-note laugh. "Maybe it's payback for all the times she says we're unfair to her."

James and I watch as she continues to tease us. Her hips sway, seducing me. Her hair catching my eyes again... The way it flows around her body...

The night's melody moves with her as if she is orchestrating nature.

I wonder... "Hey James, do you hear that?"

"Hear what?"

"Exactly." I taunt. He raises his eyebrow. "You know how you haven't been able to figure out a score for the succubus fight... What if you just did this?" I motion my hand out in a semi-circle. "The graceful eeriness of night."

James' eyes light up. "That would be perfect."

Lily places her hand on the window and pulls at the string of her robe. Slightly bending forward, letting her hair cover what's underneath.

Oh, what a tease.

She straightens, bit by bit, swinging her body around. Lily's robe falls off one shoulder and rests in the nook of her elbow. She peeps over the other shoulder and glides her hand down, pulling this side down to match the other.

In a gracefully swift motion, the robe falls to the floor. For a moment, she is perfectly still. More white lace covers her body, catching in the starlight. My blood pumps, filling me out. I adjust myself.

The lace hugs her body, exposing her voluptuous curves. I'm drawn to her hand, caressing her hip, studying the way she touches herself. My hand yearns to grasp that ass.

Lily's hand slides down her thigh as she lowers to the floor. While resting on her ankles, she seductively picks up her robe and tosses it to the side. Her ass snaps into the air and I press my mouth together.

"Our succubus is wearing lingerie," James says. "I thought she said she didn't own any."

"She doesn't..." I stutter. "At least none that I have ever washed or seen."

"Fuck... Are you certain we can't go up there?"

"With the way she's been acting..." I dig my fingers into the armrest and keep my eyes on Lily. "If I went up there, I'd have a hard time controlling myself. I'd never forgive myself if I hurt her."

"I won't let you hurt her." James' tone is confident, but I find it hard to put faith in those words. He is struggling as much as I am.

"It's been so hard to hold back. I don't trust myself to touch her anymore."

"I get it. When she brushes up against me, I want to pick her up, and take her right there." James motions the action with his hands. "The only time I didn't feel out of control is when we're with Jane and Zach."

"I think that was different. She was hurting." My eyes travel to her arm, the bruise still visible from here. "I mean, she still is. Her arm hasn't fully healed yet."

"We'll just have to wait and see what happens these next few weeks." James sighs, both loving and begrudging the anticipation. My mind screams at me, aching with the same torture.

I get lost, taking in Lily's curves as she swings her hips around to face us for the first time since losing the robe. The laced fabric is high-cut. It rests over her hipbones, emphasizing her hourglass figure. A deep V plunges down the middle, barely containing her breasts. The only thing holding them in place is the X strap across her chest. My hands clench on the chair.

I want to go to her. Touch her. Have her skin press against mine.

I catch James squirming to contain himself. Unable to unclasp my grip to nudge him, I say, "Stop playing with yourself. She'll see you."

James side-eyes me. "Is that why you're gripping onto that chair for dear life?"

I silently huff. Not wanting to say out loud how right he is.

Her beauty and grace ignite my passion. I truly hope she wants to be with both of us. James is right. It's hard to read her sometimes... She treats us the same. Looks at us the same. But she won't make a move. Is she scared? No. She is too strong. She takes what she wants. So why...

Her hand trails across the window as she walks to the edge of her room. She grabs the curtain from its place, its sheer fabric follows her like a ghost. It silhouettes her figure in the frame, obscuring the details yet framing her perfectly. It's enchanting. I lean forward as her leg lifts behind her, and she removes her shoe.

James shifts in his chair. "Is she serious—"

"Shh!" I interrupt him harshly.

We watch in silence as the next shoe comes off. My eyes trace over her curves as she lifts her arms to her neck. The slope of her breasts fills out, taking shape as the fabric moves, painstakingly slow, shimmying down her body.

I want to run my hands over her. Caress her every curve. Wrap her hair around my arm.

My chest aches as she walks to the edge of the curtains once again. The heavier, opaque curtains glide closed.

The show ends.

James strokes his goatee as he takes a few deep breaths. I brush my hand through my hair and stare at my feet.

"That was complete and utter torture," James says.

"It was the most torture I have ever experienced."

"Really?" James' gaze travels up and down. "I thought you liked this kind of thing?"

"No, I'm the one that does the teasing." I glance at her empty window. I might have to change my stance on that. *It was torture... And I want more.* I sigh. So much more.

James stands up, the bulge in his pants still very much visible. He picks up his chair and positions it in front of me. "I know we have only joked about it. But are you serious about wanting to share her?"

"Yeah, I'm completely serious about it." I lean back. "Though I'm not sure we can be with her. Even if we wanted to."

He brushes his goatee, still trying to calm his nerves. "Regardless. We have to keep working on our game. Or she'll be furious and definitely won't let us touch her. If she found us slacking off, she'd probably tie us down to some chairs and force us to work."

"I don't know?" My fingers pet my chin. "I might like that."

James lifts his eyebrow. "Seriously?"

"I'd only allow it if she tied you down and forced me to watch her ride you."

"That sounds hot as fuck." James sits back, finally able to relax. His eyes gleam. I enjoy the sight of him reminiscing over her dance.

The night's melody fills the silence between us.

I sigh, forcing the silence to shatter. *I need his help.* "James... we should come up with those body signals we joked about. We need to communicate silently. If I get too rough, you have to stop me."

"Honestly, it would be beneficial for both of us. Not just you," James says. "We both want to be with her, and we need to get comfortable with what that means."

"Communicating and controlling ourselves to make sure we give her what she needs will be harder than us watching each other. We've seen each other have sex before."

"Yeah, but not with the same woman. And definitely not a woman like her."

"When she danced for us in the kitchen, is when it hit me…" I rub my hand over the back of my neck. "She means something to me. I don't just want her. I want to make her happy."

"Me too." James massages the palm of his hand, his eyes becoming distant.

"You can't keep blaming yourself for what happened that night. There was nothing we could have done to fix it."

"I know that now, but…" James stares at his hands, his thumb digging into his palm. "It hurt not being able to help her."

"It still hurts." My stomach clenches up. "Not knowing how to reach her. Trying to figure out how one minute she can be as bold as this." I gesture toward her window. "And then the next be so closed off. It drives me up a wall."

"Tell me about it. I thought after her opening up about her gifts and her scar that she'd be able to stop putting on that bullshit smile." James eyes me. "You know the one."

"I fucking hate that smile." I clench my jaw. "Does she think we believe that lie?"

"Obviously she does. Since we're too chicken shit to confront her."

"We're not being chickens- we're giving her space," I say, trying to reassure both of us. "We can't act like those other macho dicks she knows. She has to deal with those idiots enough as it is. She doesn't need us cornering her too. If we push too much, we might lose her." I sigh. "I don't want to hurt her."

"I don't know why you keep comparing yourself to Brian. You're not him." He insists.

My gaze locks with his. "James, you know how rough I like it. For crying out loud, I'm so fucked up, I can't get off unless I can bite them. I never want to lose control with her."

"That's your problem…" James challenges my gaze. "You keep thinking that you're the monster, because of your kinks. But you're not. Brian's the monster that's pretending to be human, prancing around in his overpriced Armani suit. If I had seen him do that to her." James' eyes overflow with anger. "I'd probably have put him in the hospital."

"Guess we both need to learn some control."

"Then that's the first thing we have to do. Figure out a signal that will stop us from hurting her."

"That will be hard." My lips peek into my cheeks deviously. "But once we do, we can get to the fun stuff." I rub my hands together. "Planning her first orgasm."

"I still can't believe she hasn't had one." James' eyes glow in the moonlight. "It'll be a lot of pressure to make her first time special… Ha… No pun intended."

"Suuure…" I say and we laugh.

~~~~~~

The smell of coffee guides my groggy feet through the kitchen. Half asleep, I muddle through the mundane task of preparing a fresh cup. The loud, obnoxious sound of a protein shaker clanking grabs my attention.

"Have you had any coffee yet?" James asks as he comes into view, and I grunt. His playful smirk comes to life. "Sounds like a tough morning." I growl at his mocking, holding back the urge to kick him. He motions to the table. "Come sit and drink. I have something to show you and you need to be awake for it."
~~~~~~

I shuffle my feet to the table and sit. We drink in silence until I am halfway through my cup.

"Has the beast been tamed?" James asks me as I take another sip.

"Enough that you may speak, and I won't kill you." I wave at him to go on with whatever it is he is so eager to show me.

"Great!" James sits up straight and slides a glittery white notecard to me. "This was at the coffee pot this morning."

The textured paper is like holding velvet. I rub my fingertips over it, savoring its softness. I open it and read;

To Doug and James

I hope you both enjoyed
        Doug's early birthday present!

I look forward to dinner next Wednesday.

Lady Lily

My heart thumps hard in my chest, and I clutch my hand to it. She did plan it. That little minx. A strange sensation fills me- like I'm falling through my chair. Euphoria takes control of my senses; awakening something I haven't felt in many years.

"She just tore my heart out of my chest."

"Welcome to the club." James chuckles, hiding behind sarcasm. His eyes dull and drop to the table. And with that, I know he feels the same.

CHAPTER II

LAZY POOL DAY

LILY

SUNDAY, SEPTEMBER 4TH

A warm breeze passes over my body, carrying the smell of the pool with it. I rest leisurely, with Snowball at my feet, soaking in the sunlight. Her white coat shines brightly. Clouds trail through the sky, giving us a brief reprieve from the intense heat. My sister lounges in the pool, her 7-month-pregnant belly bobbing under the water as she talks with her wife, Alex.

The back patio doors open, and James and Doug carry out trays of food. The sight makes me hungry in more ways than one. I force my leering eyes away from their naked chests. "I thought I gave you guys the day off?"

They set the food down and Snowball perks up. She hops down and heads over to James.

"You did," Doug says.

They smile cutely at me, and I squint my eyes. "Then why are you serving us?"

"Sorry, Lady Lily," James says in his knightly accent, running a hand over Snowball as she curls against his leg. "Princess Leilani has overruled your authority today."

My sister bares her teeth in a wide, childlike grin. Doug walks to the poolside with a small platter. "Yes, we have been requested to prepare the coming Prince's favorite meal."

James sets down a full dish and Snowball barely says thank you before setting her sights on devouring the chicken. James turns to Layla. "I made homemade pickles with a side of whipped cake icing for dipping."

Layla treads the water, closing the distance between her and the platter of food. "Is this the pickle recipe you told me you wanted to make last month?!"

"Yep!" James boasts. "I started pickling them three weeks ago. I'm excited to know how I did."

"Wait..." I sit up and glare at her. "We weren't here last month. When did you talk to him?"

"I got their phone numbers from your assistant." Alex leans back against the pool wall, placing her elbows on the edge. "After that dick hurt you, Layla was manic. I wasn't allowed to sleep until I found them."

"Layla, why didn't you call me?" I place my feet on the warm stone and walk to the pool.

"I did! And you told me that you were perfectly fine and to stop worrying. Think of the baby!" She picks up a pickle and violently dips it in the icing. "I called them, and they told me what I wanted to know."

"She threatened them is more like it," Alex says, and James and Doug chuckle.

I side-eye them. "Do I even want to know?"

James stands in his best knightly stance, donning his matching accent. "We are under oath. We shall never speak of it."

"We will not break our oath and incur her wrath, My Lady," Doug says, following the charade. Layla continues eating unphased.

"Really, Layla?" I shake my head in defeat as the cool water wraps around my ankles.

"Mmmm..." Layla moans dramatically to ignore me. "These are amazing, James. Thank you!"

James bows. "You're welcome, Princess."

I squint my eyes at him. "Don't encourage her, James. Or we'll all have to call her that."

"Oh, don't be jealous, sis." Layla turns to me.

I lighten my tone to match her bratty one. "Oh, I'm not jealous."

Layla pouts at her belly. "Well, I am!"

"Why are you jealous?" I ease the water up to my knees.

"Oh, let's see." She points her finger at me. "You've lost weight. Are flaunting a sexy new suit AND... you started dancing again and didn't tell me."

"How do you know I've..." I stop walking down the steps into the pool. I glare at the boys, wishing I had Zach's ability. Sarcastic guilt crosses James' and Doug's faces. "What did you do?"

"Layla said she needed to know you were happy." James turns away. "So, we sent her a video of you dancing with the girls. For proof."

"We're sorry, My Lady." Doug waves his hands in surrender. "We were scared for our lives!"

"Oh, I'm sure you were." As the warmth of the water surrounds me, my mind drifts. How many videos do they have? My stomach flutters. I'll have to talk to Jane again. Maybe she's right, I am an exhibitionist.

"I haven't seen you dance in years." Alex moves her short, wet black hair to the side. "Not since we used to go to the clubs. You looked so happy."

"Well, I am happy." I check out James and Doug as I rest against the side of the pool by Alex. "And it's kind of all your fault."

"How is it our fault?" James presses his hand to his chest.

"You kept insisting that I meet your friends, and you reminded me how much I missed dancing."

"Then we happily accept the blame, My Lady." Doug bows his head. He and James gleam cocky grins and my cheeks grow warm. Grateful that my skin is already blotchy from the sun, hiding my embarrassment.

"Ok, princess, it's time to start your stretches," James says. "No more stalling."

Layla points to her food and whines. "But I've just eaten. I have to rest first."

"Nope. That's just a myth." Doug hops into the pool.

"Lily!" Layla's green eyes plead with me. "These two are trying to kill me. Tell them to leave me alone."

I'm unfazed. I've seen it too many times over the years. It doesn't help that we look alike. Other than our differences in height, body type, and breast size, we look very much like sisters.

"Oh, no..." I wiggle my finger. "You brought this upon yourself. You made them promise to help you keep up with exercising to prepare for your labor. I warned you and once again... you didn't listen to your sister."

Layla dramatically stabs another pickle into the dip. Alex and I laugh. She shoves the pickle in her mouth. "Fine, let's get this over with."

....

Layla and the boys chat as we relax at the patio table. Joy fills out my features. This is the first time we've spent the day together. It's nice. I'm glad Layla's chaotic personality didn't scare them off. They weren't joking when they said Heather and my sister were cut from the same cloth.

"Food's here," Doug says. "We'll be right back."

James and Doug head upstairs. As they leave, Layla is eerily silent. It's creepy. She's never this quiet.

The second they are both out of sight, she turns to me with a wicked smirk. "So, tell me... Which one are you sleeping with?"

My eyes widen as my stomach tightens. Of course, she wants to know that. "I'm not sleeping with either of them."

"Oh, come on." Alex tilts her head and puffs out her lips. "There is no way you guys aren't sleeping together. The sexual tension out here is ridiculous."

I shake my head, insisting, knowing. "They don't see me like that."

"What do you mean? They couldn't keep their eyes off of you." Layla ogles me. "But I can't blame them. You are smoking hot in that suit. When did you get it?"

"Recently." I squirm in my seat.

Alex leans into the table. "Did you buy it for them?"

"Maybe." I tuck a piece of my hair behind my ear.

"Ohhh..." Layla teases. "Ok then, which one do you wannnt to sleep with?"

I cross my leg and angle myself away from them. I want them both, but I don't know if you'll understand. Even if you did, I don't want you meddling in this. My breathing stiffens as the surprise prick of tears well up. "It doesn't matter. I can't..."

"Are they seeing someone?" Layla asks and I shake my head. "Then why can't you?"

"Because…" My eyes become wet as I stare at my empty plate. "I just can't."

Even if they don't understand, I should talk to someone. Maybe if Alex hears it too, she can reign in Layla's enthusiasm. Hold her back from trying to set us up. I don't need any of this to get even slightly more complicated…

Now just isn't the time. They need to focus on their game, not me.

My leg shakes and I hold it tight.

We're just friends. They don't want me that way.

I can't keep fantasizing.

Alex stands up, pulling me back to reality. She walks away from the table, holding her arm out. "Let me help."

The boys step onto the patio with bags full of food.

"You can tell me later." Layla places her hand over mine and I nod.

As James sets out the food, Doug grabs plates and serves us.

"Okay, I've been dying to ask you two." Layla points at James and Doug. "How can such sweet snacks be single?"

"Leilani!" Embarrassment boils through me.

"What?" She eyes me unapologetically.

"I'm so sorry." Alex animates an apology. "She has been insatiable and unruly these last few months. You do not need to answer that."

James strokes his goatee. "So, you think we're snacks?"

"Bro…" Doug elbows James. "I think that is the best compliment we have ever received."

James puffs out his chest. "Yeah, I think so."

I hold back my amusement at their comments, not wanting to fuel Layla's prodding.

"I don't envy you, Alex." Doug sits down. "I can't imagine how much she is wearing you out."

"Tell me about it." Alex sighs. "It's exhausting."

"Well, it's what you get for being so damn good, dear." Layla boasts. I place my hand over my face and groan. James and Doug laugh as Alex takes a bite of her food to hide her deepening red cheeks. "Oh, I'm sorry. Did I embarrass you, sweetie?"

Alex side-eyes her wife. "Funny, you don't sound sorry."

Doug places his hand on my arm. I lower my hands and give him my attention. "No need to be embarrassed. My family is way worse. It's all good." A sweet smile lifts my lips, and he pulls his hand away.

James pulls his chair to the table. "But to answer your question. We're single because the girls we were seeing a few months back weren't supportive of our dream and what we wanted to do with our lives."

"That's stupid. Why wouldn't they support you?" Layla asks.

"I think Lily said it best." Doug motions to me. "They were upset that they wouldn't be the center of our attention. They cared more about themselves than they did us when it came down to it."

James glances at his plate. "Honestly. They weren't the only ones that felt that way about us chasing our dream."

"What do you mean?" Alex asks.

"Sometimes we doubt if our friends and family even support us," Doug says.

"Why?" Layla asks.

"For one, they never ask us about it," Doug says with a bite of anger in his voice.

"That sucks," Alex says. "None of them?"

"The only person who does is Lily." James gazes at me sweetly and my stomach flutters.

"We wouldn't be this far along if it wasn't for her." Doug's smile sends me spiraling. I latch onto my thigh to stop myself from leaping into their arms.

"Oh, that I believe. Lily has told us all about it." James and Doug's attention snaps to Alex. "I'm honestly excited about it. The way she hypes it up is contagious."

"Really?" "Seriously?" Doug and James' voices overlap as their cheeks become noticeably red.

"Yeah, of course." Layla taunts me with her eyes. "You guys and your game are all she talks about."

My chest blazes from embarrassment.

Alex points her fork at James and Doug. "When you're far enough along, I have some marketing ideas for you guys."

Layla elbows her wife. "She also wants to play test it, too."

Alex pauses, the fork an inch from her mouth. "Yeah, that too."

As we eat, I listen to James, Doug, and Alex converse. Their eyes shine over the praise that Alex gives them. I love when they get this hyped up. But I feel so stupid. I can't believe I never noticed that no one in the group has even mentioned it. I've heard them talk about playing games. But they're right, I've never heard them talk about their game with their friends.

My nerves blaze, sparking my frustration. I'm gonna have a chat with Zach about this. At least Alex is here to talk to them. It might help them out some to get someone else's input. Someone that knows what they're talking about.

I wouldn't mind it if we had dinners like this more often. It's like we're a family.

No. Stop. They are just your friends. Don't start that now. You know you can't be with them.

CHAPTER 12

DINNER WITH LILY'S FAMILY

DOUG

SUNDAY, SEPTEMBER 4TH

A warm breeze passes through. Drifting my thoughts further away. Lily's family is amazing and so much fun to be around. I can't wait for her to meet my family.

My shoulders tense at the thought and my gaze drops to my empty plate. My stomach twists in knots as the falling sensation courses over me. I don't just want her to meet my family; I want my family to meet her. My eyes consider James. We've never talked about it, but I'm sure he'd want the same.

I tune back into the conversation. Alex is awesome. She's not a casual gamer. She knows her stuff. It's been so nice to talk to someone other than Lily about our game.

My gaze drifts across the table to Layla, wondering if we are boring her. Layla caresses her stomach. Her hand moves smoothly in large circular motions. She leans back in her chair, perfectly content. Her features are bright. Bright in the same way Lily's get, when she listens to us like this.

I turn to Lily, immediately noticing her tension.

Shit, not again.

Lily's eyes are closed, and her hand is covering her mouth as she steadies her breath. Her fingers dig into her thigh.

I rest my hand over her death grip, asking, "Lily?" Her eyes shoot open, lit with fear. "Do you need ginger?"

"I'll go get it." James' chair screeches as he pushes it back.

Lily lowers her hand from her mouth. "No. I'm ok." He pauses, studying her as her grip relaxes under my touch. James sits back down.

"What's wrong?" Layla's eyes fill with concern.

"It's nothing. Don't worry about it." Lily slides her fingers in between mine. Electricity courses up my arm, her warmth spreading through me like wildfire.

"Your face is red, and you look like you're about to vomit. Tell me what's wrong." Layla's eyes search Lily's.

Lily's fingers tighten around mine, her eyes glistening. "I can't."

So, she's hiding from her sister too. But why?

Layla sits up straight and scooches to the edge of her chair. "Are you having visions again?"

"No."

"Then what is wrong?" Layla demands and Lily's mouth opens.

She sighs and lets go of my hand. Her demeanor shifts, her face suddenly emotionless.

Lily elegantly stands, walking away from us. "I just need a moment. Please excuse me."

Layla aggressively follows her. "Lily Dawn Callahan! Don't you ignore me!"

My hand turns to ice in the absence of her warmth. I dig my fingers into my palm, willing myself to stay put. Layla will get to the bottom of this.

"What's going on?" James and I turn to Alex.

"Honestly, we were hoping you might know," James says.

Alex shakes her head. "No, this is the first I'm hearing about it. When did this start?"

"A couple of months after we started working for her." James strokes his goatee. "Around her birthday, right?"

I nod. "Yeah. I thought she might be pregnant."

"I thought so too until..." James drops his gaze, unable to keep eye contact with Alex.

"Until," I continue for him. "She told us about Jade and not being able to have any."

"So, what exactly has been happening?" Alex asks.

"She's been having these... spells." I rub my leg to calm my shaking. "She checks out. Stops paying attention. Tenses up. Winds up super dizzy or nauseous. Sometimes both."

"They have been getting more frequent, too." James crosses his arms and sits back. "It used to only be a couple of times a month. Now it's a few times a week."

"She says she's seen a doctor and, according to her, it's just stress."

Alex studies us. "But you don't believe that?"

"No," James says.

"Why not?"

"Something is off about it." James pumps his fist to calm his anger. "I know we don't have proof, but the way she looks at us makes us think she's hiding something."

I motion to where Lily was sitting. "You saw it with your own eyes. She IS hiding something."

"Yes, I did." Alex sits back. "Has anything unusual happened?"

I raise my eyebrow as I start in, my hands animating my words. "You mean besides finding out that she is part Fae, has magical powers, and has a giant white cat familiar that lives in the magical forest in the backyard?"

James elbows me. "Don't forget about her adopted dryad mother and two elven dads that threatened to turn us into fertilizer if we ever hurt their precious baby girl."

"Yes. Besides all that boring, mundane stuff." Alex flicks her wrist.

My mind reels back. She was stripping for us a few weeks ago. That was definitely out of the ordinary. But probably not what she means.

"Well..." James uncrosses his arms. "About a month ago, we walked in on her dancing on top of the kitchen island while she was baking brownies. After the timer went off, she..." James fidgets with the fabric on the armrest. "She wasn't moving right."

Alex's brow furrows. "What do you mean, she wasn't moving, right?"

James pauses and his finger motions for me to take the lead. "Lily walks a certain way. When she is baking, she is full of grace. Her smile lights up the entire castle."

Alex tilts her head and her cheek lifts slightly.

You sound like a creep. Shut up.

"Then how was she moving?" Alex asks, motioning for us to continue.

"It was like this..." James tries to imitate Lily's rigidness from that night. "All stiff. She barely had any energy to lift her arm."

"Ok. Is that it?" Alex asks. "She was just acting differently?"

"No," I say, finding my voice again. "After that, she spoke, and when we replied..." My jaw clenches up. "She didn't even realize we were there. Which didn't make any sense. We talked while she was dancing."

"The best way I can think of to describe it is that when she stopped dancing, the lights switched off. We didn't know what to do. We thought we misread her intentions and crossed the line." James' hand flexes into a fist, twice more. "So, we've been keeping our distance."

"What color were her eyes?"

"Brilliant green." "Emerald green." We say without hesitation.

"What does she smell like?"

"Peaches." We say in perfect unison.

Alex lets out a short chuckle. "Well, this explains a lot."

"What does?" I ask, my eyes looking her over in confusion.

"Yeah..." Her eyes dart back and forth between us. "You have fallen for her, hard. It's no wonder it felt so tense today." A sweet grin lights up her face.

Of course, she noticed. Even air-headed Matt noticed. Should we ask her how Lily feels? Would she know? Would it matter?

I glance at James, and he nods. I sit up straight and lock eyes with Alex. "Can we ask you something?"

"Yeah, go for it."

"We want to invite Lily to our friend's wedding."

"Ok then ask..." Alex tilts her head. "Heather?" We nod. "Ask Heather if she can come. No big deal, right?"

"I mean, yeah, they want her to come too... But..." James fidgets with his fork, and she raises her eyebrow. "We want her to be our plus one."

The tableware clatters as Alex leans onto the table too enthusiastically. "Really!"

"Yeah, but we don't know how to ask her," I say.

"What do you mean? You just ask."

"She—" Alex puts her hand up, stopping James mid-sentence. I follow her gaze to Lily and Layla who are walking through the basement to the patio.

"We'll talk later," Alex whispers.

Layla and Lily are holding hands as they walk back to the table. As they get closer, the telltale signs that they have been crying have darkened their eyes.

"You feel any better?" I keep my tone even and sweet.

"A little..." Lily says as they sit down. "I'm sorry for the interruption."

"You have nothing to apologize for," James assures Lily.

Her lips lift softly around the edges. That's the smile, the one that hides something deeper.

CHAPTER 13

WILL YOU...

LILY

SATURDAY, OCTOBER 29TH

Bold red and gold accents adorn walls and surfaces in the basement, tying together a rich medieval renaissance theme. Celtic tavern music plays quietly in the background. I scan the room for the hundredth time tonight, still adjusting to the new furniture.

Matt and Alex are playing a round of pool while the rest of the boys watch them from the new poker table. The way James and Doug lit up when their gift arrived yesterday was well worth the chore of rearranging the room.

Alex and the boys are dawning matching outfits. The sight brings a smile to my face. I stand by my opinion that the outfits are for Jedi Knights. Not casual knight attire, as they called it. But their faux axes and swords help them pull it off. They look good. I can't wait to get the photos printed from their sparing session in the field today.

I'm mesmerized by the shimmery red liquid pouring from the giant dispenser as I fill our tankards with whatever this incredibly tasty secret concoction is that Doug made for tonight.

It's been a few years since I've had a Halloween party. I'm glad the girls convinced me to make it happen this year. I can't believe they talked me into making it a whole weekend thing. The dinner, and the haunted house runs last night. The photo shoot today, and now the party. I'll need a week's worth of catch-up sleep, but it will be worth it.

I lift the tray with five heavy tankards a top of it and make my way around the bar. My purple gown flows around me as I pass between the tables. Laughter rings out as I approach. My chest expands with excitement, and I pause at the edge of the makeshift dance floor.

The girls are lounging on a couch at the edge of the room, appearing absolutely royal.

Layla lights up the space, her regal crème and gold princess dress whispering around her body. Her sweet round belly holds up the fabric as she caresses her stomach. A tiny crown sits atop her head, with a beautiful veil trailing behind. Heather, Susan, and Jane surround her in matching gowns of red. A princess sitting with her ladies-in-waiting.

I hope the pictures capture the grandeur of this moment as vividly as I see it now.

My chest warms at the sight of my family, fitting in with James and Doug's friends. I set the drinks on the coffee table, grabbing the two virgin drinks for me and Layla. I settle in next to Jane on the couch and turn toward Heather. "Did you decide what to do for your bachelor/bachelorette party yet?"

"We narrowed it down to two options." Heather picks up her tankard and waves her other hand around enthusiastically. "We're all going to do dinner beforehand, regardless. If we split up, each group would need a driver. Unless we hire drivers and if I have to do that, why not get a party bus and do everything together?"

"Ok, so, you guys haven't narrowed it down. Got it." I take a sip of my drink to avoid rolling my eyes.

"What does Bill want to do?" Layla asks.

Heather sits up straight and deepens her voice. "Whatever you want to do is fine by me, dear."

We all groan.

"I don't know how you have done all of this wedding planning on your own," Susan says. "I'd go nuts and call the whole thing off."

"I love it! Being in control of all the choices suits me perfectly. Plus, it's not like we don't communicate. If he doesn't like something, he tells me. Actually..." Heather leans closer as if to whisper, but doesn't. "Last week, when I didn't think he was listening to me, I told him I was going to have the guys wear kilts. He laughed so hard beer shot out his nose."

Heather bares a bright grin, and we bust at the seams with joy.

"Yesssss," Jane says. "Let's put them in kilts next Halloween!"

"Hey guys," Layla shouts over the music to the boys. "You are wearing kilts next year."

"Seriously, babe?" Bill gives Heather a sweet glare.

"Oh, I'm so down for that," Zach says.

"Hell, yeah," Matt says. "It will make it easier to flash you guys."

"Oh, god no..." Bill points at us. "Take it back right now."

The girls and I laugh, Alex and Zach's voices chiming in after a moment.

"We'll be back." Doug's voice booms, getting everyone's attention. He and James open the patio doors.

"Where are you going?" I ask.

James beams at me and Doug winks. Without a word, they close the doors behind them. I blink rapidly. Ok, that was weird. I set my drink down and turn my attention back to the girls. Their faces share matching grins, and Heather clasps her hands in her lap.

I glare at Layla. "What did you do now?"

"Huh..." Layla places her hand on her chest. "I didn't do anything. Why do you think it's always me?"

"Because it is always you." I retort.

"Well, this time it was all their idea."

"She's right." Heather bounces with excitement. "It's a surprise!"

The room goes silent, and I peep over at the table. The guys stand close together, all wearing the same smiles.

"I don't like surprises." I stand up and cross my arms. Heather, Susan, and Jane stand up as well. Layla scooches to the edge of the couch. I sway from side to side as Jane helps Layla stand. "Why did you let them do this?"

"It's ok." Layla rubs my arm to comfort me. "They ran everything by me first."

"That doesn't make it any better! If anything, that makes me worry more." I scan their faces as they all crowd around me. "Do all of you know about this?"

They all concede, nodding in unison. I sweep my hair in front of me. My fingers brush through my hair as Jane rubs my back. My mind reels with anxiety.

What are they planning? I don't like this.

The whispered chatter of excitement swirls around me. Jane's soothing touch does nothing to help me. I close my eyes and take deep breaths to calm my racing heart. Focusing my attention outside, I hear Doug and James' feet tittering outside.

What could they possibly have planned that everyone knows about except for me?

Seconds tick by.

It feels like an eternity.

How long do I have to wait?

I focus on the music playing in the background to distract myself from the noise of everyone shuffling around the room.

Layla kept this a secret? She's never been able to keep a secret. Not ever.

A knock at the window jolts my senses into overdrive. My eyes fly open, my stomach drops, and my breath catches in my throat. Everyone has moved. They pair up, each holding hands with their lover.

WHAT IS GOING ON?

"You ready?" Layla intertwines her arm with mine, and Alex positions herself to stand on the other side of me.

Matt and Susan each step out onto the patio and hold open the doors. Zach steps through the threshold with Jane by his side and leans down to kiss her on the cheek before taking a step away to stand next to Matt. Jane stands next to Susan. Heather and Bill follow suit. Layla takes a step forward, making me follow her through the door.

A hush falls over my mind as I step out the doors. Warmth fills me as I pass Jane and I breathe in deeply.

This is gorgeous. Breathtakingly, gorgeous.

White candles trace a path on the ground. Purple icicle lights are strung across the patio awning. My eyes follow the path the lights make. Beautiful fauna colors of orange, red, yellow, and green adorn and surround the patio table.

The purple lights cascade behind the layered plants and maze around the arrangements on the floor.

Layla and Alex stop and take a step to the side, letting go of me. James and Doug stand on either side of a large sign centered on the table. My body freezes. My heart races and my legs want to give out.

You're supposed to keep walking. Come on feet, move!

Two hands press against my back, Layla and Alex nudging me forward. My legs comply, and I make my way down the aisle of lights. My eyes trace over the scene before me. James and Doug each hold a red, single-stem stargazer lily.

My eyes glisten with unshed tears as I force myself to look away from James and Doug's captivating smiles, to the words written especially for me.

Joy floods my senses. The tears fade, replaced with racing adrenaline. My face and chest warm, turning my skin pink against the cool evening air. Doug and James present the lilies to me.

A smile springs across my cheeks, and it takes all my self-control to refrain from leaping into their arms. I reach out, accepting the lilies, and their invitation in the symbolism. They lean in and kiss my cheeks. Their lips are warm and gentle. The softness brushing against my skin. Fire burns between my legs.

The sound of joyous cheering erupts behind us.

"I... I..." I am at a loss for words. This is too much. I hug the lilies to my chest. "Thank you."

"No. Thank you" "We should be the ones thanking you." They stumble over each other's words; A hint of my nervousness reflects in their voices. Radiant excitement shines from their eyes.

Hug them. Come on, you can do it.

I caress their cheeks with the back of my fingers.

Kiss them and show them... You want this!

The sound of clacking heels echoes across the patio. James and Doug peer over my shoulder and sigh. I don't need to look to know the girls are bounding toward us. This moment belongs to more than just us; I realize.

I turn around and am bombarded by red fabric. James and Doug step away from me to be surrounded by their own gaggle of male excitement. My gaze scans for Layla and Alex, but I can't find them through the excited hugs from Jane, Heather, and Susan.

This is too much.

My breathing becomes labored as Heather's exhilaration overflows. I hear too much. My sight is fuzzy. My stomach twists into knots.

I have to get away. I desperately need time to process this... alone.

My mouth opens, but nothing happens. I can't speak.

Where are the boys?

I think I might actually throw up this time. My vision blurs as my breathing becomes shallow.

Of all the times to not notice me, why does it have to be now?

Crap! Crap! Crap! Please, someone help—

"Excuse me, ladies, may I borrow my sister?" Layla's hand comes into focus and is all I see.

I grab her and they move aside to let me through. "Excuse me." Not letting go of Layla, I catch my breath, steadying myself as we walk inside the house. "Thank you for the rescue."

"Yeah, they were so intense. Even I needed a break from them." Layla jokes as we head up the stairs. "Now let's go find a place to put those beautiful silk flowers."

Did they plan all of that themselves?

They couldn't have, it's too good.

They make gorgeous backdrops in their game. They could have.

Yeah, but you had to decorate for the engagement party because they didn't know what to do.

Layla had to of helped. Possibly Heather too. She and the girls are the ones that decorated. Was this why I wasn't allowed to help?

"Any ideas where to put them?" Layla lets go of my hand as we step inside my room.

"How much of this was your idea?" I ask, not caring how harsh it may have sounded.

Layla's smile is small and sweet. "None of it was my idea. Alex and I told them not to do anything fancy. We told them to just ask you. But they insisted they wanted to do something big. Honestly, it was sweet to hear how much effort they wanted to put into this."

I shake my head, bewildered. "But, why?"

"I asked the same question. What they told me made me cry. Which isn't hard to do since I'm pregnant and all." She rambles. "I couldn't help but jump in. Their ideas were wonderful and romantic. I was so giddy about it. I get it now, what you see in them. They—"

"Leilani, please..." I lock my gaze with hers, my shoulders tensing unbearably. "What did they say to you?"

"Oh, sorry. I guess I'm still excited." Layla takes a breath. "They told me it was time for you to be treated special. That you go all out for others but are rarely on the opposite end of that generosity. They said they wanted to show you, in front of everyone, how it feels to be wanted and appreciated."

I grip the lilies tighter to my chest. "Really? You're not just making that up?"

"Nope! According to Alex, Heather told them what you shared with her about never attending prom. Then they told me they hadn't gone to prom either. They thought it would be fun to pull a bit of the magic from that, make it as over the top as they've heard you're supposed to."

I exhale an exuberant laugh. "Well, they did that. I haven't felt that giddy since I was in high school." I point at the flowers. "What about the lilies? Did you tell them that red stargazers are my favorite?"

Layla shakes her head. "No, I told them to get you a bouquet of roses. Regardless, they picked out some flawless silk flowers." Layla touches the rim of a petal. "They went above and beyond. It was more elaborate than I imagined it would be. They are good to you."

"Yeah, they are." My mind wonders at their choices. How did they know? I don't think I shared my favorite flowers with them before...

"Now, back to my question. Where do you want to put them?"

"In my bed," I mumble.

"No, it's not big enough." Layla wiggles her eyebrows.

"It's a king. Of course, it's big enough."

"It's a twin at best, thanks to all those pillows."

"Hey." I point at her. "You leave my pillows out of this."

"Oh, I know." Layla faces the bed and spreads her arms out. "I should design you an obscenely enormous bed. One of those wall-to-wall ones."

I dramatically clap my hands with enthusiasm, squealing playfully. "Yes, then I can get more!"

"NO!" Layla grabs a green square and turns to me. "No more pillows."

She throws it at me. I dodge it, tittering.

"Humph." Doug's voice huffs out. I turn to find him clutching the square to his chest.

"Sir Douglas, it appears you have been shot with a pillow," James says in his knightly accent.

"Yes. And it was a mighty fine shot." Doug's smirk lights up his eyes. I clutch my side, aching with glee.

"Does thy Princess detest these?" James points to the weapon.

"No, Sir James." Layla's arm waves over the mattress. "I detest that there are more pillows than there is bed."

"Agreed," Doug says curtly, and my laughter ceases.

"I concur with the Princess, My Lady. Thou hath too many," James says.

I place my hand on my chest and scoff. "How dare ye!"

A pillow whacks against my side, and I face my sister. "Oh. No, you didn't."

I pick up the small round object of my demise as my sister grabs another from the bed. As I prepare to throw it at her, I whip around and chuck it at James. I run to the bed, placing my lilies on the nightstand as I do. Layla throws another at them. We grab more and prepare ourselves. The boys display their hands in surrender.

"Now ladies, this is quite unfair," Doug says.

"We can't hit a pregnant woman," James says.

Layla throws her weapon and hits James. "Ha. I win by default!"

"You heard her." I lower my primed arm. "The Princess is victorious. Now, may I have my pillows back?"

"No!" Layla takes mine from my hand and tosses it to the floor. "No more pillows." She grabs more and throws them behind her. "You need more bed space."

"Why is my wife chucking pillows across the room?" Alex asks as she enters, standing between the boys.

"There has been a catastrophe, Sir Alex," James says.

"That ended in the least fair pillow fight I have ever witnessed," Doug says.

"Let's give you a fair shot, then." Layla grabs an assortment of armaments from my bed. Her baby bump giving her resistance to hold on to so many. "Downstairs! Pillow fight. Round 2!"

"Now that sounds like fun." Doug picks up the weapons on the floor, grinning.

"Great! Ok! Everyone out." I motion with my hands for them to leave as they all rush to grab some.

Picking up the lilies, I walk to my floor-to-ceiling window where the sitting area overlooks the garden. On the side table sits a colorful faux floral arrangement. I take out the old set of flowers, leaving only the cascading green foliage, and arrange the two lilies in the center of the glass vase.

"Lilies look beautiful in the moonlight," Doug says.

As they approach me, I take a step to the side and shine for them, just the way they like. Once they reach me, I grab their hands. My small hand attempting to wrap around each of their palms. "Thank you. This meant a lot to me."

"You're welcome, My Lady," James says with a slight bow, followed by Doug.

"I wanted to show you my gratitude downstairs, but we were interrupted."

"That we were." Doug bends down to my ear. His warm breath escaping onto my neck. "Unfortunately, Matt followed us up here."

I glance at the door. Part of a sleeve is peeking through. A tempting idea floats through my head. I stand on my tippy-toes and whisper, "Follow my lead."

"James," I squeak as I lead them to the bed. "Stop that... Someone will see us."

"I'm sorry, My Lady, but I can't keep my hands off of you." A grin lights up his face.

I giggle as I reach the bed and grab a few pillows. "Sir Douglas, could you remove your sword? It is very hard and long against my back."

"Of course, My Lady. I'll be happy to unsheathe it for you."

My legs warm at the wordplay as their gaze thrills me. The urge to follow their words, the temptation to truly unsheathe them, hits me, hard. My eyes instinctively drop to their groins as I hand them each one and motion throwing it.

I turn to the door, leading them to it. "Please, don't tease me. You know I can't be quiet."

"Who said we want you to be quiet?" James bends and whispers sensually in my ear. "Moan."

"No, don't... not there..." I pant and let out a loud moan.

Matt jumps into the doorway. "Huh, caught you—"

Three pillows hurl their way to him, muffling his screams as they smack into him. Bill and Zach laugh as we grab more weapons and chase them through the house.

Chapter 14

We have to go NOW

James

Tuesday, November 8th

The smell of chicken and roasted vegetables wafts through the kitchen. I open the oven door and heat blasts me in the face. It's almost done. Making my way to the cabinet, I grab the plates and set them on the counter. I glance past Doug to the kitchen table.

Lily's water and her phone are still on the table where she left them. She hasn't come back yet. I join Doug at the sink and dry the dishes he has cleaned. She said she was putting her paperwork away. She should have been back by now...

My gaze flicks to the hallway, then the empty table. Where did she disappear to? I tilt my head to the side, cracking my neck. A soft pop resounds in my ears. I exhale in relief.

"James." Doug elbows me as he washes a bowl.

"Should I go check on her?"

Doug's jaw flexes. "I know you are anxious about asking her to join us for Thanksgiving, but you need to relax. She's under enough stress preparing this twenty-million-dollar real estate deal. She doesn't need you running around like a chicken with its head cut off."

His eye twitches and I smirk. "Look who's talking. You're just as anxious as I am."

"Yes. But unlike you, I can keep my emotions in check." Doug shoves the steaming bowl into my chest.

"Oh, you have those?" I dry the bowl and goad him. "I didn't realize, under that manly bitch face."

Doug rests his hands on the edge of the sink. His right cheek sucks into his mouth and his eyebrow raises. His lips make a smacking sound as he picks up another dish and ignores me.

I chuckle and dry the measuring cup. "You think she'll be ok tomorrow, dealing with those sexist pigs?"

"Hell Yeah! Lily is strong." Doug's eyes shine and his voice deepens. "She'll sweep that deal out from under their fat asses and laugh at them all the way to the bank."

"Uh huh..." My gaze sweeps over him. "Seems more like you are just excited to see that fiery spirit of hers when she gets home after kicking all those men in the dicks."

"Damn, straight," he says, mimicking my voice. I chuckle, shaking my head at his dorky grin. He hands me the last dish to dry, then dries his hands, frowning. "Should we still ask her tonight? I don't want to distract her."

I point my finger at him as we lean our backs against the counter. "We have been stalling since Halloween. No more excuses." I dramatically point at the floor. "We are doing this tonight."

He puts his hands up in surrender. "Ok, ok."

"Do you want to ask her at dinner or while we play pool?" I ask.

"I don't think it mat—"

"Shit! Shit! Shit!" Lily comes running down the hall and heads for the foyer. "Where's my phone?"

"It's on the kitchen table," I yell to her, raising my eyebrow at Doug. He shrugs.

She briskly stomps her way to the kitchen table. "Layla's on her way to the hospital! We have to go."

"Isn't it too early for her to be in labor?" Doug asks.

"She's not going into labor." Lily bites at him. She nabs her phone off the table. "Damn it." Lily's voice cracks. She turns to us, and I push myself away from the counter at the sight of the silent tears streaming down her cheeks. "I need to leave now. Will you come with me?"

"Yeah, ok," Doug says. "Of course."

"Let me turn everything off." I head toward the stove.

Doug follows Lily to the foyer as I remove the food from the oven and cover it up as best I can. I briskly make my way to them. Lily is pacing and mumbling to herself. Doug stands up from tying his shoes and eyes me. Fuck, this is bad. I've never seen her this manic.

Doug places Lily's slip-on flats on the floor in front of her. She ignores them. Her pacing doesn't falter. Doug steps in her path, forcing her to pause.

"Lily." Doug's delicate tone pulls her eyes to his. His body stiffens up, fighting the urge to touch her. To whisk her up and carry her somewhere else. Somewhere safe. "Get your shoes on. We are almost ready to go," He urges gently.

"Shoes?" Lily drops her gaze to the floor. "Shoes." She steps into her flats and stands still, staring at them.

I step to Doug's side in front of Lily. "Where are we going?"

"I don't know." Lily glances over at her phone, lying on top of her purse. Fear consuming her eyes. "Alex hasn't called yet."

"Does she not know where to go yet either?" Doug asks.

"Umm…" Lily closes her eyes, and her chest quakes. Crap, she's hyperventilating. I grab her shoulder to calm her, but her breathing does not match her chest's movement. After a moment, she responds, "Alex hasn't calmed down enough yet to call me."

I lower my arm and blink a few times, studying her. Lily's eyes dart around under her eyelids, her leg shakes, and her hands lay across her stomach. "Damn it, Alex. Call me!"

"Why don't you call her?" I suggest.

"We can start heading to the one by her house," Doug says.

Lily nods and opens her eyes. Her eyes change from brown to her usual green. She grabs her phone and it immediately buzzes. Alex and Layla's picture pops up on the screen. Lily's hand trembles as she taps the speakerphone icon. "Alex. We're heading out the door now."

"Lily… It's Layla…" Alex says in between hyperventilating breaths. "A car…"

"I know, sweetie." Lily holds back her tears. "You need to breathe. Take a deep breath. Layla needs you to stay strong right now."

My chest tightens at the sound of the pain in their voices. Doug swiftly moves past us as Alex audibly breathes.

"Which hospital is she going to?" Lily asks.

"Um… Saint umm… Crap… the one she is supposed to give birth at."

"Ok, we're on our way. Text me when you get to the emergency room."

"I'm grabbing the car." Doug places Lily's coat over her shoulders.

"I'll lock up," I say as he leaves.

"Alex sweetie," Lily's voice holds steady. "I'll call Grandma. You just focus on getting to Layla safely. I love you. We will be there soon."

"Ok... Yeah... I love you..."

The phone clicks off and Lily takes a deep breath.

I lead Lily out the front door and hear her take another. We wait for the car, and she takes another. And another.

....

We wait in the Blue Family Waiting Room. Gray-blue walls and deep blue chairs offer a note of peace underneath the landscape photography of mountains and lakes. But they do nothing to help Lily as she paces. It's just us three, in this room meant for ten.

I massage the nape of my neck and put my phone in my pocket. Doug's leg is bouncing as he scrolls on his. I want to hold Lily. She needs to be comforted. But should we?

"Course... hap.... Blood moon." I only catch half words and phrases as Lily mutters to herself. Something about Grandma Barb and Walter now.

The lost look on her face decides for me.

I elbow Doug and stand up. Two steps are all I need to reach her. Doug stands too, and I put my hand on her shoulder. Lily immediately embraces me. With her body pressed against mine, her lungs heave. I gently brush her hair out of her face. Doug frames the side of us, caressing her back.

Our touch soothes her. She loosens, just a little, as her body melts against me. Her breathing calms.

Lily shifts on her leg and peers up at Doug and me. Her lips peak gently into her cheeks as she squeezes me. We smile back and Lily's grip around me loosens. Not wanting to let her go, I stop petting her hair and hold her tighter.

Fingertips graze my forearm as Lily glides them across, taking Doug's hand. Their fingers interlock as she shifts closer to him. Lily closes her eyes, breathing sweetly. I pet her hair, surrounding us with the scent of peaches. Doug's muscles soften along with mine. He rubs circles over her back.

Embraced together in the empty room, we wait for news.

....

Lily's head shifts on my chest, a question written on her face. I gaze into her green eyes, waiting.

"Alex will be here soon." Her voice weakly whispers.

I comfort her, not letting my hold loosen.

I won't let you go.

"Ok," Doug says while caressing her back.

He won't let her go.

A soft, genuine smile crosses her face as a tear glides down her cheek.

We wait.

....

The door opens and Alex steps in. Without hesitation, Lily steps away from us to enfold her into an embrace. Alex tucks her head into the space at Lily's neck. Her hands shake against Lily's back, tightening and ringing the fabric on her shirt as she holds on.

I patiently wait, not wanting to interrupt.

Alex untucks her head and her gaze lands between Doug and me. Her red puffy eyelids give everything away.

"The baby is fine." Her voice cracks a little. "But they both need to be monitored. They gave Layla something to help her rest. So, she can heal. Thankfully, she doesn't need surgery and has no internal bleeding. I think that means she's ok. All her wounds will heal on their own. In time. She just has to stay here."

"For how long?" Doug asks.

"She won't be able to leave till Eric is born at the earliest."

Lily steps back. "Are we allowed in yet?"

"Yes, but they asked that we not disturb her, that we keep it brief," Alex says.

Lily kisses Alex on the cheek and, without another word, leaves the room.

"How you holding up?" I ask.

"I don't know." Alex rubs her arm and stares vacantly at the floor. "I feel like I haven't slept in days. And I doubt I'll be able to tonight."

"No, probably not." Doug lays his hand on her shoulder, and she meets his gaze. "But even if you don't sleep, trying to rest is better than nothing."

Alex holds onto Doug's forearm to steady her shaking. "I'll try."

She inhales and closes her eyes. Doug and I don't speak as she takes a few deep breaths. Her shoulders slump, relaxing her posture, she opens her eyes. I give her a comforting smile. Her roving gaze sweeps over us.

"So…" A mischievous grin breathes life into her face. "You tap that yet?"

Doug's hand falls from her shoulder as he chortles. I shuffle my foot against the floor, unable to meet her gaze.

"Are you asking because you need a distraction or to make us uncomfortable?" Doug chokes out.

"Yes!" Her brown eyes gleam with joy.

I stroke my goatee to hide my warming cheeks. "No."

"No, you haven't? Or no, you won't tell me?" Her eyes twinkle.

"No, we haven't." Doug's chin drops, shaking his head.

Alex squints at us. "Why not?"

"Um... Well..." I rub the back of my neck, avoiding her glare. "You know..."

"You guys are hopeless. When Layla finds out you guys haven't taken care of her sister, she is going to kill you." Alex's posture slacks as she pretends to scold us.

"Well, Doug." I turn to him and adorn my knightly accent. "I guess we have no choice. We can't let the Princess down."

"Plus..." Doug pretends to shake with fear. "The Princess is scary when she is mad."

Alex's laughter fills the small room. Doug and I take in the beautiful sight. Hopefully, she released enough stress to sleep. Even if only for a bit.

"We probably shouldn't leave Lily alone for too long," I say.

Alex nods in agreement. "No, probably not."

We follow Alex out of the waiting room and say goodnight to Princess Layla.

......

With her neck propped at a weird angle, Lily stares out the window on the drive home. Her eyes fighting to stay open. The streetlamps strobe golden rays through the car, highlighting her tear-stained face. Her hair is dull, and her eyes have grayed-out bags underneath them.

Layla is going to be furious when she finds out how much energy Lily gave in her healing spell. ...At least I think it was a spell. Maybe it was a ritual? She did some weird thing with a plant.

Turning back to the road, I catch Doug looking at Lily in the rearview mirror again. This is the fifth time in the last minute alone. His forehead is sketched with lines, deep and worried. When we get home, I'll ask him how he feels about sleeping in the basement tonight. To be closer. At least that way she won't be in the house alone.

...

Lily's voice sounds from the backseat. "I know I've been a bother, but can I ask for one more favor?"

The seat belt digs into my shoulder, baring me from turning any further to face her. Doug glances back. Goosebumps spread across my skin when I notice the color coming back to her face. Rosy cheeks and gleaming eyes shine out of the darkness, captivating me.

"You aren't a bother," I say. "Whatever you need, we will do it."

"Can you spend the night with me?"

My body stiffens.

Crap.

My hand crumbles into a fist.

No. We have to tell her no. Right? But I can't say no to her, she needs us. What do I say?

Doug's body locks up, grasping the steering wheel tighter.

Shit, he doesn't know what to say either.

My heart aches. Emotions mix and swirl in my stomach.

Lily rubs her hand over her thigh. "Please... I don't want to be alone."

We don't want you to be alone tonight, either. But how...? Sharing a bed is out of the question. If she asks us to touch her, I don't know if we could say no.

Compromise. We have to compromise.

"Ok, how about..." I lock my questioning gaze on her despondent eyes. "Doug and I set up the guest mattress downstairs for us. We'll watch your favorite anime till you fall asleep on the couch. AND we promise we will be there when you wake up in the morning. How does that sound?"

Holding my breath, I keep my eyes on her.

"I'd like that." She peers out the window. "Thank you."

As I turn to face the road, I silently exhale my relief as Doug's grip loosens. He catches my attention and mouths the words thank you to me. I nod and rest in the leather seat.

...

The car creeps through the autumn trees. The sound of leaves crunching under tires whispers through the night. Deer trot along the side of the car, flanking us as we make our way home. Lily's giant white cat familiar is patiently waiting by the front door when we arrive.

I step out of the car and greet her. "Hello, Snowball."

Snowball nuzzles my leg as Doug opens Lily's door for her. She doesn't move.

"Lily?" Doug's trembling voice pulls my feet to him.

"Quickly, get her inside," Snowball says. "I'll go get Mother and her fathers."

I lift Lily into my arms. "Doug... grab the doors," I insist, trying to stay calm.

She gazes at me. "I'm sorry." Her weak voice whispers.

Doug and I rush her to the basement. I ignore the sight of the backyard now littered with animals, keeping my focus on Lily. Her chest lifts with a steady rhythm.

I lay her on the couch and snap at her. "Damn it, Lily! You overdid it."

"You gave her too much energy." Doug bites out.

"If you..." Lily's voice shakes, and the muscle in her arm twitches.

I grab her hand. "You can't even lift your arm. What were you thinking?"

"Why can't you ever think of your needs first?!" Doug's vexed tone explodes. "You won't help anyone if you push yourself past these limits."

Lily's inhale cracks and her eyes flutter. Fear takes hold of my chest, digging its claws into my gut.

Her hand finds the strength to lift off her stomach. She reaches for Doug and squeezes my hand. "Shh..." Her soft voice breathes out, sounding ever so slightly stronger than it did before. "If you had the power to heal the ones you love, you'd do the same thing."

I'm stunned by her words. Doug and I remain silent as she closes her eyes, unable to keep them open any longer. Her chest rises and falls, keeping a steady, slow rhythm.

The patio doors open, and Doug stands. "Good, you're here." He nods to Jade, Liam, and Greyson. Snowball nuzzles against Doug's legs. She purrs as I pet her, trying to calm us all.

Jade moves to Lily's side and brushes fingers over her forehead. Her green skin makes Lily look paler. Her silver hair falls on Lily's faded red hair as she kisses her cheek. The dire state Lily is in, becoming more apparent. I feel so helpless.

Her eyes shift between the two of us. "She just needs rest. She'll be fine in a few days."

My voice cracks. "That's not soon enough."

"The deal to secure the land for the fae sanctuary is tomorrow," Doug adds for me.

"There is nothing we can do," Liam says, and my temper boils.

"If the Moirai Sisters of Fate and Goddess Faya have willed this delay. Then we must be patient." Greyson's calm tone and gray eyes do nothing to soothe the heat rising in me.

"FUCK THEM." Doug's rage spurs my own.

"Nothing you can do? BULLSHIT... LILY WOULD NEVER ALLOW THEM TO INTERFERE. **SO WHY SHOULD WE?**" I snap.

Their eyes harden and I realize we crossed a line, but for the moment, I don't care. I hold my gaze steady.

"You would defy the will of the Gods?" Liam's stern tone and warrior appearance spur my braveness.

"Damn right, we would!"

Doug steps beside me. "We would do anything for Lily! She needs help now. Not in a few days."

Jade dances to Lily's feet, her voice inspired with urgency. "If you had the power to restore her energy..." Her golden eyes testing us. "Would you?"

"Yes." We say together, without hesitation.

The three of them stand there in silence, the tension rising between us as they study us. Greyson points his tanned finger at Lily. "Place your hands upon her."

It takes me a moment to understand what he means. Snowball pushes into the back of my knee. I quickly kneel beside her, placing my hand on her shoulder and stomach. Doug rests one of his hands next to mine on her stomach, and the other on her thigh. We turn to them, waiting for further instructions.

"Think of your intent." Liam's green eyes hold my attention. "Will yourself to give her the energy she needs to make it through tomorrow."

"And only that much. No more. No less." Greyson warns.

Jade grabs hold of Lily's feet. "I'm going to help your energy flow from you to her and control where it goes."

I close my eyes and inhale deeply, controlling my thoughts. Trying to find some strand of hope or faith to hold onto for strength. I need this to work. On my exhale, a warming sensation flows through my arm.

The warmth gathers inside of me and pours into Lily. I inhale again, ignoring the strange sensation, trying to maintain focus. My breath blows out of my lungs and this time, I am lighter. Doug's intentions mix with mine, perfectly in sync. We breathe together.

I am struck by a wave of emotion. That we could both take hold of this confidence so quickly... Set aside our doubts and insecurities to come together and try this thing we have never done before. Our feelings for Lily could push us to do anything. It's what fuels us now.

A hand grasps my shoulder and Doug and I stop. We gaze up at Liam and Greyson. The smiles on their faces beaming proudly.

"Now we wait," Liam says.

I sigh. Again? That's all tonight has been... Waiting.

...

Doug and I stand silently by Lily's head, willing her to wake. Jade remains on the end of the couch, holding Lily's feet, and Snowball is curled up next to them. I ignore the pointed looks Liam and Greyson send us from where they sit on the coffee table. Choosing instead to focus on Lily.

"Did you know humans cannot heal?" Jade asks, breaking the silence.

Doug and I quickly glance at each other and shake our heads. "That can't be true." I point to Lily and notice the bags under her eyes dissipating. "Lily can heal."

"And we just healed her," Doug says, stating the obvious.

"She can heal because of her heritage. Her blood is fae," Liam says.

"You have no such bloodline, nor have either of you been blessed by the Gods," Greyson says. "You should not have been able to heal her."

"Then how did we?" Doug asks.

"I don't remember what Lily said you humans call it in this century," Jade goes on. "But did she explain to you what a pod is?"

"Well…" I stroke my goatee, trying to remember. "We were told it's what you three are."

Doug sits on the arm of the couch. "It is an old elven term for mates or life partners."

"Extremely simplified- but yes, that is accurate," Greyson says.

"Only a pod can heal their pod." Liam's eyes dart between Doug and me, sharing a quizzical expression with Greyson.

I observe Lily, trying to understand what they are getting at. Relief fills me and distracts me. Her skin is pinking up, the roots of her hair darkening. She's looking more like herself with every passing second.

"We aren't Lily's pod though…" Doug's voice wavers. "We aren't—"

"You must be," Liam interrupts. "There is no other way you could have done what you did."

My eyes widen with realization. They think we are sleeping with Lily. "No, we aren't sleep—"

Lily takes a sharp ragged inhale as her eyes flutter. Doug quickly stands as Jade places her hand over Lily's ankle.

Snowball sits up. "She's waking."

Her beautiful auburn locks wave to life and her cheeks pinken. She sits up and instantly I'm relieved. Doug's body relaxes next to mine. Her eyes touch each of us.

Lily sternly glares at Jade, Liam, and Greyson. "Why did you heal me?"

Her angry tone and question throughs me off, confusing me.

"We didn't —" Liam starts, but Doug swiftly steps forward, cutting him off.

"They didn't like seeing you like that." Doug grabs Lily's hand.

I glide in next to Doug and her brilliant green eyes shine on me. "So, of course, they would heal you."

"So, don't go getting all pissy about it, My Lady," Doug says.

"They knew what the Princess would do to us all if she found out what you did for her." I match Doug's sassy tone. "And we can't have that, now can we, My Lady?"

Lily's giggle settles the ache in my heart. She turns to Jade. "You didn't have to do this."

Jade rubs Lily's leg, her eyes on me and Doug. "It was no problem, darling."

Greyson comically pushes us aside. "Anything for our baby girl."

Liam pinches Lily's cheek, and she swats his hand away. "Stop that, Pop Pop, you're embarrassing me."

"Come on, sweetie." Jade stands. "Let's get you into bed."

"I'm not going to my bed tonight."

I stiffen up and my eyes widen at her bluntly innocent statement. Liam and Greyson stare daggers at Doug and me.

"Then where will you sleep, my child?" Jade asks.

"On the couch." Lily gestures to Doug and I. "They are going to bring down mattresses to sleep on the floor."

"Ok." Jade offers Lily her hand and helps her up. "Let's get you changed."

They head upstairs as Snowball follows behind. Doug and I don't move; Liam and Greyson's gaze still holding us captive.

Their eyes soften. Oh, good... It was all part of the act for Lily's benefit. I release the breath I had been holding in from the tension.

"How are you feeling?" Liam asks.

"Not too different, honestly," Doug says, and I nod in agreement.

"It will hit you tomorrow," Greyson says.

"Next time..." Liam pauses. "And there will be a next time. Don't wait till she passes out to heal her."

"There's a better way to do it." Greyson looks us over. "One that won't leave you two drained the next day." Their smiles are too bright. It makes me anxious.

I proceed cautiously. "What way is that?"

"Intercourse," Greyson says matter-of-factly. My throat catches on the air, making me cough.

"We aren't having sexual relations with your daughter," Doug says stiffly.

Liam snorts. "That's very apparent."

I squint my eyes at his snide remark.

"Once you do, though..." Greyson wiggles his eyebrows. "You'll delight in the other benefits of being in a pod."

"Other benefits? What other benefits?" I ask, my voice a bit too eager.

The two of them chuckle as Doug lets out an exasperated sigh.

"As thanks for what you did, we'll help you get set up down here," Greyson says, ignoring my question.

"No." I wave my hand at him. "That's ok, we got it."

Liam turns to the stairs. "Oh, it's not up for debate. We're helping."

Doug and I bite our tongues as they head upstairs.

"Now we know where Lily gets her attitude from," Doug mumbles under his breath to me.

We collapse on the couch together for a brief rest, laughing away any remaining stress from the night.

CHAPTER 15

THE BRIDAL SHOWER

LILY

SATURDAY, DECEMBER 10TH

The repetitive task of setting tables is comforting to me after the exhausting month I have had. Everything has been in a constant state of excitement... And not the good kind. I was a revolving door, going in and out, in and out of that hospital every day. The machines beeping, terrorizing me even in my dreams.

Today is no better. I haven't quite woken up. The gloom in the sky isn't helping.

Still, the soothing piano music makes for a pleasant background as Heather, Susan, Jane, and I decorate for the bridal shower. It's nice to be here with the girls, but I wish Layla could be here too.

My attention draws to the large window. The Beaufort Country Club is covered in fog. Peeking through the mist, an array of lights shines. Multicolored strands wrap around the trees and fauna. The courtyard fountain twinkles with tiny orbs of white lights.

I take a deep breath and let the sight soothe me. Denise did an amazing job with the lights. I pull out my phone to take a picture, sending it to Doug and James.

It's beautiful here!

MMS 9:57 AM

The familiar speeding of my heart and warming of my body washes over me as I think of them. I wonder if Doug's mom is coming today. My eyes widen. *Does she know I'm coming as their date?* Heather said it was ok to introduce myself as their—

"Lily!" Heather says loudly, getting my attention. "You didn't hear a word I said, did you?"

"No, I'm sorry." I turn to her and point at the view behind me. "The alluring gloom distracted me."

"Oh, that's right," Susan says. "This is your first time at Doug's family country club."

"The lights are beautiful, but I'm so ready for the sunshine I was promised today." Heather's buoyant tone shines. "Anyway... I wanted to ask you, how is Layla doing?"

"Are they home yet?" Jane asks.

"Yeah, they went home on Tuesday."

"That's good," Susan says.

"Can we see pics of the baby?" Jane's grin spreads like wildfire to the others.

"Oh, yes, please." Heather pleads with her hands. "I've been dying to see him!"

I grab my phone, and my own secret joy springs up through my body and across my lips, mirroring the girl's giddiness. I read the messages waiting for me.

Doug

Only you could find beauty in all that gloom. I'm glad you're enjoying it!

MMS 9:58 AM

James

You can tell us all about your adventure when you get home. See you soon.

MMS 9:58 AM

I shake away the distraction and get back to what I was doing, opening my photo gallery. "I thought you got pictures already?"

"James said he would send me pics on Thanksgiving," Heather says, while the three of them make their way through the maze of tables. "But apparently, he forgot to take them. He claimed they weren't allowed to stay long."

"They lied to us both, then." I gingerly shake my head and pull up the photo album. "They were there for two hours, and they told me they'd send the photos to the three of you."

Heather scoffs and crosses her arms, perking up her subtle cleavage. "They are so gonna get an ear full when I see them next."

I pass Jane my phone and Heather and Susan peer over her shoulders eagerly. I watch their expressions while they coo and ahh at every photo they scroll through.

The sight of them huddled together makes me truly happy. Their friendship shines, blooming an image of how beautiful the bride and her bridesmaids will be on the wedding day.

I silently giggle, remembering Susan's annoyance at not being able to dye her hair. Her blue hair has faded; the light blonde roots grown way past her tolerance level. But it will be worth it once she gets the lavender color that Heather picked out. It will match the wedding colors and compliment the bridesmaid's mauve dresses beautifully.

Heather chose a surprisingly simple satin white dress. I was sure she would pick a ball—

"No way!" Heather beams at me with bright eyes. "How did you get them to hold the baby?"

"Oh... It wasn't by choice." I chuckle. "Layla forced them too."

Susan hides her eye roll under a flutter of her lashes. "Of course she did."

"Layla must be persuasive," Jane says. "They don't want kids at all."

"Yeah, always said they would never hold one either. But look at them." Heather coos. "They would make great dads. Do you have any more pics of them?"

"Sorry ladies, that's all the photos I have of the boys together." Jane hands me my phone and I smile, listening to them go on about baby Eric.

Heather groans. "Guess it's time we get back to work."

The girls head back to a set of tables and continue decorating. I check the time. We still have an hour till guests start arriving.

Eucalyptus green, mauve, and lavender blend, weaving in and out of the scene, allowing the white dinnerware to stand out beautifully. The white stemless wine glasses are my favorite addition. They boast an enchanting half-white, half-clear vertical design. I take a step back from the table and admire it all. Heather has excellent taste.

"Oh... they would make the cutest babies," I overhear Heather say to Susan as they place a tablecloth down.

"Don't you go pushing your fantasies off on Lily!" Susan points at Heather.

"Oh, don't act so innocent." Heather points back. "You're curious too."

"I can hear you," I shout at them, and they stop to gawk at me.

"Oh... I..." Susan mutters, embarrassed to be caught, and Jane chuckles.

"Good!" Heather gives me her full attention, her face beaming with bold excitement. She leans over the back of the chair in front of her. "So, which one do you want to knock you up first?"

My body stiffens, my face flashing with heat.

"Heather! Control yourself." Susan gives Heather her signature motherly glare. Her body language betrays her words, though. She's showing just as much interest. Even Jane's usual calm, silent demeanor shifts in favor of curiosity. All eyes land on my face in anticipation.

"One..." I hold up my finger. "We aren't having sex. And two... I don't want kids either."

"What? Why not?" Susan asks.

"Why don't you want kids?" Heather asks.

"Well, I've been raising Layla since I was fifteen, and that was hard enough. So no, not interested."

"Really?" Heather tilts her head.

"But you'd make an exceptional mother," Susan says.

I huff in irritation. Of course, they'd think that. Most women don't understand. Or they pretend to, while impatiently waiting for me to shift my stance on the subject.

"I don't doubt that." I stay calm, covering up the heat boiling in my stomach. "Even so... I don't want any. Plus, I have a nephew now. I'm going to be the most amazing auntie ever. And I'm content with that."

My shoulders tighten. Please, don't push the matter further. I hate being lectured. Explaining my choices is so irksome. I just want to relax.

"For now." Heather glares at me, and I challenge her gaze. Jane and Susan laugh, and I smile when Heather joins in.

Good, they're going to drop it.

"You know, Lily, we haven't seen them this happy in years." Susan grabs a faux candle centerpiece to place on the table. "I'm glad that you guys found each other."

"Yeah, you guys are so cute together," Heather says.

"It's too bad you weren't able to go with them to their folks for Thanksgiving," Jane says.

"Their family is a hoot!" Heather places a stack of plates on the table. "You would have had a great time."

I tilt my head. Was I supposed to go? I don't remember them inviting me. I stop setting the table. "What do you mean?"

"Doug's family is amazing. Never a dull moment in that house," Heather says, and I don't interrupt her babbling to correct her. "We used to go there for Bar-B-Q's every summer. It was a riot. I miss going." She pauses and looks to the side, her eyes reminiscing. "I hope we get to go next year."

"When Doug's family took James in after high school, they all became even rowdier." Jane goes on. "James was a bad influence on them. Wait till the New Year's Party, you'll have a blast."

Susan bursts with the most energy she has had all morning. "I can't wait to go to that!"

"You'll see what we mean when you're there," Heather says to me.

I raise my eyebrow. "I'm invited to that too?"

"Yeah, they text the invites on Christmas. It's torture waiting." Heather dramatically slumps. "But you'll, for sure, get an invite."

"I just thought of something." Susan sets down a box of decorations and locks gazes with Heather. "Have the boys ever brought anyone over before?"

"Of course they have." Heather points between her, Susan, and Jane. "We go all the time."

"No... I mean... I don't think they have ever brought home someone they were dating before."

Heather's eyes get bug sized. "Oh, my God."

"Yeah..." Jane says. "You're right."

They turn on me. "I don't understand." I keep my eyes focused on Jane to steady the spinning in my mind. "If they have never brought anyone to visit their folks; then why do you guys think I was supposed to go to their place for Thanksgiving?"

"Because they said they invited you," Susan says as if that is obvious.

"No... I..." I glance at the floor. "I didn't even know they wanted me to go."

There is an awkward pause, then Heather shakes a fist in the air. "Oh, those jerks are really going to get a piece of my mind!"

"Well, maybe because your sister was in the hospital, they didn't want to take you away from her," Jane says, trying to assure me. My mind spins faster. I face the table, and without another word, I resume decorating.

I mean, maybe?

But why...?

Of course, they wouldn't invite me. Right?

They knew you'd say no cuz you wouldn't leave Layla's side all month. Duh.

The girls shuffle and murmur behind me. I try to distract myself from their gossip while the war in my head continues, by keeping my hands moving.

Would you have gone if they asked?

If Layla knew I hadn't gone because of her, she would have been furious.

So why would they invite you?

If they've never invited anyone else... then... why would they invite me? I'm not special. Obviously, that's why they played it off with the others.

My hands quake and I set down the centerpiece. I press my thumb into my palm, just like James taught me, and will myself to calm down. I close my eyes and take a deep breath. It doesn't help. Crossing an arm under my breasts, I grab my forearm and take another.

But I mean, they told the girls that they wanted you to go.

They wouldn't make that up... Would they?

Of course not.

Then why? I'm not...

Why would they invite you?

I don't know.

Would you have gone?

I don't know.

"**WHY**?" My body tenses as I stare at the table, frozen. The silence that follows my outburst fills me with dread.

"Why what?" Heather asks.

"Why…" My voice grows weak. "Why would they invite me?"

The sound of whispered voices rings in my ears. No, I take it back. Don't tell me.

"Lily…" Susan's motherly voice opens my eyes, pulling my gaze to her. "They care a lot about you."

"Why do you think they invited you to my wedding?" Heather says.

They walk toward me, and I rub my forearm. "Because they knew I wanted to go, and I didn't think I'd get an invite, and…" I take a step away from the table and brush a lock of my hair behind my ear. "We hadn't known each other that long. There was no reason that you would invite some random woman you just met."

Heather's walk falters, her eyes steaming with rage. "Did they tell you that?"

"No," I say, barely carrying the word out. They appear relieved.

"I was going to invite you." Heather's voice is sweet and calm. "But when I called them to ask how to spell your name. They asked me not to cuz they wanted to bring you as their plus one."

"Oh… I didn't… I just…" I fidget with my hands. "I thought they just wanted to invite me since they found out I've never been asked to a dance before."

"Really?" Heather scoffs. "You believe they would go through six-plus weeks of planning something that extraordinary just to play out some dance proposal fantasy?"

I drop my gaze to the floor. "Layla said that they said they had never been to a dance either and wanted to share the experience, too."

"Well, yes, that's true," Susan says. "But you can't believe that was all there was to it?"

"I have to."

"Oh, sweetie." Heather hugs me.

"We know you care for them," Susan says.

I pull away from Heather, not returning her touch. "It doesn't matter how I feel."

"Why not?" Heather asks.

"I can't be with them."

"Is it because they work for you?" Susan asks.

"No."

Heather crosses her arms and puts on her best bitch performance. "Then... Why?"

"I can't ruin our friendship!" My irritation explodes. "For crying out loud, I had to give them the month off and demand they focus on their game because they wanted to take me to the hospital every single day. I refuse to get in the way of their—"

"YOU LOVE THEM!" Jane yells and my sight glues to hers.

The girls freeze, staring at me. I hold my breath and press my lips together.

No, it's not like that. I don't...

One lonely tear falls down my cheek. My legs urging me to collapse. Jane grabs my hand, holding me steady, and blots a napkin to my cheek. "You love them." She repeats, quieter now.

I search her eyes and find the answer reflected back at me. The answer I haven't been able to admit. Even to myself.

"Yes... I love them." My voice cracks as I hold back the dam of tears, wanting to escape my eyes. "But it doesn't matter how much I fantasize. I can't choose between them." My voice straightens up, finding its backbone. "And I refuse to distract them, just because I desire to be with them."

"Why do you believe that you have to choose between them?" Jane's warmth spreads through me.

I grab the napkin from her to rub it under my eyes to stop more tears from escaping. "What do you mean? Don't I?"

"She means…" Susan lays a comforting hand on my shoulder. "We don't think you have to choose."

"We see the way they look at you, the way they talk about you." Heather caresses my cheek and lifts my chin.

"Did you notice that they no longer say 'I' when they talk to you?" Jane asks.

I pause. She's right, they only say 'we' when they talk to me. "Yeah… but…"

"But nothing." Heather lets go of my chin, talking with her hands now. "If they expected you to choose, you'd know it. There would be obvious tension and jealousy. They feel the same way you do. Everyone knows it. Your sister knows. Hell, even our oblivious boyfriends have noticed."

"Talk to th—"

"Heather, can you help me?" A feminine voice calls out, interrupting Jane. She stops walking as she takes in the sight of the girls comforting me. "Oh, I'm sorry. I didn't mean to interrupt."

"It's ok mom, what do you need?" Heather walks to her mother.

"I'm going to go freshen up."

I step away from Jane, but her grasp gently tightens. Her eyes gleam with unshed tears and a small, delicateness lifts her lips. Jane walks with me to the restroom, holding my hand as we go. I sit in the showroom-ready seating area and collect myself as Jane talks about nothing and everything to comfort me.

The cold room warms- I can tell it's her doing. I glow in its radiance. She is becoming more powerful. I'm happy Jade could help her. She'll be a remarkable healer when she turns.

CHAPTER 16

WE NEED TO TALK

LILY

SATURDAY, DECEMBER 10TH

Breath in, 1... 2... 3... 4... 5...

Breath out, 1... 2... 3... 4... 5...

Breath in... Breath out...

I open my eyes and descend the stairs to the basement. The sight of James and Doug fills me with joy as I step into the room. Enthusiasm radiates from them as they enjoy playing Mortal Kombat.

"Hey, Lily." They say in unison.

"Hey."

Breath in... Breath out...

Soft suede rubs against my palm as it glides along the back of the couch. I nestle myself into my favorite spot.

Breath in... Breath out...

Relax. You can do this.
No, I should wait.
Stop that, you promised yourself you'd—
"How was the party?" James asks, his eyes never leaving the game.

"It was nice," I say, willing my backbone to kick in. "I'm less anxious now that I've gotten some of the introductions out of the way."

"That's good." Doug's fingers clash violently with the controller's buttons. "Did you guys do anything special?"

"Yeah! I showed off **ALL** my pictures of Eric! The girls loooved them."

The game pauses. I tilt my head to the side and gleam at them.

"You didn't?" They object in unison.

"Oh, I did!"

"Nooo." James racks his hands down his face.

Doug elbows James. "We'll never hear the end of this."

"You're not alone. They teased me too."

James' back straightens. "What?"

"Why?" Doug asks, his voice barely audible under James' response.

"Well, according to Heather, that's gonna be my baby next." I move my hands, miming myself with a pregnant belly. "The girls wouldn't listen when I told them I don't want kids. But... they kept insisting I'd change my mind."

"Yeah, we went through that too." Doug points between them. "They don't believe us when we say we don't want kids either."

"I am well aware. They wouldn't let it go. Heather said, and I quote. 'We have ruined their fantasy.'"

James raises an eyebrow. "How?"

Their gaze rakes my body and I fidget with my hair. "To put it bluntly... They are mad that I won't let you guys put babies in me." Color darkens their cheeks, and their eyes grow wide. "Yeah, they have shipped us so hard; and according to them, so has my sister." I place my finger on my chin. "Which does NOT help my case... I honestly don't know who is worse, Heather or Layla?"

"Shit." James rigidly nudges Doug with his elbow. "Prepare yourself... Heather is definitely going to make sure we never hear the end of this."

"Oh, no." I shake my head. "She wants to yell and kick you both in the shins. Technically, they all do." I wave my hand. "But that's beside the point."

"Why?" Doug asks. "What did we do?"

"It's what you didn't do... Honestly, I'm surprised Heather hasn't jumped down your throats already."

"They want us to have a baby that much?" James asks.

"Well, Yes... but no."

Their foreheads rumple in confusion.

"Are you going to warn us?" Doug asks.

"Or watch them kick us in the shins?" James' chuckle sounds forced.

"I thought about it the entire ride home." I steady my gaze. "Why did you tell the girls you invited me to your folks' for Thanksgiving dinner when you didn't?"

Their shoulders slump and they turn away from me. My stomach churns in the silence.

Breath in... Breath out...

I sweep my legs out from under me and position myself on the edge of my seat, wondering if I should retreat. They look at me, and I pause.

Doug brushes his fingers through his hair. "We're sorry."

"We were going to, but with everything going on with Layla." James' hand rubs the couch cushion between us. "We didn't want to take you away from her."

I twist my head away, not wanting them to see my sorrow. "I figured as much."

I rub my clammy hands across my thighs.

Now ask them.

Breath in... Breath out...

"What's wrong?" The concern lies heavy in Doug's brilliant blue eyes.

"Did Heather upset you?" James reaches out, then pauses, letting his arm fall back down to the couch.

I stare at his hand. The hesitation in his movement sends an icy wave flooding through me, leaving me cold. Aching for the warmth of their hands.

Why won't they touch me? After the girls pointed out the obvious, I was hopeful. But things never went back to normal between us. There has been so much distance. I almost had hope, believed... but how could they feel the same if they won't even...?

They only touch me causally and when we have company now. Their hands polite. Platonic. They haven't truly touched me since Brian hurt me, and I told them about my past. Emotions clash inside my heart. My eyes flash rage at them.

Calm down. Don't yell. You need to stay calm. They already look worried.

I close my eyes. Breath in... Breath out... Ready, I ask, "How would you have introduced me to your family?"

"What do you mean?" James asks.

"They already know who you are," Doug says.

My nostrils flair. "That's not what I asked."

I hold my breath to stop myself from saying anything else. I don't want to snap at them. Was I wrong? Doubt flickers through me. I wonder if I am only making a fool of myself. I sigh. My feet help me stand, though they don't step with strength. I stare at the floor as I walk behind the couch. The sound of them shuffling echoes behind me.

"Lily." "Please, don't go." Their voices pleading with me.

I stop walking and slowly turn around. Damn. This is hard.

"We don't understand what you mean?" James says as they move out from behind the couch. "Maybe if—"

"Stop." I straighten my palm and they freeze in place. I can't figure them out. They truly don't know what I'm talking about. I'll change the question. "Today, Heather introduced me to her friends and family as your date. Is that what you wanted?"

"Well, you are our date," James says.

"So why would that bother us?" Doug asks.

They are truly sincere. The girls are wrong. They don't feel the same way. They are just being nice, just entertaining me. I retreat, tucking my emotions back inside.

"I'm sorry. With all the baby talk and the girls teasing, I got emotional and worried that you would get upset that they didn't introduce me as just your boss." My emotions won't quite stay tucked in, they threaten to spill out and overwhelm me. I turn around and head up the stairs. "I'm going to take a bath to relax before dinner."

Silence fills the air as I force my hearing away from them. I don't want to know what they'll say about my freak-out. Their pause already told me everything I need to know.

Stay strong. You can cry in the shower.

Heavy footsteps pound the stairs behind me as I step onto the bedroom floor landing.

"Lily..." James' voice shakes. "We're sorry. We didn't understand."

"We're stupid and overly cautious..." Doug adds, their words seamlessly pass back and forth between the two of them.

"You aren't just our boss."

"We do want to introduce you as our date."

I stare at my bedroom door. My breath catches in my throat. A soft pause vibrates between us. Tired of waiting and unable to hold back my desperate curiosity, I ask. "And if I wished to be more?"

"Whatever you want," Doug says, his voice gentle and urging.

"You just have to ask." James' voice layers over sweetly.

Their soft tones wash over me. Convincing and strong. A bittersweet mixture of relief, fear, and dangerous hope courses through me. I turn to face them. I smile, wary and nervous. Anticipation rises in me like a raging storm as they slowly walk toward me.

They stop, and my heart aches, burning me. Doug's hand balls up. James clenches the banister. Their eyes advert away from my body.

What is wrong with them? Why do they keep acting this way?

Anger melts over my lips and my forehead vein pulses. "How can I be your date if you won't touch me?"

"We want to touch you," James says as Doug presses his lips together.

"Then why won't you?!" I snap, not caring that my voice breaks on the words.

Their chins drop to their chest. Their eyes fall to the floor again.

"Because..." Doug starts.

"... we're scared." James finishes.

My anger dissipates as confusion slips in between the cracks of the walls I was building.

Why do they sound ashamed?

Something in their tone urges me to speak sweetly. "Why are you scared?"

Their heads bow further toward the stairs.

Doug's shoulders shake. "We're worried that we'll hurt you." His tone deepens. "We don't trust ourselves to be gentle with you."

"To take it nice and slow, like you've asked us to... Like you deserve." James' apologetic tone fuels me.

My perspective shifts. My mind reeling. Really? That's it? They're worried about being rough with me... Why? That's so stupid.

"Are you sure that's the reason?" I ask, wondering if they are holding something back. But they both nod. A weight lifts off their shoulders in the wake of their honesty.

I've been fretting this whole time about distracting them from their work- afraid to want too much. Stupidly believing that I might have to choose between them. AND... and all they were concerned about was this bullshit.

They stand there staring at the floor. Their breathing uneven and deep.

I slip my shirt over my head, my hair falling beside me. I crumple my shirt and throw it down at them. It hits Doug in the arm. It falls to the floor, getting their attention. They give me what I crave. Their posture straightens and their eyes smolder. My emotions rage as my nipples harden and my clit pulses with excitement.

"For 7 months, I've fantasized about us cracking the kitchen table to putting holes in my shower wall. I don't need your caution. I am not so fragile that you need to shield me. I have gone over and over scenarios in my head, convincing myself..."

Water wells in my eyes. "But it doesn't matter. My hesitations were bullshit, and yours are too. Jane had to yell at me, to help me face the truth." My eyes close and a tear falls. I place my hands on my stomach. My voice boldens. "I want to be yours. Not just your date. I want to show you how much I love you..." My voice cracks. "I need to—"

A coarse hand trails across my cheek as his fingers glide into my hair. I lean into James' hand as his lips press against mine. Tension bleeds out of me, and I go weak from our kiss. Doug brushes past us, their bodies framing mine in this tender moment. His fingers stroke my bare neck, making their way down my arm. He intertwines his fingers with mine. James pulls away and I open my eyes.

"We're sorry we kept you waiting." James' voice feathers over my skin, enchanting me.

Doug takes a step back, pulling my arm with him. The sound of the bedroom door closing behind us sends my desire to a height I've never reached.

Chapter 17

This isn't Talking

Lily

Saturday, December 10TH

The intensity of radiant anticipation overwhelms my senses. I long for their touch, long to hear them whisper in my ear. Months of torment, the years of dissatisfaction-built up within me, yearning for release. We reach my bed and Doug turns me around, pulling me close to him. Goosebumps dance across my flesh as his fingertips lightly glide along the curve of my neck.

Carnal desire burns in his eyes. I rise onto my toes and meet his lips. The subtle smell of citrus surrounds our sensual embrace. Fingers slide into my hair. Our kiss blazes with passion. James steps closer, his warmth whispers across my flesh. The hunger in his touch dances over my skin. I muffle a hum against Doug's lips.

Doug releases his hold on me and steps back. As James reaches for my bra clasp, Doug removes his shirt. The sunlight shines through the window, magnifying his features. His blue eyes twinkle in the light.

I place my hands over my breasts to hold my bra as James unclasps it. The relief of pressure is thrilling, inspiring. Playfully, I slide one strap down my shoulder. Doug's gaze sets me on fire. The need to seduce them, to tease them, overwhelms me. I slip the other strap down. James' hand tightens on my waist. I tilt my chin to my shoulder and gracefully pull the bra away. It drops to the floor.

Doug beams and I glance down at the protrusion in his pants, pressing to be set free. A wave of joy floods over me. They no longer hide their desire from me.

Firm hands caress my stomach and make their way to my breasts. I lean back against James' brawny chest and voice my pleasure as he massages me. Doug kneels in front of me and claims my hips.

Kisses pepper my stomach, and I trail my fingers over Doug's shoulders. James gently squeezes my nipples and I tilt my head back quickly from the sensation, snapping my hand into his thigh. My lips press together, a moan escaping. Fingers slip into the waistband of my leggings and Doug pulls them down my thighs. Careful not to take my panties with them.

James' lips graze over my neck as Doug lifts my leg with a light touch. The soft fabric skims across my foot, intensifying my pleasure. A soft kiss presses against my inner thigh above my knee, sending a shiver up my leg and into my core. I didn't know being spoiled could be this incredible.

I present my other leg to Doug and close my eyes. The sensation magnifies under his mouth and hands. They stimulate every one of my senses. Lost in my bliss, the heat of their bodies shoots through my palms as I explore them. I no longer have to imagine what it's like... to caress Doug's shoulder... to have James' muscles under my hand.

This is real now.

Doug's mouth climbs my leg, his stubble scratching me. James' kisses descend to my shoulder. His soft facial hair is erotic. Like being brushed with a feather. I open my eyes and squeak at the sudden aggressive possession of my hips as they collide with Doug's lips. The muffled sound of Doug's primal need washes over me.

James leans me forward, stepping away. My fingers intertwine in Doug's hair as his kisses move up my body. James walks around us, his gaze lingering on my naked chest.

I press my nails into Doug's shoulder as James removes his shirt. The sunlight sends highlights over each line of his defined muscles. The sight of his broad shoulders and powerful arms makes my knees buckle. Doug's arm swiftly holds me steady.

Teeth graze the side of my supple breast, and I shudder in his arms. An electric energy vibrates through me. My fingertips drift along his warm skin. He trails kisses up my neck and cheek. His grip tightens when our lips meet. I whimper and arch my body into his.

Our passion turns savage as Doug's erection presses deep into my stomach. The taste of him wraps around my tongue as he indulges in me. My breath quickens. I hunger for him. His arm shakes behind me and as he pulls away, I open my eyes.

"You ready?" Doug straightens up and releases his hold on me.

"Yes." I breathe out the word.

Doug pivots to the side of me, and without hesitation, James takes his place. He pulls me close, his desire sending an ache straight to my clit. Our lips embrace and my arms wrap around his neck. I caress the curves of his muscles. James slides his hand tenderly underneath the wave of my hair, lifting and wrapping it around his arm.

I squeak in shock as my eyes widen. Did he just?... He moved my hair the same way I do. No one has ever moved my hair.

James lifts my leg to his hip and our lips part. He shines with excitement. In one swift motion, he lifts me, and I wrap my legs around him. Pleasure whispers from my throat as his arousal presses against me. I hold tight to him and tuck my head into the curve of his neck. James lays me on the bed and rests my hair next to us.

The heat from James' body pours over me, his woodsy scent surrounds our embrace. His kiss is like a drug.

I unwrap my legs and reluctantly allow him to stand up. He slides his fingers under my panties. The smooth fabric has never felt so good sliding off my thighs. James kisses my stomach.

With my legs trapped under him, his lips dab across my scar and down my thigh. The sweet, sensual act fills me with overwhelming bliss. James removes the last bit of fabric, leaving me fully exposed.

Doug and James stand side by side and gaze at me with longing. I let my seductiveness shine. My small hands glide down my stomach and, as my arms perk my breasts up, I reach for my thighs. I open my legs and present myself to them. The bare-chested men of my fantasies flare with desire at the sight of me.

I've never felt so wanted. The need to have them inside me ravages my mind.

Doug takes a step to the side, making a gentle motion with his fingers. I recognize the gesture as one I was not meant to see. James kneels and grabs my knees, holding my legs open. Kisses trail up my inner thigh. The sensation is delicious, making me crave more.

I run my palm along the smooth sheets and purr. His grip tightens, he stops. Lust builds between my legs, his smile hypnotizing me. James tilts his head to the side to kiss my other thigh.

"Oh, you're going to regret that."

James' chuckle vibrates against my leg, and I whimper. I focus my gaze on Doug and enjoy the sight of him watching. James' lips tease me as fingertips glide up the inside of my other thigh. Doug undoes his belt as James' hand explores my shape.

My legs tremble under his touch. Doug pushes his pants down to his thighs and I'm flooded with anguish. My eyes plead. But Doug doesn't notice, his gaze riveted below.

James applies more pressure with each stroke through my hair. Two of his fingers press open my lips. My body reacts to his touch, an undeniable elation commanding me. His wet fingers glide to my clit. I dig my hands into the bed and arch my back. He presses in and I cry out.

My back is pushed down onto the bed as James moves over me. He lies next to me, his teasing touch never ceasing. I wrap my arm around him to hold his shoulder. His mouth embraces my nipple.

"James…" I hum. His touch is agonizing. I catch Doug's gaze and plead. "Please."

Doug stands in his briefs, and I stare at his erect penis, praying for it to escape its fabric prison. He smiles, reading my wish, and guides his fingers into his waistband. James glides his fingers down and Doug's gaze follows his movement.

Fingers push inside as Doug unveils himself. The sight of his arousal and the pressure of James' fingers are enthralling. I close my eyes and pant as he thrusts into me.

The pleasure intensifies as I bathe in the sounds they make. I open my eyes, and, for the first time, I take in what it's like. The sight of someone enjoying me. Adoring every moment of pleasure meant just for me. I savor every touch and nestle my body into James, forcing myself not to squirm. Doug touches himself in rhythm to the show we provide him.

My eagerness explodes. I want Doug's thick cock. The yearning devours me. I crave to see the shape of James' arousal.

I place my hand under James' chin and lift him to kiss my lips. Fingers slip out of me and immediately press into my clit. The circular pressure is too intense, and my legs clamp around his wrist. I scream my pleasure at the ceiling.

James leans into my ear. "Relax."

I shake my head and moan. I don't know how. It's too good. What do I do? He sits up and grabs my knee. My legs won't give in to his demands.

Doug grabs James' shoulder and my thigh. James' finger finally relents as Doug jerks his head. My breathing slows as Doug caresses my thigh and I unclench my legs to free James' hand. Hypnotized by his gaze taking in every curve of my body, a rush of excitement flows through me.

As I try to sit up, Doug traps me beneath him. My eyes beg. "Please, I want you in my mouth."

"No, not yet. It's all about you right now. AND right now, my cock wants to give you what you deserve. I'm going to please you till you have no breath left in your lungs. So be a good girl and arch your back so I can carry you to the middle of the bed."

I can form no words. My mind surrenders- follows his commands. My hair cascades across the pillows and the spell breaks. Pure instinct takes control as he climbs over me.

My tongue ravishes his, trying to make him regret not letting me take him into my mouth. I push my breasts into him as I rub him against me. He tenses and growls. The sound fueling me. Our lips part and his eyes waver, fighting to gain control.

He leans into my ear. "Look at James."

I bite my lip at the sight of James licking his fingers, savoring me. Doug's teeth graze the curve of my neck as his hand moves between us. The tip of his penis strokes across the length of me. He gets wetter with each controlled motion. My fingers grip his arm as he presses against my opening. Every deliberate thrust lets another inch of him inside me.

My scream overshadows his muffled moan as I fully engulf him. The sight captivates James. I turn my head, forcing the heat of Doug's breath off my neck. My body quakes under his gaze. I make the first move, grinding into him. Doug lifts my leg above his hip and thrusts deep into me.

My moans fall in sync with each powerful stroke. Wrapping my leg and arms around him, I relax into him, into this ecstasy. The smell of him. The taste of him.

Time passes and my mind is pulled in a new direction. A shock of realization. We're still going.

An unfamiliar sensation awakens within me. I want more.

James is watching us. His pants undone, and his thumbs are ready to remove them. I reach for him. He smiles and bares the shape of his arousal to me. My moan changes, grabbing Doug's attention.

Doug snatches my outstretched hand. "You can't have him yet." He leans into my neck, and his thrusts become savagely sharp and hard. "You're still mine."

His teeth press into my neck, and I wince from the sudden pain. His tempo falters as he pulls away. I dig my nails into his back and force him to stay put. "Yes, right there. Fuck... That feels so good."

I lock eyes with James and turn into the pillow, presenting my gift to Doug. He releases my hand and swiftly cups the back of my head. He nibbles on my neck and ravages me. Noises escape from my throat as I rock with Doug while James strokes himself, enjoying the show.

My senses drift, adoring everything he has to give me.

The bed shifts beneath us, and Doug slows his thrusts. Sensual kisses trail from my neck to my mouth. My legs shake as we stop. Doug straightens and grabs my knees, helping me open them wide. As he gently pulls out of me, I grasp the sheets, press my lips together, and weep.

James crawls over me, playing with my breasts. His touch is fuel to my desire. This sensation is one I've never experienced before. The act of being spoiled and taken care of is better than I could have imagined. And they enjoy it. I don't want it to stop. I crave more.

I shift my hips, urging him to take me. James grabs his erection and teases the tip of himself at my opening. I press my hips into him, sliding the full length of him inside me. He moans as he enters me, and I cry out.

"Fuck you're tight."

Without letting me respond, his soft lips connect intensely with mine. I caress James' back as he takes long, deep strokes. I relish every curve of his muscles under my palms. We find our rhythm and I press my hands, one into his lower back and the other into his shoulder, holding tight to him.

The woodsy smell of his beard balm is an aphrodisiac that I lose myself in.

I have always been able to distinguish between their scents. Their touch when I could not see them. I know the sound of their footsteps. Their voices. Everything. But now,

I can feel the difference pressing against my body. Doug is primal and rough. James is sensual and cherishing.

My eyes open and I unlock our lips. A tear escapes my eye as his sweetness beams at me.

James is making love to me. This is what it's like.

His hand embraces my cheek, brushing the tear away. I tilt my head into the curve of his hand.

My eyes blaze, desiring more from him. "Take me."

I brace my feet on the bed and push my hips hard into him. My back arches and his arm reaches under me to lift me off the mattress. I brace my arm against the headboard and take him as deep as I can.

James grinds into me lovingly, taking his time to savor every inch of me.

"Damn Lily, you are so sexy." Doug's husky tone grabs my attention. I swoon as he caresses himself. "I want to hear you speak. Tell us what you want."

James slows down and I unbrace myself from the wall. "I want to wrap my hand around your cock as James fucks me. See the desire in your eyes until you make me scream your names to the heavens."

Their eyes shine in the sunlight. The bed shifts as Doug joins us. James pulls out of me without warning. My moan weeps at the suddenness and my legs clamp up. James grabs my ankles and puts my feet on his shoulders.

Doug takes my hand, placing it just where he wants it. My fingers wrap around his erection, squeezing his shaft. James grabs my waist and thrusts into me. My throat cracks as a scream of bliss escapes from my lungs.

They don't wait for me to catch my breath. James gives me everything I asked for as Doug trains my hand to move the way he likes it. I relax into the pleasure, into them, intensifying their touch.

I pout at Doug and push his hand away. He obliges. I softly caress his shaft, my grip tightening around the tip. Slowly, I tease him as they enjoy me. My pace steadies as James slams my body into his. I close my eyes and keep myself from moaning. I'm weightless, euphoric, and safe with their rough pleasure.

Fingertips drift across my chest and linger above my nipple. I open my eyes and tighten my grip in response to Doug's teasing.

"Lily," James says as Doug glides his fingertips up my neck. "Won't you sing for us?"

I press my lips together and shake my head. Doug stops my hand from pleasing him and grabs my chin. The passion in his eyes is thrilling. That's what I want. I clench my walls around James' staff and tighten my grip on Doug's cock. They moan and James' tempo falters, his fingers gripping my thighs.

Doug's devilish smile enraptures me. He removes my hand from him and leans over me. His face is an inch from mine, his eyes challenge my resolve. My passion is ruthless. I press my lips to his, and immediately my tongue enters his mouth. I quickly take advantage of his shock to suck on his tongue.

Now unable to scream out, I squeeze James again, but he is unphased- controlled. Doug caresses my neck and takes over my kiss.

They are rough with me. This passion- it's addictive.

Unable to move my hips, I grip Doug's back and twist the sheet in my grasp with the other. Doug's hand bares down my neck to my breast. He squeezes my nipple and twists. I rack my fingernails into his shoulder, down to his hip.

The pleasure is intense. The pain is unbelievably amazing.

Doug releases my nipple and rubs his hand down my stomach. James slows his assault and I squeeze my walls around him. There is no response. He doesn't falter. I thrash under them.

No, please don't touch me there. I can't handle it.

Doug cups his palm over my hair as his middle finger finds my clit. With every powerful thrust James gives me, Doug's finger pushes into me. I rack my nails back up and dig into Doug's shoulder blade. But his kiss is unrelenting.

I surrender my body to them. Doug releases my mouth and I scream. "DOUG... JAMES..."

I shake my head, unable to handle it anymore. My chest heaves and I collapse under them. They stop our pleasure and gleam triumphantly. My eyelids tip closed as I catch my breath. They shift around the bed. The thrill of what more they have to give me sends a burst of energy through my muscles.

Hands clasp my ankles, and my eyes snap open. Heat pours over me at Doug's lustful smile. He pulls me to the edge of the bed, where he stands. He takes my hand, lifting me. I kneel in front of him to stop him from pulling me off.

His hard-on presses against my stomach. I nip his breast muscle and he whispers a moan as he cups my nape. He pushes me into him, and I take a bite. My hair shifts to the side as James kneels behind me, his coarse hands exploring my back. Doug lifts my chin to kiss him.

With my legs in between James', Doug pushes me back onto James' lap. I grab Doug's cock and bend my body in half. James' hands shift to my hips, holding me tight as I ready myself to take him in my mouth.

A hand wraps around my wrist. "No, Lily." I peep at Doug through my lashes. "Until we make you cum, we are unworthy of this mouth."

"Then hurry up."

"Oh, no." James pulls me up to rest against his chest. "We plan on savoring every delicious detail of you."

Doug kneels, trailing kisses from my cheek to my chest as he goes. James' hands tenderly capture my breasts as Doug's hands caress their way to my knees. My knights' sensual touch is a soothing balm after the roughness they offered.

Fingertips skim across my thigh, barely touching me. The sensation sends a chill over my skin and Doug smirks. His hand disappears between my legs, and he unforgivingly pushes his fingers into me. I cry out from the sudden switch in sensations.

With his fingers thrusting up into me, his palm slams into my clit, causing a burst of pleasure to radiate through me. James plays with my breasts as his erection glides between my cheeks. My nails dip into Doug's shoulder. I reach for James' cheek, to pull him close as I twist to kiss him.

My cries are muffled in his mouth. Our passion is fire underneath hunger. There is nothing to cool this intense pleasure. James' mouth. Doug's fingers. It's too much. I can't relax... I don't know how. I can't take this.

"I... I can't..."

Doug catches my pleading gaze and stops. My body grows weak, unable to hold myself up any longer. James clutches my chest as I fall forward. Doug's fingers pull out of me, and I clench up, trapping his hand between my legs.

The edge of my vision blurs. They lean me up against James' chest and I barely make out the motions their hands make beside me. The burning in my lungs fades out into a calm between storms.

"Do you need a break?" Doug asks as he forces his hand out from between my thighs.

He stands up and I can't take my gaze away from his erection. "No, I need you inside me."

Doug tilts my chin up, his gaze studying me. His lips lift, satisfied, as he helps me stand, twirling me to face the bed. James' eyes captivate me as he motions for me to come to him.

I crawl and powerful hands firmly pull on my hips and glide me back to the edge of the bed. I turn my head back, and Doug's eyes send me over the edge as his cock readies to take me.

James' gentle touch guides my gaze to him as he pleasures himself. Doug guides my hair to the side, pushing into me. Lust fills me. I scream out. There is no reprieve. Unable to keep up with Doug's fast and powerful thrusts, I fall forward.

The ragged noises we make echo in my ears. I enjoy being taken, being dominated. I lose myself in the bliss of his roughness.

My mind wonders with a renewed thrill at all the pleasures I could have. The things I could try. They are so good to me. I want to make them feel wanted. To give them a taste of this pleasure.

My elbows protest as I straighten them. I push back into Doug, gaining the confidence to match his power. Gradually, he lets me take control.

I pull James' hand to me and hold his eyes captive. James stops caressing himself and watches me intently. I lick the fingers he used on me. The taste of me is gone, but the light that flickers into his eyes keeps me going. He moans deeply. I rotate my hips into Doug while I push James' long, callused fingers into my mouth.

Those deep brown eyes flood over me. I squeeze my walls around Doug in excitement. His fingers twitch on my hip and I smirk.

As I grind and suck, they let me go at my pace. But I know they're holding back. They want more.

Soft hands rub along my skin, caressing my curves. I hold on to James' wrist and thrust him into my mouth. My rhythm extends through me, and I take Doug in deep. I clench around him and cry out. James glances at Doug as he tightens his hands around my waist and moans.

Doug's grip is tight, and I can't move my hips any longer. His hands are shaking. I remove James from my mouth and lick his fingers as I clench myself around the thick cock inside me. Doug growls and lightly smacks my ass.

I let go of James to peer over my shoulder. "You stay there. It's my turn now." Doug lets go of my waist. I smile at James and point to the top of the bed. "Lay down."

I press my lips together, glance down at the bed, and drag Doug out of me. The sensation is just as fierce as when they do it. I seductively crawl over James and fix my hair to the side, giving Doug the perfect view of us. My clit tingles at the sight of James wanting to devour me.

I brace my hands on his chest and gleam at him. "I'm going to take you deep inside me and have my way with you." James' cock pulses between my legs and I hum. "Doug, can you see me?"

"Yes, Lily. Every curve of your sexy body."

"Good." I press James' attentive hardness to my opening. "I want you to watch."

"You like it when we watch you. Don't you?" Doug asks.

I push the tip of James into me and moan. "Yes."

My hands clamp onto James' ribs as I bounce on the tip of his cock. The thrill of being filled overwhelms the discomfort and soreness. My moan crashes out as I fully take him into me. James' moan rumbles. He grabs my hips and grinds into me.

Pleasure rocks through my core. James' hard, muscular chest is alluring under my hands. His long, hard cock deep inside me sends me to a place I've never been before. I lay on his chest and kiss him. I moan in his ear as we rock together.

"James, please don't stop." I kiss him. "This position..." The words tease out of me. I prop my hands on his chest. "You feel so good."

"You've never been in this position?" James asks, his voice tender. I shake my head. "You like how deep I get in you?"

"Yes." My ecstasy weeps. "Please don't stop."

"I can go deeper." James' sultry voice whispers. My clit shudders with excitement and my eyes widen. "Lean back and place your hands on my thighs." Those brown eyes hold me captive. I do as he says. "Now bounce on my cock, Lily. Take all of me inside you."

Instinct takes control and I lose my mind. Pleasure is all I know. I tilt my head back and sing for him. James' grip glides up my waist to my breasts. His strong hands capture them and euphoria shoots through me like a drug. He pinches my nipples, and my voice responds to his touch.

I'm set afire. I want more.

My hips stop, and I turn to Doug, motioning for him to join us. "Kneel behind me."

"No, Lily, you're not ready for that."

"I know." My gaze falls from his. "I'm sorry. But—"

James caresses my cheek. "You have nothing to apologize for."

"But..." I bat my eyelashes. "I want to play with Doug while I ride you."

The bed immediately shifts under Doug's weight. I squeeze my vagina to tease James. He smirks and bucks into me. I squeak and tease him again as I gather my hair to make room for Doug. James pinches my nipple and I press my lips together to conceal my moan.

We stop toying with each other as Doug gets comfortable behind me. I offer my neck to him, and he nibbles on it.

The three of us rock together. I grind my hips into James as Doug's penis strokes my back.

The smell of the forest blends with Doug's citrus scent, bewitching me. The carnal desire to have them both is overpowering. Their hands vigorously caress my flesh. Desire radiates from them. It mixes with mine. Every ounce of pleasure that I bring them returns to me.

I glow from the passion and grab James' wrists, directing his roaming hands to hold my hips. I take Doug's soft hands, place one on my breast and the other around my neck. Arching my back, I reach behind me and grab his thick cock.

Doug's groan vibrates on my neck. I stroke the tip of him and gently wave my hips. "James…" I hum sweetly. "Doug…"

Elation devours me. I lead, exploring the pleasure in the rhythms we make.

Doug sighs as I let go of him to grab his wrist. I guide his hand down my chest to my scar and glide James' hand to my breast. I place James' fingers in my mouth and brace a hand on his chest. My fingers glide through Doug's hair, pushing him further into the curve of my neck. His teeth devour me, his kisses reprieve the ache.

Fingers thrust into my mouth as they each caress a breast. Doug's gentle massage is sensual and sweet; contrasting with James' calloused fingertips roughly pinching my nipples.

Their touch sends me into a spiral, a euphoric trance.

With my eyes closed, I take in everything through my other senses.

Muscles sore. Throat hurting. James inside me. Doug against my back. Hands on my breasts. Bites on my neck. Fingers in my mouth.

I'm elated as I rock back and forth, letting them ravage my body.

An overwhelming sensation shoots through me, heating me. My eyes shoot open as I stifle my labored screams on James' fingers. I squeeze his ribs.

James' eyes widen, glowing. "Come on baby, cum for us."

A thunderous storm bellows inside me. James' wet fingers escape my mouth and Doug releases my neck. I rest my head on Doug's shoulder.

Captured by ecstasy, my lust explodes. I sing my bliss to the ceiling.

My body quakes between theirs. Doug twists my head, kisses me passionately while James keeps me cumming. The pleasure doesn't end. They stoke the storm raging within me.

I pound my hands on their bodies, and they stop. I fall limp in their arms. My vagina twitches around James' long, hard cock.

Doug brushes my hair as James caresses my arm. They wait for me to collect myself. My breathing calms and Doug moves to the side of us, taking my hair with him. His fingers make a gesture I don't understand. I sit up, but James wraps his arm around me, stopping me.

James pulls me close to his chest; he rolls us, pinning me on my back in one smooth motion. He braces himself over me, leaning in close. The passion of his kiss pours into me. I tighten my legs around his sides. His thrusts deep... slow... hard... The motion consumes my senses.

Doug's fingers twirl through my hair, his gaze rejoicing. I brace my hand on James' shoulder and push up into each powerful thrust. His eyes waiver for control. I know he is close.

A thrilling sensation courses through my body as his excitement heightens. His pleasure is intense and exhilarating. I express my arousal. His moans deepen.

"JAMES." I squeeze him tight.

James roars and shoots his heated release deep inside me. We moan, sharing in his pleasure.

As he twitches and pants, my legs quake, clenching his ribs tight. After a moment, I let go of him and grip the sheet. James places his hand on my knee. I arch my back and close my eyes, willing myself to relax for him. My body protests as James pries my legs open and tenderly pulls out of me.

The bed shifts around me, and Doug towers over me. His soft touch is erotic and if I didn't know better, I would call it romantic, but those eyes tell me I'm in danger.

He grabs my knees, holding my legs open as he watches himself. A quick thrust pushes seamlessly into me. Just as swiftly, he pulls out of me and thrusts back in again. My legs tremble from the punishment. He is in complete control.

My scream cracks. "Doug, please."

"Please what?" Doug repeats my torment and I whine. My eyes plead with James as he lies next to us, enjoying the sight. Doug enters me and turns my chin to face him. "He can't help you. You're mine."

I spring a smile and wrap my free leg around him. I squeeze my walls. He growls and braces himself over me, holding my wrists down. "Yes, DOUG... Please... take me."

My walls clench around him again. His eyelids slam shut as he growls. Doug tucks his head into the curve of my neck. He holds nothing back, pounding fast and deep into me.

I'm addicted. Intoxicated. In love with this surrender. I let him take me with every deep thrust. It makes me see stars.

Arching my body, I press my chest into his. Doug's grip tightens around my wrists. My pulse pounds against his palms. I lower, my back touching the smooth sheets again. Pain shoots up my shoulder from the motion. My breath catches in my throat.

A dull pain lingers as the pleasure continues. My mouth opens, wanting to get Doug's attention, but my voice betrays me. I moan blissfully. The passion in each thrust is overwhelming my will. I can feel how much pleasure I bring him. I can't stop.

Pain and arousal fight for dominance. It opens my mind to the other ways Doug could bring my body to dance like this again. I glance at James and wince as the pain shoots through my shoulder.

James' enjoyment of the show Doug and I perform is written across his features. Our gaze meets and that changes in an instant. His hand latches onto Doug's wrist. Doug's eyes shoot open, fear consuming them as he freezes.

Doug lets go of my wrists. "I'm sor—"

My palm clasps over his mouth, and I wrap my legs around his waist to stop him from pulling away. I cup my fingers around James' palm and defiantly stare at Doug, digging my nails into his shoulder.

"Stop teasing me. I want to cum again."

I pull him close and grind into him, running my nails down his back as hard as I can. He lets out a thunderous moan that vibrates straight to my clit. His kiss is sweet as his body relaxes into mine. Unsheathing my claws, I glide my fingertips along the welts I've left behind.

He stops kissing me, and his eyes gleam once more. I sing for him. This time he doesn't take his gaze off me, and I make sure he sees every ounce of pleasure he gives me.

No one has ever been so rough with me. How can it bring this much pleasure?

Not caring about my sore throat, I continue to express my joy.

The pressure builds and my body tenses up again. I dig my nails into him and squeeze James' hand. "Doug." My eyes challenge him. "Harder!"

Doug increases his speed, thrusting his power upon me. His moans pant out with me. The excitement in his eyes is captivating. It throws me over the edge. I tilt my head back and scream out. My body melts. I pulsate around Doug's cock as he ravages me.

My climax floods me with adrenaline.

I brace myself on my elbows and expose the other, untouched curve of my neck to present my offering to him. His tempo falters as his gaze lingers on my neck. "Take it, it's yours."

Swiftly, his hand grips my nape. His teeth latch around my neck. Once again, pain and pleasure mix. I hum as he takes me. All I can do is hold on. His passion fuels me.

I moan louder as he tenses up. He lets go of my neck and grunts his fierce release. His thick cock pulses inside me, causing me to clench around him. We rock together, savoring the finish. Soon, our breathing slows, recovering our senses.

A cocky grin forms on his face and his cock flexes inside me. I squeak and pulsate around him. He does it again and I moan, squeezing so hard he almost falls out of me. I playfully smack his chest. "Stop that!"

He laughs and grabs my shaking knees. He forces my legs to stay open as he pulls out of me. James leans over and places a warm washcloth over me. The heat soothes my ache. Doug closes my legs and James hands him one.

I smile, not knowing how to handle this new experience. No one has ever cared for me like this, let alone help to clean up the mess they leave.

I hurt so much, yet am so euphoric.

How long were we at it?

CHAPTER 18

WANNA BUILD A FORT?

JAMES

SATURDAY, DECEMBER 10TH

Lily stares at her nightstand, studying the clock. I smile as she calculates.

"Two minutes," Doug says, getting her attention. "Give or take."

Her glow is beautiful. I could stare at her all day. We waited too long for this.

"Is it normal to not be able to move your legs?" Lily asks.

"Yep," I say, proud of our achievement.

"I guess I really shouldn't be skipping leg day then, huh?"

"NOOO!" Doug says. "Are you trying to kill us?"

"Your legs are like a vise," I say. "I'm surprised you didn't crack our ribs."

"I would say sorry, but I have a feeling it's your fault."

"Yeah, it is!" Doug says.

"We accept full responsibility." I kiss her shoulder.

Doug soothes her shaking leg. "Did we fulfill any of your fantasies?"

"No! Not a one." Lily smirks at us.

"Guess we'll just have to try again." Doug taunts.

Her eyes scream at us. "Now who's trying to kill whom?"

"Good point." I caress her arm. "So..." Her brilliant glowing green eyes gaze at me. "Any chance you plan to share these fantasies you've had?"

"I'll tell you if you tell me how long you guys have been working on those body signals?" She smirks.

"I don't know what you're talking about." I feign ignorance and glance at the ceiling.

Lily points at both of us. "Don't play cute. I saw your hand signs and head nods."

"Eight months." I shyly admit.

"Well shit, that explains a lot."

"When did you figure it out?" Doug's tone weakens as he stares at his fist. Lily swiftly kneels in front of him before I even have a chance to react. She covers his hand and turns his head to face her.

"You weren't subtle. I recognized it right away. You've been using some of those gestures around the house for a while. I just didn't put it together that they were specifically for me until I saw how you reacted when James grabbed you."

"I didn't mean to hurt you."

Lily shakes her head. "You didn't hurt me." Her warm, honied voice gently coaxes him. She studies his face as his expression shifts from sorrow to confusion. He opens his mouth to speak, but Lily places her hand over it. "It wasn't your fault. I just moved my shoulder wrong." Lily peeks over his shoulder and cringes. "I think I hurt you more than you hurt me."

"You didn't hurt me." Doug's blunt tone makes me huff out a short chuckle.

Of course, she didn't. You fucking love that shit.

"Tell me that after you lay down. However, I'm going to fight you for the ice pack. I don't know if I'll be able to sit down like a proper lady once my endorphins take a nap."

"You're welcome!" I say, and her laughter fills the room, sharing her joy with us.

I'm glad we could make her happy. She even got Doug to smile. Maybe he'll let this go? She is an incredible woman.

"Shit!" Lily grabs her stomach. "I shouldn't have laughed so hard. I'll be back."

"Hey," I yell out to her as she gets to the bathroom. "Bring back those cookies you owe us."

She shakes her head as she walks into the bathroom, leaving the door open. I get off the bed and gather our clothes.

I catch Doug flexing his hand. "You didn't hurt her," I say as I get dressed. "She doesn't blame you."

"She only said that to make me feel better."

"No, she didn't. She's being honest. Personally, I don't think this phased her in the slightest. Your reaction is the only reason she brought it up. I watched her when she wouldn't let you go. You didn't scare her." I hold his gaze. "Couldn't you feel how happy she was?"

Doug steps off the bed, contemplating my words. "Yeah, I could but—"

"But nothing dude. You gave her a second orgasm. So, get over it. She has."

"You better not be lying to me."

Leaning up against the foot of the bed, I stare at the bathroom door entryway, yearning to see her again. "That was... way better than we imagined. She is amazing."

"Yeah, she is." Doug leans on the bed next to me to put his socks on. "You were smooth on the stairs, the way you swooped in on her. I fucking choked when she said she loved us. I was still processing it by the time you were on her."

"Those words forced me to move. I wasn't expecting them and hearing them just lit a fire in me." I turn to face him. "Listen, bro... We both love her. AND, I know you don't like to say those words. Neither of us has had much practice using them. But when you tell her you love her, say I. Not we."

"Was already planning on it. She deserves that much from us." Doug rubs his neck. "I can't rely on you to do it for me. I have to tell her that I love her myself."

A loud bang echoes from the bathroom. Doug and I rush to her.

"I'm fine. You don't need to rush to my aid. I just dropped my brush." Lily steps into the archway as we reach her. Her beauty is distracting, her hands hypnotize me as she runs the brush through her hair in smooth waves. "Some assholes knotted up my beautiful hair."

"I'm sure they could have made it much worse." Doug's cockiness seeps past his lips.

"Are you teasing me or challenging my hair?"

"Oh, definitely challenging your hair." Doug strokes her copper locks and she eyes him.

"Careful Doug." I nudge him with my elbow. "This one bites back."

"Speaking of biting... What are we ordering for dinner?" Lily asks.

I lift my eyebrow. "I thought we were doing leftovers?"

"We all need more than leftovers after that vigorous workout." Lily's eyes sparkle in the light. "Plus, I was thinking we could watch a movie and fulfill one of my fantasies."

I rub my neck. "I don't think we have more in us."

"Oh, you will for this one."

"Oh, yeah?" Doug's gaze washes over her.

"Yeah, this fantasy is easy. I promise." Lily's cheeks flush as her voice lightens. "I mean, you have to put in some effort, but I think you can handle it."

"What is it that you want?" I ask.

"Remember when we came home from the hospital and we all slept downstairs?"

"Yeah," "Of course," Doug and I say together.

She stops brushing her hair, tilts her head, and smiles. Oh, I hate it when she does that. She's so beautifully seductive, and she knows I won't... can't say no.

"That night I fantasized we built a fort around the TV and couch. Had dinner and watched anime. Till I eventually fell asleep in your arms."

"That sounds like a pleasant fantasy." Doug leans closer, his gaze toying with her. "You sure that's all that happened?"

"Yeah." Lily goes back to brushing her hair, unable to look at us.

"Ah ha, sure..." I say and she hides her grin.

"So..." She breaks the silence. "I know we haven't been on a date yet, but I was wondering if you wanted to spend the night in a fort with me?"

"Yeah, I think I'd like that." Doug's eyes travel up and down, taking her in.

"Me too." My gaze follows suit.

"Ok, well let me know when you two are done eye fucking me so I can finish cleaning up." We follow Lily's bratty command. We stare at her breasts, yearning again. I will never tire of this sight. She stops brushing and laughs. "Fine... I guess I have to give you a limit." She holds up her hand. "You get five more seconds."

Five.

Doug and I take in her every curve.

Zero.

She guides her hair to cover her front and turns around. Her ass sways as she takes a few steps back into the bathroom. She stands there motionless, giving us another five seconds. A vine wraps around the door handle and softly pulls it closed, ending the show.

CHAPTER 19

PJ PARTY

LILY

SUNDAY, DECEMBER 11ᵀᴴ

A sliver of light peers through a gap in the bedsheets. I stretch my sore, groaning muscles. Doug's hand tightens around my thigh as I sit up. I awe at the adorable sight of his feet hanging off the end of the mattress.

Yep, we need a bigger bed.

My gaze roams over the inside of our tent. James is gone. I softly kiss Doug on the cheek and gently unwrap my braid from around his arm. The change from my usual morning routine is jarring. I'm not used to waking up outside of my bedroom.

Sunlight streams through the windows. I bask in its glow, loving the way the morning lights up the front of my home. The smell of coffee travels down the hallway and pulls me to the kitchen. James is leaning over the counter, staring into his mug. I've seen him do this before. He is either deep in thought or angry about something.

I study him as I approach. He still hasn't noticed me. Ok, deep in thought it is. I lay my hand on his shoulder. "Good morning, James."

His face lights up at the sound of my voice. He spins around and picks me up. The passion is immediate. My clit tingles. My face warms as his coffee-flavored kiss slips into my mouth. I moan and his arms tense up around me. The kiss ends, and he walks me to the kitchen island.

He caresses my cheek. "I'm sorry. I meant to use words."

"That's ok, I got the 'good morning to you too' message loud and clear." My legs squeeze his ribs.

"I meant to just touch your face and kiss you gently." His eyes soften, his voice sultry. "And tell you… I love you."

"Oh…" My heart pounds. "Would you like a take two?"

Fingertips graze my neck as he drags his thumb across my jawline. His lips hover over mine. "No…" He turns my head to the side. "I'll try again tomorrow." His warm breath breezes over my ear. "And the next day." He caresses my arm with a firm touch. My body craves him. "And the next day."

I whimper and press my crouch into his stomach. He kisses my neck; my fingers get lost, roaming over his muscles. I hum with delight at his touch.

He turns my head and presses his hard cock against me. "Are you sure we can't have one-on-ones with you?"

"You're making it very difficult to say no."

"All right," James lifts me off the counter and walks away with me in his arms. "Then let's go wake Doug up."

"Wait," I say as we pass the coffeepot, and he pauses. "We can't wake the beast up without coffee." James laughs and sets me down. I squint at him. "Don't make fun of me. You're the one that calls him that."

"True, but it will be fine. He can handle one morning without it."

"No way…" I tilt my head to the floor. "I'm still sore. I won't be able to handle the beast."

"Oh, I doubt that." James lifts my chin. "You're still walking after everything he put you through. I think you could take him."

"That was different." I place my hands on James' chest and caress his muscles. "You don't know what it's like. You've never had him look at you like he wants to rip your clothes off and eat you alive."

James shifts his hips, and his erection grazes me. "That sounds like a fantasy I'd like to hear about."

My eyes and lips seduce him. I grab his cock and stroke my hand over his smooth gym shorts. "Sometimes I'll catch Doug in the kitchen when he hasn't had anything to drink yet, and he gives me this look that sends a chill right through me. Then he'll pounce on me, taking me to the table to eat me."

"And where am I?"

"Watching…" I kiss his chest. "Patiently…" I kiss his stomach. "Until I beg to be fed sausages for breakfast." I peer up at him as I press my breasts into his hard cock.

James bites his lip. "And do we feed you?"

"Oh, yes." I kiss him over his gym shorts. "You give me everything I crave." I stand and kiss him. "I take you both until the table cracks."

"You must really like that look." James' hands caress my arms.

I moan. "Yes."

James grabs my wrist and swiftly turns me around. I fall back on his hard body. Doug stands there, his erection begging to be set free. My heart pounds in my chest as my breathing labors. I instantly melt against James.

"You mean that one?" James' tone deepens, pulling me in as Doug's gaze roams my body. My nipples harden and my knees quake. I press my lips together and whimper.

Doug gently grabs my chin and leans down. With his mouth an inch from mine, he says, "You're not ready for the beast yet."

Lust and anger explode in me. My lips ravage his mouth as I press my ass on James' cock. I pull down Doug's pajamas and stroke his thick cock hard and fast. James' hand reaches up into my nightgown. I moan as his fingers roam over me.

Doug takes a step back and covers himself. "Let me have some coffee." Doug palms my cheek and runs his thumb over my lips to keep me quiet. "I promise you we will give you anything you ask for today."

"And here I thought James was the only one to make boasted promises." I challenge Doug's gaze as James' chest quakes against me.

"Oh, but I mean it."

"Hey…" James stiffens up. "I take offense to that."

"I'll make everyone's cup and bring it downstairs." Doug glances at the clock. "It's almost lunchtime. So, why don't you think about what you want while we drink?"

"Ok." I lift off James gracefully and make my way to the basement. I pause before I disappear into the hallway and peer over my shoulder. Their gazes fixated on me. "I am going to hold you to your promise."

Once in the fort, I remove my gown and wait for them. I know James followed me.

He enters, and his eyes are drawn straight to my breasts. "Well, hello My Lady."

"Good morning, Sir James. I have a request."

"Ask and it shall be done."

I kneel beside the couch and pat the seat. "Take your clothes off and sit."

James bows his head and happily removes his clothes.

I let my seductive side take control as I run my hands up his thighs. My breasts press together, and his gaze falls on them. His cock hardens in my hand, filling me with excitement. I lean forward and run the tip of my tongue along the length of him. His moan sends a twinge of lust through me.

It's been a long time since I've even wanted to please someone this way. I forgot how exhilarating it is to toy with a man. Watching him, I wait for his eyes to beg for me to take him fully into my mouth.

I don't have to wait long. As Doug's soft footsteps approach, I take James and guide him to the back of my throat. His moan is deep and makes me want more. I hold on to his shaft and suck on the tip of his cock.

Doug steps into the tent. "James, I thought we were supposed to give Lily what she wanted today?"

"I assure you, Sir Douglas..." James' words falter, melting into a groan as I shove his shaft into the back of my throat. "I am only doing what Our Fair Lady has requested."

"Is that right?" Doug's voice questions.

I take James out of my mouth and stroke him. "Yes, it is so. Today I want to roleplay, and you will only call me My Lady or Lady Lily."

"Of course, My Lady." Doug hands us each a thermos and I smirk at the clever idea.

"Um, coffee and blowjobs for breakfast. You guys realize how spoiled you are, right?" I take a sip.

"Yes," Doug says.

"Yes, Lady Lil—" I place James back in my mouth, interrupting him. He draws in a sharp breath. "Fuck. That's hot."

James pets my hair and moans as my mouth consumes him. My hand glides over the soft material of Doug's pants as I tease his contained erection. I take my time as I explore what James likes and get to know the shape of his arousal. I am enchanted.

Doug's eyes wake, ready. I stroke James and drink more as Doug gets undressed. "How may I serve you today, Lady Lily?"

"Sit."

Doug smirks and sits. I take another sip before giving James my attention. His moan is music to my ears and makes it easy to ignore the pain in my jaw. I stroke Doug and let myself enjoy having them both.

The way each of them feels. The sounds they make. Learning how they like to be touched and the way their eyes light up when I gaze at them.

My mouth can't handle anymore. I sit up and smile at them. "It's my turn."

Doug sets his thermos down. "Lie down, My Lady."

I place my thumbs in my panties. "Oh, no," James says. "Allow me."

My lashes flicker and I stand. Not waiting for an invitation, James grabs my hips and kisses my stomach. The fabric slides across my skin as his lips explore. My panties fall to the floor, and I step out of them. James sits back on the couch, and I lay down, keeping my eyes on Doug. He swoops in over me.

His soft, caressing touch barely grazes my skin. It's electrifying. Hunger radiates through his eyes. He opens my legs and gently brushes the inside of my thighs. His fingers dance playfully, mesmerizing me. Heat floods my body. I crave him.

Doug bends down between my legs and my heart races. His mouth is warm against my thigh, and it doesn't take long for his teeth to latch on to the supple, tender flesh. It's just as intense as yesterday. I purr. His smooth fingers trail closer to my center.

"Nice and slow." My voice cracks from the anxiety-stricken pain in my chest.

Those shiny blue eyes ensnare me as he releases my thigh. Pressure pushes against my opening, and I twist my hand into the velvet blanket. Fingers glide into me and I vocalize my bliss.

Doug's teeth latch onto my thigh again, escalating the pleasure. I fist a small tuft of his hair and cry out. I glance at James as his hand makes smooth strokes across his shaft. The intensity magnifies, making it hard to relax. I hold myself steady, deeply enjoying this attention that I've craved for so long.

I tilt my head back and close my eyes. I squeak at Doug's sharp nibble and rivet my gaze to his faux pout. "Please, Lady Lily," he says. "Don't deny me your beauty."

"I can't help it, it feels—" I yelp at the sudden change in pressure as Doug's fingers push in, hard, and press up. They circle inside me, and my mind goes blank. I sing for him.

James' smile is the last thing I see as my eyelids slam shut. My hips buck up and Doug shifts over me. His hand trails along my thigh and through my coarse hair. His fingers spread my lips and my eyes fling open. The look he gave me in the kitchen returns, darkening his features. I melt.

Doug's head dives between my legs and consumes me. My voice cracks as I scream out. I dig my nails into him, as I cannot hold myself steady. Doug holds my legs open as they unwillingly strain to clamp around him. James holds my gaze, his strokes continuous, never faltering.

Doug revels in my pleasure. I clasp the blanket. "DOUG."

His moan vibrates against me, and I can't handle it anymore. My hand latches onto his forearm and I frantically shake my head. Doug releases me and his eyes study me. I turn away from his gaze and sit up.

"My Lady?" James' tender voice coaxes me to peer at him. "That wasn't your first time, was it?"

I nod, unable to speak my embarrassment at not being able to handle my first exploration with oral. James motions for me to come to him, and I kneel between his legs. His fingertips caress my cheek and glide down my neck.

His lips sweeten, and I melt into his hand. "Doug and I are going to give you many more new experiences."

Doug gets behind me, his warm breath drifting over my ear. "We promise... we are going to make you cum over and over." His erection rubs in between my legs, and I moan as I press my ass into him. James' fingers graze across my supple breasts.

"We want to make you sing for us every day." James squeezes my nipple and I cry out.

Doug kisses my neck. "To taste you every day."

"Please..." I grind my hips on Doug and his hand moves between my legs.

"Please what?" Doug teases the tip of his cock against my opening. I cry out as I stare at James and take him in my hand.

"I want you to fill me with your big, thick cock."

Doug eases into me, and we moan together. I bounce on him, taking him fully inside me. I scream as Doug takes control. James' hard cock lures me in. I crave more.

"I want you to fill me with your long, hard cock." Leaning over James' erection, I lick the tip of him. I tease him as I did before, and they both vocalize the pleasure I bring them.

"Fuck, Lily, do you know how sexy you are?" James says, and I hide my delight as I devour him.

My senses are overwhelmed as I enjoy every touch and every sound we make.

A trumpet sounds over the house speaker and we freeze in place. "The royal family has arrived," NASS says.

"Shit, I forgot they were coming today," James says as I remove myself.

I grab my nightgown as we rush to get dressed. "We all did." I turn to them. "How's my hair?"

James ogles me. "It's hot."

"You have that sexy 'I just woke up' look." Doug lovingly runs his hand over my high ponytail braid. "This is what brings the beast out in the morning."

My cheeks heat and I quickly make my way to the bathroom, forcing myself not to melt into his hands again. The mirror reflects the picture they painted. For the first time, without dancing or trying; I feel sexy.

I rush upstairs to the front foyer, just in time for the front door to open. A trumpet sounds over the house speaker as NASS is triggered again. "Announcing the arrival of the royal family."

Layla holds the door open for Alex as she comes in with baby Eric. Alex shakes her head as Layla's excitement explodes. "That was the best! Who changed it?"

"I did," James says, and Layla sets down the bags to hug him. Alex sets the car seat down and I go straight to my nephew, undoing his buckles.

"I love it." Layla jumps with joy. "Thank you."

"We hoped you would. We've been waiting weeks for you to hear it." Doug leans down to hug her.

"Would you guys like coffee?" James asks as I stand, holding Eric to my chest.

"It seems like you need it more than us." Alex's gaze sweeps over the three of us. "Was this supposed to be a pajama party?"

"We forgot you were coming over," Doug says.

"It was a late night," James says.

"We didn't want to adult today." The three of us say in one jumbled mess.

"Ah huh…" Alex's eyes settle on James. "Your shirt is on inside out."

She smirks as James pulls at his shirt. "Well, this is awkward." He glares at Doug. "Were you ever going to tell me?"

"Nope," Doug says nonchalantly, but I can tell he is lying. He didn't notice either. "Anyway, how about some coffee?"

"Yes, please." Layla walks to the kitchen. "Can you make that blend you made on Halloween?"

"Absolutely!" Doug follows her. "I could use the zombie blend myself."

I stand in the hallway and glare at Doug's back as Layla, Alex, and Doug disappear into the kitchen. James giggles beside me and my eyes snap at him. "What?"

"You can't force choke someone without the hand. Like this." James mimes how to do it right.

I huff. "That's a stupid rule."

"So, why are you trying to kill Doug?"

I listen to the voices in the kitchen, waiting to make sure Layla won't overhear. She speaks and I softly ask. "Who's a better wake-up call, me or the coffee?"

James leans into my ear. "Since I've had both, I can tell you that you are the winner by a landslide. However, Doug hasn't had the pleasure of your mouth yet, so don't be too harsh on him."

"He would have if he hadn't denied me yesterday." I poke baby Eric's nose. "Isn't that right, my little prince? He should know better than to deny me."

James gets behind me to rub Eric's head. "Tell your aunt that's harsh." James kisses my neck. "But that's ok. Doug likes your bratty behavior."

The sound of the grinder echoes in the hallway, startling Eric. I bounce him. "Shh... Shh... It's ok."

James steps around and holds us. Eric calms, and James tilts my head up. His eyes glisten. "I love you."

"I love you too." I lift onto my toes and kiss him.

James leans down, kissing the top of Eric's head.

...

Layla regales us with stories, glowing with the blessed emotions of motherhood. Doug pours the last bit of coffee into his cup and sits beside me on the bench, sandwiching me between him and James. I hide delight behind my cup, sipping from it slowly.

My tastebuds wince, the strong flavor choking me. James holds my thigh as I recover. I snap my knee at Doug as he chuckles under his breath. He pushes the raw sugar closer to me and I enthusiastically scoop more into my cup. I take a cautious sip. It's not great. Pushing the drink aside, I decide this is not for me.

Across the table, Alex leans back in her chair. Her eyes adoring her wife as she brushes her fingers through Layla's hair. She loves doting on her. My sister is so happy. It fills me with joy. I relax next to James and Doug. We listen to her gab on and on.

Baby Eric pulls on my shirt, his nails scratch my breast. I smile at him, rocking back and forth. My attention is pulled to Alex as she makes faces at James and Doug. I glance between her and the boys, trying to decipher the silent conversation. My knight's cheeks are pink and their posture is stiff.

Alex's deviousness shines as she winks at me. She places her hand over Layla's, a gesture that pulls her back to the present moment.

Layla's gaze sweeps over us. "I'm sorry I got carried away again, didn't I?"

"It's ok sweetie, but I'm sure Lily would like a chance to talk too." Alex motions toward me.

"No, it's ok," I insist sweetly. "I enjoy listening to Layla."

"Oh, come on, tell us." Alex's eyes creep over me. "How was it?"

I stare at Eric cradled to my chest. "How was what?"

"Oh, that's right," Layla says with renewed excitement. "Heather had her bridal shower yesterday. Tell me all about it."

"Yeah Lily," Alex says. "It must have been quite the time. I mean, you're positively radiant."

Alex and the boys chortle as my eyes throw daggers at her.

Layla's gaze bounces between us. "Am I missing something?"

Alex pats her hand. "Sweetie, look at your sister."

Layla studies me. "What? She's happy."

"One might even say she's glowing." Alex sweeps her hand between the three of us, smirking.

"She better be," Doug says under his breath.

I hide my embarrassment behind a defiant glare. "I'm not glowing."

"Yes, you are, My Lady," James says, drawing my ire.

"NO WAY." Layla's eyes light up. "WHEN?"

James and Doug beam proudly as I answer. "Yesterday, after the bridal shower."

Layla points at the boys. "You gave her an orgasm, right?"

"Yes," James says while Doug holds up two fingers.

Layla hops up from the table. "This is so exciting. Where's my phone?"

"Why do you need your phone?" Doug asks.

"So, she can call all your friends and tell them the good news," I say.

"Oh..." James says.

"Oh, no..." Doug says.

"Oh, yes..." I shake my head, nuzzling baby Eric's nose. "Isn't that right?"

"Layla, don't forget to remind Matt that he lost the bet," Alex says loud enough to let her voice carry to the other room.

"What?" Doug raises his eyebrow.

"There was a bet?" James asks.

"Yep. Matt started a bet on when you guys would finally hook up."

"You know, I really shouldn't be surprised." Doug takes a sip from his mug.

"So, who won?" James asks.

"Jane."

I titter. Of course, it was her. I lean over Eric and poke his nose. "What a cheater."

Layla screams with joy, and I hear Heather rejoicing through the speaker with her. Ahh, that hurts my ears.

"Alex," Doug says. "I think you lied to us."

"Yeah." Alex raises an eyebrow. "About what?"

"Layla wasn't just insatiable during her pregnancy, was she?"

Alex chuckles. "I didn't lie about that. I just didn't warn you it runs in the family too."

"A warning would have been nice," James says.

"Why?" Alex furrows her brow. "Can you honestly tell me it would have changed things?"

"Nope." Doug rubs his hand over my leg.

"Ok, so now that you have taken the plunge, I have two pieces of advice." Alex pauses for dramatic effect. "Strap in and enjoy the ride."

We wait for her to continue.

"And the second?" Doug asks.

"That's it." Alex holds up one finger. "Strap in." She holds up two fingers. "Enjoy the ride."

James bows to Alex. "Thank you, oh great and wise sage, for your advice."

"But..." Doug says. "You know our dicks are attached, right?"

"Oh, yeah... That must suck to only have the one." She winks at them.

We laugh, and I turn an ear to listen to Layla talking in the other room. "Hey Alex," I whisper. "Don't tell Layla I said this. But she was right."

"What about this time?"

"We need a bigger bed."

"TOLD YOU!" Layla shouts from the other room, and Alex giggles.

"She designed six different rooms for you while she was in the hospital. So, trust me, she's got you covered. The three of you will have a blast picking one out."

"Of course she did." I shake my head and tune them out, focusing on Layla and Heather's conversation from the other room. My lips lift into my cheeks as I overhear them planning a party. I open my mouth to interrupt the conversation happening beside me, but stop. Why are they talking about a swing? I elbow Doug and tilt my head.

He chuckles and kisses the top of my head. "Don't worry, we'll explore that too."

My eyes widen as I put together what a swing is. "Oh..." He smiles and I turn to James, embarrassed. "Somewhat off-topic, but how do you guys feel about having a 'coming out' party today?"

"A what now?" James asks.

Alex stands up. "Please tell me she isn't?"

"Yep, she's making plans to have everyone come over to celebrate our union."

Doug peeps over my head at James. "Guess that means we should go tear down the fort in the basement."

Layla lets out a loud squeal and rushes down the stairs with Alex.

"Too late now. She's taking pictures." I pause and glance at James, then Doug. "You're still bound to your promise today, My Dear Knights."

"That was only supposed to be for sexual things," Doug says.

"Oh, was it?" My bratty tone pours past my lips. "I don't remember you specifying those terms."

"They were implied." Doug's eyes insist.

"Well, that's too bad. You'll just have to service me differently today."

James reaches over me and playfully pushes Doug. "You need to stop making promises to pretty ladies. They always get us into trouble."

Doug brushes his fingers through his hair. "Sorry, I can't help it."

We harmonize our joy, laughing.

I suddenly stop. "Oh, shit." I turn to James. "Where did you put my underwear?"

James' eyes widen. Doug leans into my ear. "Well, aren't you a naughty girl?" His hand reaches up my leg, pushing my nightgown up.

"Not while I'm holding the baby." I smack his hand. Doug smirks and James' hand glides up my thigh. I glare at James. "That goes for you too, mister."

I peer down at Eric cradled against my chest, avoiding those mischievous smiles. "Tell your uncles to behave themselves. You need good male role models." My heart pounds as I still. Blood drains from my face as I grow clammy and cold. I place my hand over my mouth and choke back my tears. "I'm sorry I—"

"Don't you dare apologize." Doug lifts my chin and his voice softens. "I like the sound of that."

James' hand rubs my back and leans into my ear. "Me too."

Doug kisses me and my heart happily pounds in my chest. Eric reaches up and grabs Doug's shirt. His gaze falls to Eric, and we chuckle at the interruption.

"Don't worry, you're still your auntie's favorite little prince." Doug rubs Eric's head and the sound of baby joy rings out.

"Hey! Who made my sister cry?" Layla points at the boys as she steps around the table to face them.

James and Doug place their hands above their heads and point down at Eric. "The baby did it."

I burst with laughter, and my heart quells.

CHAPTER 20

MEETING THE BEAUFORT'S

LILY

SATURDAY, DECEMBER 24TH

Rows of cookie-cutter homes line the street, dressed in colors and lights. All the flavors of holiday cheer.

Doug and James are eerily silent as we approach the house. I guess they are trading their verbal warnings for inner worries now. They've been repetitive and nervous all week, and especially so for most of the car ride today. They have told me many stories about their father and his antics, how eccentric his mother and brother can be.

We pull up to a house tucked into the middle of a cul-de-sac and I admire the change in the style of homes here. I can tell where the original brick home began and where they added the modern additions, but the transition is seamless. Had it not been for my insider knowledge and training in architecture, I wouldn't have noticed.

Traditional Christmas lights connect the three homes; a Rudolph the Red-Nosed Reindeer reenactment plays across the lawns. These decorations should be on the cover of a home design magazine. Too bad it hasn't snowed.

James opens the car door for me and calls over my head to Doug, "How much you want to bet that mom is showing off to impress Lily?"

"We don't need to bet. That's a given." Doug and James chuckle, and happiness fills me as they relax. Hopefully, being home is enough to help them past their nerves.

They grab our overnight bags, and we head for the front door. The only thing keeping the cold out is a frosted-covered screen door. I can't tell if the frost on the windows is real, and I dare not touch it. The sound of barking spills out as James enters. He steps to the side, letting me in, and I'm bombarded by two large dogs.

Doug bends to pet a long-haired black dog with a white chest. "This is Coco."

"And that is Benedict," James says as I pet a long-haired, gray dog.

I introduce myself to them both. They lick my hands and sit beside me.

White and silver cascade around me. It's mesmerizing. There is so much to take in. When Doug told me that his mother would redecorate her entire home for Christmas, I didn't think he meant it like this. I'm pretty sure that she has replaced every item; none of these are part of her usual home décor.

When I think- winter wonderland, this is what I picture. It's perfect and again, I can imagine her home pictured in a magazine. This just gives me another reason to introduce her to Layla.

"Which set of my boys just came home?" A feminine voice shouts from another room.

"It's me, Mom... Your favorite son," James says, making Doug snort as he bends down to take off his shoes.

A woman steps into view and the first thing I notice is her smile. It's warm, inviting, and just for me. Her short, curly blonde hair bounces as she walks toward me, her eyes filled with excitement. I step forward as her arms outstretch to hug me.

"Hello Denise," I say as we embrace. Her touch is light; she is careful so that her red sequined shirt doesn't catch on my white lace dress. "It's wonderful to see you again."

"It's wonderful to see you, too. You look stunning." She takes a step back, taking me in. "The silver under the white is breathtaking. The pictures didn't do it justice."

"It really didn't." I ogle her skirt. "Is that a white leather skirt?"

"Yes." She spins, showing me the back of her outfit. The red top delves into a deep v, exposing her back. "Isn't the back gorgeous? Paul picked this out for me."

"Oh my. How very risqué. It suits you," I say. Denise shines as my eyes scan the house. "This winter wonderland theme is spectacular. Is the entire house like this?"

"Just the common areas. Would you like a tour?"

"Yes, please."

Denise links her arm in mine and whisks me away. A wide smirk adorns my face, taunting James and Doug. We leave them standing there, stunned. Denise's plan to get back at them is working perfectly.

The dogs follow us as Denise leads me on a tour of her beautiful home.

"You know Denise, I'm grateful that Heather invited me along to your lunch date."

"Me too, darling." Denise pats my forearm and chuckles. "You think they liked our charade?"

I giggle. "They have no idea what just happened."

"Good! That's what they get for keeping you all to themselves."

As we walk through the house, I place my hand over hers, enjoying the touch of a mother's love.

......

I relax beside Denise on the couch. The tension from the day dissipates. Coco lays at my feet and Benedict's head is on my knee. I pet him mindlessly, as Denise boasts about Paul's upcoming Drag show they'll be hosting next month.

A commotion in the kitchen grabs our attention, and the dogs leave my side. As they bound away, I pick up the voices of two men. Doug and James step into the living room, and Denise and I stand up. I recognize the two joining us from photos.

Doug motions toward his father, Fred. "Lily," he says as Fred reaches his hand out. I grab it, smiling. "I'd like you to meet—"

"Well, isn't she stunning?" The youngest of the men pushes his father out of the way, forcing our hands apart. His short, curly blonde locks bounce as Paul steps in to hug me. Fred steps back, his lips lightly lift.

"Hello Paul, it's a pleasure to meet you."

"Likewise. My, your hair is flawless." Paul fondles my hair, examining it. The blue eyes he shares with his mother shine and the light shimmers against his cheeks.

"Not as flawless as that makeup." I compliment.

Paul sweeps a lock out of his face and poses as if he was taking a selfie. "I could give you some tips."

"Oh, no, that's all right." My hand waves the idea away. "I don't wear makeup. I prefer the skin I have."

Paul's jaw dramatically drops, and he bats his eyelashes. "I must be the one to do your makeup for the wedding. My man Dusty can do your hair and we will make you a star."

"Paul." Doug bites out his name. "She is not a doll."

"Ah…" Paul quickly lets go of my hair, his eyes dart to Doug then back to me. His features turn formal, similar to the gaze of his father. "Of course not. My apologies Lily."

"It is all right. I understand your passion. Actually, Denise was just telling me about your upcoming show. I'd love to hear more about it."

"Have you ever been to a drag show?" Paul motions for us to sit on the couch.

"No. My sister and her wife and I keep talking about going to one, but then we'd forget about it and miss it."

"Oh… We have to correct that. It's a spectacular event! A must see." Paul bounds with animation as he goes into the details, painting me a picture with words. What it's like backstage, the glitz and the glam. The drama and music and the fun.

Doug, James, and Fred stand by the fireplace mantel in their gray suits, sipping from whisky glasses. Fred's posture hasn't relaxed since he got home. He looks stern, almost angry. This must be the side of Fred they refer to as the 'hardass'. I silently chuckle. Doug gets that expression from his father.

James catches me staring and smiles. Warmth fills me. I haven't been to a family Christmas like this one in over ten years and am glad it's just us. I needed the quality time.

…

Denise and I light the candles in the dining room as Doug, Paul, and James set the table. The chandelier dims and the room dances with glitter and light.

My gaze floats, taking in the sight. "It's beautiful."

"I'm glad you like it," Denise says. "I hope it makes up for not finding a yule log to incorporate your traditions with ours."

"You found one, though." I motion my hand around the room. Denise tilts her head to the side, confused. "A yule log is a representation of bringing warmth to a winter gathering. You light the fire and enjoy the time with your loved ones."

"That sounds like a beautiful tradition." Paul sets a basket of biscuits on the table. "But... you still brought the yule log cake you made, right?"

"No. I'm sorry..." I shake my head, teasing him. "Didn't they tell you? They ate it all."

"You did not!" Paul places his hand on his hip and points at them.

Doug mirrors Paul's body language. "Oh, yes, I did!"

"It was soo good." James rubs circles over his belly. James and Doug chortle.

"However, that's why I made two more," I say, ending the charade. "One for tonight and then one for you to take with you tomorrow to Dusty's family."

"Oh. That's sweet of you!" Paul gushes. "You didn't have to."

"It was no big deal. I had to make nine. So, what's one more?"

Denise leans into Doug. "She is too sweet."

"Yeah, she is." James and Doug say. Their gaze travels over me. My cheeks and chest warm up as I brush a lock of hair behind my ear.

"Dad will be out in a moment." Paul's tone deepens. "It's time to take our seats." Paul holds out a chair for Denise and motions for his mother to sit. He pushes her in and kisses her on the cheek.

James and Doug lead me to the bottom end of the table. I sit, ignoring the awkwardness of being pushed in. They take off their blazers and rest them on the back of the chairs before sitting down on either side of me.

"You outdid yourself." Paul removes his blazer and sits across from his mother. "This spread looks wonderful."

Paul and Denise talk about the food as we wait for Fred to join us. Doug's leg bounces as James fidgets with his fingernails. I reach for each of them, holding their knee and wrist. They take a deep breath and I listen for Fred.

Soon, I hear a door close and say, "He's coming."

The room falls silent as I hold up four fingers and count down.

"Sorry for the wait." Fred enters the room in his suit top and boxers. His features are softer than they were earlier. "I had a fight with my pants."

I hold in my giggle as James and Doug stiffen up. This is exactly what they warned me about.

Fred removes his blazer and rests it on the back of the chair. The red button-up has an undone button in the middle and his silver tie is gone. His boxers have an ugly Christmas sweater pattern on them that matches his ridiculously high socks.

"It seems you lost the fight, Father," Paul says.

Fred pulls at his shirt sleeves and puffs his chest out. "It was more of a mutual understanding." Denise scoffs as he sits down. His eyes shine at me, mischievously. "Are you all right, dear? You're beat red."

"It's nothing." Dismissively, I wave my wrist. "I'm Irish. I'll be pale as a ghost again shortly."

The room fills with laughter.

Denise puts her hands together and bows her head to begin grace. Her prayer of family and blessings is sweet and brief. Grandma Barb would approve.

We pass the food around the table as Fred talks about golfing tomorrow. As he drowns on, James fusses with the cuff of his sleeves. I pass the biscuits to Doug and help James roll them up.

"I've been trying for years to get James into a button-up," Denise says. "None of them would fit right, thanks to those ridiculous muscles." Her fiery spirit is alight in her eyes as she pokes her fork through the air at James. Then, in an instant, her gaze sweetens as she turns back to me. "How did you manage it?"

"I took him to my tailor and had a suit custom made for him."

"That had to of cost a pretty penny," Paul says.

I side-eye Paul. "I'm not allowed to talk about that."

"No, you spent too much on a suit I'll only wear once." James glares at me.

"You'll wear it more now that it fits comfortably." I take a bite of ham, ignoring his eyes.

"Why do you have a tailor?" Paul asks.

I take a moment to swallow. "Because they don't make clothes for curvy, short women. So, whenever I find something I love, but know won't fit me right, I send him photos of it. Or I have him alter the things I purchase. He custom-made this dress for me."

"He is very good. It fits you perfectly," Denise says.

"Lily," Paul says. "Can Pauline ask you a question?"

"Of course."

Paul's features brighten, and his tone lightens. "How do you hide your bra in a dress like that?"

My gaze travels over each of them. Fred is enjoying his meal, and James and Doug are no longer on edge. Ok. This kind of talk is normal, then.

I relax and answer her. "Since this was custom, it has bra pads and the wire built in. But if it wasn't, I could easily hide it with one that fits. Bras are another thing that I have him make for me. The standard size at the stores aren't made with the shape and slope of the breast in mind."

"Maybe that's the problem. Because when I put my set in the cups, there's always a gap. Then they move around too much."

"At least you guys can wear a bra." Denise pouts at her petite chest. "All I have are pasties."

Doug chokes on his food as James covers his mouth. Doug takes a swig of his drink.

"Well, I like them, especially this one pair." Fred wiggles his eyebrows at the boys. Pauline, Denise and I laugh.

"You should consider yourself lucky that you've never had to feel the pain of having your lungs crushed," I say to Denise.

"Tell me about it." Pauline leans back in her chair and mimes the size of her breasts. "I ordered a chest size too big and thought I broke my back."

I feign a toast to her. "Welcome to being a woman." Pauline lifts her glass, and we drink.

"Can we change the subject?" Doug asks.

"Why?" Denise's tone teasingly asks. "Don't you like talking about your woman's well-endowed chest?"

"Are Grandma and Grandpa still in Arizona?" James asks.

"Thankfully." Fred perks up, replying too fast.

"Fred!" Denise glares at her husband, and I smile.

"What? You said so yourself just this morning."

The table fades into normal boring conversations, but I am still intrigued. I listen, learning about the family and the latest gossip at the country club.

A brief silence fills the room. "Uhm…" Paul moans with a mouth full of food. "This apple sweet potato casserole is delicious."

"Yes, it's divine." Denise glances at James and Doug. "Thank you for bringing it."

"You're welcome," Doug says.

"We're glad you all like it," James says. "It took us a while to get the recipe just right."

"You know, boys." Fred's tone shifts to the stiff one I heard before dinner. James and Doug's postures go rigid. "You would be brilliant chefs. It would be an excellent career choice."

The table is quiet. Doug's eyes waver with a hint of rage. James grinds his teeth. Paul hasn't exhaled and Denise won't look up from her plate. This is the Fred they were hoping I wouldn't see.

"They are amazing cooks!" I lift my voice, adding a hint of innocence to it. I grin. The tension in the room breaks. "But why do you think that would be a good choice for them?"

"It's an honorable and rich profession."

"That it is!" I straighten my spine, mentally preparing to talk down a stubborn man with a narrow focus. I deal with men like him all the time when I'm negotiating real estate deals. "It's a wonderful career. However, unless they owned the restaurant, the demands of others would stifle their creativity."

"Then even better." Fred puffs out his chest, proudly. "They should own something."

I place my hand on their knees to stop them from interrupting. "If that is what they wish, then I will happily drop half a mil to buy them a restaurant." I turn my gaze to Denise. "But would you truly be ok with never seeing them again?"

Denise's forehead wrinkles. "What do you mean?"

"In that line of work, they would work fourteen-hour days and every holiday. Not to mention how their culinary efforts would be drawn away from us. We would never again savor one of their dishes prepared especially for us. And that... That would be a travesty."

"Oh no, Fred." Denise grabs Fred's forearm. "That's not for them. I want to see my boys."

"As you wish, dear." Fred holds his wife's hand. They share a passionate glance with each other, and his posture relaxes. Fred turns his attention to me. "Lily, please forgive me for getting worked up. It's just a father's pride. I can't help but offer advice."

"I understand completely. A great father should boast with pride about their children." I gesture around the table. "I can't imagine the overwhelming joy you must have. Paul is taking over the family business. Whereas Doug and James own their very own design studio. I only wish you could see what I do."

Joy consumes me as my eyes shine at James, then at Doug. "It's the most beautiful sight. Every day they pour their hearts into their work." I choke up at the gleam in Doug's eyes. I hold back my tears and turn to Fred. He stills as my teary eyes hold his gaze. "Though I'm sure Denise understands what I mean. She sees you do the same. I'm sure she is proud that you set a good example for her boys."

Denise dabs a napkin under her eye. "It is true. My boys are amazing."

"I'm glad they found a strong woman to rein them in." Fred places his hand under Denise's chin. "Just like Denise did for me."

Paul grins and elbows Doug. "It's too bad they waited so long to bring her home. We could have had this beauty in our lives so much sooner."

I smile as Denise scolds them through her tears for being selfish and how she will disown them if they hurt me. I lean into James as Denise goes on. "Is this what a normal family is supposed to be like?"

"Yes, My Lady." James squeezes my hand.

"So, boys," Fred says, getting our attention. "How is the game coming along?"

Doug and James stare at Fred as he cuts a piece of ham. I nudge Doug's foot and he finds his voice. They proceed cautiously, testing the waters. Not quite sure how to deal with this attention. When Paul joins the conversation, James and Doug relax a little bit more. I sit back in my chair and listen happily.

...

James' firm chest presses into my back as he wraps his arms around me. He holds me as Doug and his family take another round of photos, this time without James and me. I don't know how they can take this many photos. My eyes hurt already from all the lights. I can't wait to get the photos of us, but Paul is going overboard.

"I love you," James whispers into my ear.

"I love you too." I rest my weight on him and relax.

"What's wrong? Are you upset about the photos?"

"No, it's nothing."

"Lily, don't give me that." James turns me around. "You're doing that thing with your face. You're thinking too much."

I lift my eyebrow. "I don't make a face."

"Yes, you do. You just don't see it like I do. Just like how you say my lip twitches when I'm concentrating on something."

"Well, it does."

"Exactly." James brushes his finger under my chin, not letting me drop my gaze. "So, tell me what's wrong."

"Why does Doug only tell me he loves me while I'm sleeping?"

"Oh… You know about that?" I nod and he gently caresses my cheek. "Short answer is, he's working up the courage to tell you."

"That's all there is to it?"

"Yep."

I squint my eyes at him, unconvinced. "Fine, but tell him that if waits too long, I'll put his balls in a cage."

James winces and nods his head.

……

I follow Doug up a second set of stairs, and he holds the only door open. I step into their old childhood room, a loft above the garage. The room is sparse. Old band and video game posters adorn the walls. Two queen-sized beds lay on the floor, taking up most of the floor space. The mismatched blankets and pillowcases are an eyesore to the already crowded room.

Doug lifts me into his arms and cradles me against his chest, taking us to a futon next to the mattresses. He sets me down and swiftly kneels before me, to place his head on my lap. His face is planted between my thighs.

Confused by his behavior, I turn to James. He is as befuddled as I am. James gestures to give us alone time as Doug's hands hold my thighs. I rub my fingers through his soft brown hair as James makes his way to the bathroom and closes the door.

"You ok, sweetie?" I ask.

Doug's mutter vibrates between my thighs. His grip tightens and his shoulders tense. I continue to caress his head while he takes a few deep breaths. He calms down, lets go, and sits back on his feet. "Thank you, Lily."

"For what?"

"For the way, you talked to my dad. That was the first time I believed it when he said he was proud of us. I didn't think we'd ever have that moment."

I caress Doug's smooth cheek. "I was worried that you would be upset that I intervened."

"As James would say." Doug mimics James' voice. "'That was hot as fuck.'"

James walks back into the room. "That's not what I would say... That is what I said."

"I believe it!" I brush my hair to the front of me and expose my neck to Doug. Just the way he likes it. I bat my eyelashes. "I was wondering. Have you ever had a girl up here before?"

Doug grins. "No."

"Sooo..." I tuck my hair behind my ear, pretending to act shy and innocent. "What should we do now?"

"Do you have something in mind?" James' eyes glint in the light.

"Maybe." I inch to the edge of the futon, letting my skirt ride up my thighs.

"Tell us." Doug circles his finger over my exposed skin. "It's Christmas and you've been a good girl, you might get your wish."

"I want you to give me a new experience."

"Yes, My Lady," they say in unison.

Chapter 21

At the Gym

Lily

Saturday, December 31st

The strobe lights are blinding. I scan through the droves of people, but I still can't find our friends. I squeeze James' hand as he and Doug lead me down a closed-off hallway. My ears delight with the pleasure of relief to be away from the thumping music and hordes of people.

My stomach flutters, and my chest tightens. Doug peers back at me and a giddy grin brightens my face. We turn a corner and the lights dim dramatically. I stay close to them, trusting that after spending his entire life in this country club, he knows where he is going.

We stand before a framed, frosted glass door. Doug taps a keycard on a pad and the door clicks open. He turns the lights on and James motions for me to enter. A large hotel-style exercise room spans before me. The walls are wrapped in a picturesque view of a hiking trail. One wall, in front of all the big equipment, is a mirror.

I'm surprised by my reflection. I didn't think I was this sexy and stunning at home. My short bell skirt, the backless halter top with no bra, and my hair done up just the way Doug likes it. Their request that I wear this makes more sense now. They planned this night and wanted easy access.

"I feel like I'm in a porno." I turn to ogle my ass in the mirror, ignoring their wanting eyes. James removes his shirt and I grace him with my attentive hands.

"Well, you mentioned some interest in being in one." Doug takes off his shirt.

My cheeks and chest warm up at the thought. "I did."

James wastes no time picking me up to wrap me around him. His favorite way to kiss me. The thrill of having them here and now courses through me like a raging fire. James' aggressive possession of my body, his hot, fervent kisses on my lips, and his arousal make my body scream for him. He moves and our lips part.

Tenderly, James lays us down. The thick padded mat is cold against my bare back. James grinds his contained erection between my legs. I hear Doug undoing his zipper. My lust for them skyrockets. I need them inside me now. James caresses me and shifts his weight to make room for his hand to please me.

I grab his wrist. "No." He raises his eyebrow. "Please don't treat me like you do at home. I want to be fucked."

I gaze into Doug's greedy, willing eyes and provoke him. The corner of his mouth twitches. James pushes my skirt up and hooks his fingers into my thong. He teases the fabric over my flesh, and I purr for them. James stands, giving Doug the space he needs to devour me.

"Turn over." Doug grabs my hips as I turn and lustfully draws my ass to him. The back of my skirt flips up and I keep my eyes on our reflection. He rubs his cock over me, teasing me. "Is this what you want?" His voice is deep and husky, coated with the honey of desire and control.

"Please, DOUG..." I whimper as he strokes my folds open.

"Your so wet, Lily." Doug presses his tip at my opening. "You want James and me that badly?"

"Yes. I crave it." I gasp as his tip slides in. "Please, I need to be filled with your thick cock." I press back into him, consuming more of him. "NOW!"

His fingers dig into my hips as a growl escapes his throat. James hums, catching my attention. He glides his zipper down. Doug pulls himself back, the tip of him thrusting at my entrance. I pant in the heat of agonizingly pleasurable torment. James reveals himself and Doug slams into me.

My scream echoes out, surrounding us. They moan with me. None of us care if we are heard. They are enjoying it as much as I am. The thrill of spontaneity, the risk of being caught. The way we sound in this small room. It's exhilarating.

Doug's passion assaults me. My lungs get no reprieve.

We are perfectly reflected in the mirror. I love how James strokes his shaft as he delights in our performance. The elation in Doug's features as he watches himself thrust into me.

My lips press together, and I hold back my moans. I squeeze around Doug and hear the groan that I love to tease tremble out of him. Those eyes give me what I desire, the threat I've been building to. I'm in danger of releasing the beast. I squeeze again. He slows his thrusts and lets go of my hips.

"You're being a naughty girl tonight, Lily..." Doug's fingertips glide across my back. "It's almost like you want to be punished."

Yes, please.

I squeeze him again. His eyes shift, awakening. His beast howls in confirmation.

Punish me! Push me down. Pull my hair. Bite me.

James grabs my attention, shifting a bench around at an awkward angle in the room. "Why don't I get Lily ready for dinner?"

Doug twitches inside me and James' words finally click. Doug leans over me and whispers in my ear. "I'm going to eat you alive."

My clit jumps into overdrive. Doug holds me tight as he pulls out of me. James helps me to stand and pulls me close to him. I peep through my lashes up at James, his brown eyes shine with excitement. "Take my clothes off," I demand.

James turns us to face Doug. He sits down and watches. I will my gaze to stay on him, resisting the urge to scan the room as curiosity fills me. James puts on a show, sensually sliding my clothes down my body. The heat from James' chest presses into my back as he holds me close to him.

Doug lays down on the bench and motions for me to come to him. I crawl over him and ready myself to take him into my mouth.

"No, Lily." He motions for me to keep coming. "Higher." I crawl to his lap and he grabs my wrist as I sit. He hooks his finger again, motioning once more. "Higher." His beastly eyes will me to defy him. I glance at James; His eyes are just as hungry. I crawl higher, placing myself over his face.

My lips press together and hum at his exploration of me. His warm mouth takes what he wants. The intense sensation, like every time we try this, is immediate and unrelenting. I still don't know how to relax.

My thighs ache. I don't know how much longer I can hold myself up. I tilt my head back, crying out.

Doug's moan electrifies my clit as he buries his fingers deep within me. I turn my attention to James, hoping he can help me relax. James' hand embraces his hard shaft, his strokes hypnotizing me. I crave the taste of him.

I want you to shove your cock down my throat.

James stops his caress as Doug's moan vibrates beneath me. My eyes widen as I realize I said that out loud.

"As you wish." James walks to me and Doug slightly pulls his mouth away from me. He watches as I grab James' hips. I take all of him into my mouth without hesitation.

"Fuck, Lily." Their deep, rough voices fill me with gratification.

Doug's fingers circle inside me and I stifle my pleasure on James' cock. Their delight spurring me on. His mouth consumes me, and I squeeze James. He holds me steady, relieving the ache in my thighs.

The sounds we make heighten my arousal. Euphoria takes control of my senses.

James sweetly caresses my hair, holding himself back from wanting to grab the back of my head. I take him to the edge of my mouth and peer up. He tells me what I want to hear. "You are so damn sexy."

I swallow him and his hand grips into my hair. A small taste of James drips into my mouth. It makes me hunger for more. My body melts, relaxing.

Pure bliss shines on James' face as I thrust my mouth over him. Doug moving in sync with me. An addictive sensation that I've grown to love rocks through me.

The storm inside me escalates, threatening to break. My skin blushes. I make the noise that inspires them most. Their faces lit up with anticipation and determined passion.

"Come on Lily. Cum for us." James' husky tone sends me over the edge. I captivate the tip of his cock. James holds me steady, so I don't fall, Doug never ceases. The pressure cascades through my body, I scream my release. It consumes me, ravaging its way to them. The pleasure of my orgasm washes over us all.

I slide James out of my mouth and steady my breathing as my orgasm fades. I run my fingers over James' muscles. Doug bites my thigh, getting my attention. I squeak, making him chuckle as he gets out from under me. James lifts my chin to him. His kiss is generous and loving. Doug kisses my shoulder, caressing my hips.

"This is one of our fantasies," James says. "And we have one more thing we want to do to you." His thumb strokes my lips. "Promise us you will use our safe word this time."

I keep my gaze locked on his. "I promise."

Doug walks to one machine as James helps me to sit. James joins Doug and guides some things on the machine around. Doug digs into a duffle bag next to it.

My anxiety flares as my mind races, wondering what they have planned. James pulls on the handlebar, and it doesn't budge. Doug pulls out some restraints and attaches them to the bar. Excitement consumes me as I put together what they want.

James motions me over. I sway my hips as I walk, taking my time, letting them take in the sight of me. Doug turns me to face the mirror and James lifts me. I grab onto the bar and Doug expertly binds my wrists. With my legs wrapped around James' chest, my weight rests on him. Notably, it doesn't hurt this way.

I look in the mirror, longing for Doug as he lubes himself up. James shifts us, pressing against my opening. I fill with passion and kiss him, relaxing in his arms. Doug sticks his finger in me to prepare me for him. I hum my pleasure.

Doug kisses my neck. "Are you ready?"

My eyes lock on to his reflected gaze. "Yes."

The tip of Doug enters me as James pushes me down further on them both. The tips of their cocks fill me. My body rages from the sensation and I scream. They pause, observing my reactions. I kiss James to temper my body into submission. Their thrusts are kind to me as they ease themselves in.

I fully embrace them, and immediately I am elated. We moan a beautiful melody together. I lean my head on Doug's shoulder and breathe just like he taught me to. Their eyes gleam at me.

Not wanting to break this sensual moment with words, I lift one finger to signal that I'm ok.

The sight of us in the mirror as they thrust into me is hypnotizing. I don't want them to stop. This is our first time doing this, and it hasn't hurt. Sharing in their pleasure gets me high.

James captures my breast in his mouth, caressing my nipple with his tongue. Doug's dance of pain and pleasure moves along my neck. My body sings with pleasure, and I make sure they know it, echoing the song with my breath and my voice. Their groans are music to my ears.

Doug's soft hands tantalize my flesh. His fingertips trail across my scar, gliding to my center. He is close and wants us to cum with him. He presses into my clit and I cry out.

I love watching us. I love to see the rapture in their eyes as they get close. Knowing I please them, feeling them enjoying my offering.

Doug's bite falters, his grunts telling me what we already know. He is ready. It causes a chain reaction in all of us. Cumming with them both is intoxicating. Their fierce release fills me as my storm continues to rage. Even with my body collapsing, I still want to keep going. I don't want the magic of this moment to leave.

They hold me as we relax in this euphoric state together. I whimper when Doug's soft touch pulls away from me.

"Shh..." Doug's warm breath blows in my ear and I unwillingly tense up. "Breathe."

I listen and let him leave. Doug unbinds me and James sets me down on the floor. He kisses me to distract me as he pulls out. A soft cloth presses between my legs and I smile at Doug. He kisses me on the forehead and heads to the bathroom.

"We didn't hurt you, did we?" James caresses my cheek.

"No, honey... Honestly, I kind of want this set up at home now."

"I think we could do that."

I scan the room enthusiastically. "So, where are the cameras?"

James smirks as Doug comes back into the room. "Told you she'd figure it out."

...

We return to the hoard of people. Music fills my senses, and it is as if we never left. Jane and Zach join us shortly after, their faces etched over with pure thrill and delight.

"Are you having fun?" Jane's voice strains over the music.

"Yes, very much so. And you?"

"Oh, yes. I had an exhilarating time." Her caramel eyes gleam at me. My stomach flutters, elated that she and Zach watched. "Did you enjoy your first public outing?"

"Yeah, I did. But I didn't get that feeling of ever being caught. At least not how you described it."

"After this experience, are you still interested in being watched?" She asks.

"I'm not sure…" Zach catches my attention as he passes something to Doug. "I'm still interested in going to the club, but not sure if I'm ready to give live performances."

"I think you'll like it… The club, I mean." Jane fidgets with her hands. "They'll be having the open house event soon and I already talked with Tara about sending you an invite."

"Is this the same event you're in charge of planning?"

"Yes, but I'm nervous." Her eyes waver, unable to hold eye contact.

"You have nothing to be nervous about." My gaze wanders over her, confused by her behavior. I've never seen her this anxious before.

"I think I'm being tested." Her nerves flash alive, cascading over her body. Energy radiates around her.

I hold her cheek, and her gaze eventually locks with mine. Her shoulders relax and I ask, "How so?"

"Tara wants to train someone to take over as the event coordinator. Rumor is… that someone will be me."

"Sweetie, that's awesome."

"It is, but I wouldn't be the lead photographer anymore. And I'm not sure I'm willing to give that up. I love what I do."

"Oh… I see." I place my hand on her arm and sweetly say, "But you know… You may not have to give it up, at least not completely. Tell her you don't want to give up being a photographer. That you want it to be a part of your new role. You may lose being the lead, but you could still do both."

"You think so?"

"It doesn't matter what I think. If you have the confidence to do it, you'll do it. Just remind her, and yourself, why she's choosing you in the first place. I'm sure she trusts your judgment and ability."

"Speaking of confidence." Her eyebrows wiggle. "If you like the video as much as we did, we can post it to the 'member's only' hub."

"The Rabbit Hole lives up to its name, huh?"

"You have no idea." Jane shines under the dancing lights. I listen to her enthusiasm as she tells me about the event she's planning. I smile. She genuinely enjoys her work.

CHAPTER 22

THE INVITATION

THE NOTECARD

WEDNESDAY, FEBRUARY 1ST

One year ago. I met two amazing men. To celebrate this anniversary, I have decided to grant a wish. Something you both have been asking for.

On Wednesday, February 8th, I will grant each of you the honor of having me all to yourself. I will be yours to take. Whenever and wherever you please. Do whatever it is you command of me. For one whole day. I will be at your beck and call. Eager to pamper and please you.

I only have two requests. I want everything you both plan to be a surprise. And obviously, I'll still be allowed to use our safe word.

With all my love,
Your Lady Lily

One year ago, I met two amazing men. To celebrate this anniversary, I have decided to grant a wish. Something you both have been asking for.

On Wednesday, February 8th, I will grant each of you the honor of having me all to yourself.

I will be yours to take. Whenever and wherever you please. Do whatever it is you command of me.

For one whole day, I will be at your beck and call, eager to pamper and please you.

I only have two requests. I want everything you both plan to be a surprise. And obviously, I'll still be allowed to use our safe word.

With all my Love,
Your Lady Lily

Chapter 23

No Touching

James

Wednesday, February 8ᵗʰ

Chocolate coats my throat as I finish my protein shake, stepping into the kitchen. Lily lies on the table and moans as Doug's fingers plunge into her. Her deep purple lace top hides under the matching garter belt, clipped onto sheer black thigh-high stockings.

Why did Doug have to put her into that outfit? He knows that I have a weak spot for it. I'm gonna have a hard time asking her to take it off later so she can dance for me.

Doug sets down his phone as I make my way to the table. "Morning."

"Morning." I stand behind Doug to get the best view of Lily as he takes a sip of his coffee. She leers at me and bites her lip to stifle a moan.

"I think she likes you shirtless. She's tightening up something fierce." Doug thrusts harder into her.

"JAMES." Lily arches her back and screams out.

"I take it you haven't had any luck?"

"No." Doug gently shakes his head. "She's still being stubborn."

"That's too bad. Will you be punishing her today, then?"

"Yep."

Lily whimpers at Doug's words. She looks forward to her punishments now. I smirk and step to Lily's side. So do I. My fingertips glide up her stomach and across her breast. I tease her nipple long enough to hear my favorite moan.

I bend close to Lily's lips as I say to Doug, "I'm gonna rinse off in the shower, so send her up when you're done." I kiss her cheek and leave.

...

The water beads slide down my chest, their heat soothing my muscles. The familiar creak of the bathroom door hits my ears. I gaze through the shower glass as Lily comes toward me. The lace contours her curves, and I can't pull my eyes away from her. She twists her braid into a bun.

Anticipation builds as I wait for her to strip. Blood rushes through my veins, filling me out. But the moment never comes.

She opens the shower door and steps inside fully clothed. The water splashes onto her lingerie and drips down her breasts. She caresses my chest, her eyes glued to my body.

"Did Doug tell you what I wanted you to do?"

Her hands slide down. "Yes."

"So, since you haven't gotten changed to dance for me, I'm assuming that he told you to come in here instead."

"Yes." Her voice drips with honey as she teases the length of me.

"And let me guess..." I lift her chin, craving the gaze of those glorious green eyes. "You can only do what he said, no matter what I say."

"Yes, Sir James." Lily turns and cuffs herself to the wall bar. She kneels on the bench and bends her ass out to me. Her arms stretch out above her, pressed against the wall.

The lace is soaking wet. Smooth and soft underneath my hands. I caress her hips as I ease into her. Her enchanting voice echoes beautifully as her tight pussy wraps around me. It's intoxicating. I take my time to savor every sensation, every part of her.

Sensually, I thrust inside of her. My hands glide over the lace. They can't get enough of her curves. I want to rip these clothes off. Have her skin on mine. She arches her ass as I massage her breasts. Her moaning is music to my ears.

My hands cup her breasts as the water beads on my back. The water is cool. Our passion burns. I pinch her stiff nipples and she screams out. Her walls tighten around me, magnifying the sensation.

"Fuck, Lily. You are so sexy."

"JAMES. HARDER."

I kiss her shoulder as I unhook her wrists and turn the water off. "I want to take you to bed." She whimpers as I pull out of her and step out of the shower. As I grab a towel, I motion for her to step toward me. "Come here. I want to take your clothes off."

Lily glows and steps under the heat lamp with me. I caress her flesh, adoring the sound of the wet fabric sliding and snapping as I carefully pull the lace off her. I pat her skin dry with the plush towel, kissing her body as I go. She purrs with pleasure and caresses my shoulders as I kneel in front of her.

My lips make their way to her breast and her hand tenses in anticipation. I tease her nipples. The heat between us grows, intensified by the heat above us.

She lifts her hands to her hair and pulls her bun apart. Her braid falls and I want her now. I lay back, taking her onto my lap as I go. My fingertips glide over her divine skin, listening to the pleasure my touch calls from her.

I rest my hand on her cheek and gently kiss her lips. "Lily," I stare into her emerald eyes. "I love you."

"I love you James."

Our kiss is electric and quakes through us. She rubs against my cock, and I groan as I shift underneath her. Lily wastes no time taking what she wants. Her tightness envelops my tip. I take in her beauty as she gently bounces till I fill her. She cries out. I moan.

I love watching her. The way her face reddens. The glow in her eyes. How her breasts move. The way she sings. She is captivating.

I grab her hips and hold her tight to me as I buck up into her. She lies on my chest and we passionately kiss as I take her. I glide my hands over her ass and grab her cheeks. I delve in deep and her scream cracks out. Her back arches, tempting her nipple to my lips so I can suckle it.

She takes control and grinds her hips into me. Her breathing changes and she's quiet for just a moment. This is the moment I devote my efforts to. The moment I have been waiting for. She closes her eyes, raptured by pure bliss. I love that look, knowing she is right there.

"James," she says, her honied tone asking for what I know she needs to hear.

"Come on, baby." I pinch her nipple. "Cum for us."

Lily's pure sound echoes through the room. I keep her going as she flexes around my staff, prolonging her orgasm.

She collapses on my chest, and I hold her tight to me as she collects herself.

She kisses me. "I came for you." She sits up and her eyes hold me captive. "Just for you."

"I said us, didn't I?" I caress her cheek. She smiles and nods. "I think it's a habit now."

Lily is bright, beaming. Her palms massage into my pecks as she bites her lip. "How may I please you, Sir James?"

"Um…" I glide my fingertips over her heated skin. "Can you still dance?"

"Yes!" Lily grips my ribs and stands, pulling me out of her. "I just need ten minutes to get ready."

...

The view outside the bedroom window is dreary and bright. I close the curtains and dim the lights. The soft velvet of the chair does nothing to soothe my nerves. I fidget with the edge of my briefs, waiting.

Images flood my memories, remembering last month's celebration. That one was to commemorate the day her bedroom was redone. A makeover that changed the room from being hers, to being ours.

Doug and I sat in these armless chairs while wearing the suits she requested. That was the first time she danced just for the two of us around a pole. I can still clearly picture her in the shiny black top with purple neon fishnets. Her smile as she teased us. A beautiful night sky framed our window, creating a dramatic backdrop for her show.

A familiar sound vibrates out of a speaker, and I sit up straight. That's my music. I wrote this soundtrack for our game. Her heels clack and it takes all the willpower I have to not turn.

Lily heads straight for the pole and circles it. Her clear heels lift into the air as she twirls. The simple black dress holds tight to her curves and shimmers in the light. Her high ponytail trails behind her.

I'm addicted to her. The way she dances. Those eyes when she teases me. I press my hands into the chair, forcing myself to stay put.

This surprise thrills me. The lengths she will go to please us are always surprising, inspiring. I press my lips together as her glorious hips distract me with their hypnotic sway. She did all this for me. I did not intend my song to be danced to, but here she is.

She makes her way to the floor as another song starts. Her legs dance in the air and she radiates with pure elation. Her hands caress her skin and I whimper. She pays me no heed, continuing her dance routine until, mercifully, the song slows. Her eyes turn on me; she crawls toward me.

Those eyes spell my demise. This little enchantress has me wrapped around her finger. Her hands brace themselves on my knees as she drags her breasts across my legs and up my chest. She licks her lips and I reach out to stroke her hip.

Her lips smolder as she slaps my hand away. "No touching."

I smile, more than eager to submit as she has her fun. Her breasts brush against my skin as she bends between my legs. Her hands press firmly into my thighs as she stands, dancing in front of me. Just out of my reach.

Another song begins, and she presses her back into the pole. "This one is my favorite."

"Really?"

"Yes." Her hands caress her legs, drawing my gaze. "Over the summer, when I heard it for the first time, a fantasy played out in my head."

"And what might this fantasy be?"

Lily saunters to me and turns around. Her hips gyrate as she sits on my lap. "A fantasy that won't be able to be satiated till summer." She moans as my hardness rubs her cheeks. "Every time this song plays, the vision gets steamier... I'm worried you won't be able to live up to it anymore."

"Then Doug and I will just have to try again, and again until we get it right." I push my hips up and she whimpers.

Her head snaps back at me. "No touching!"

"I was just adjusting. I swear."

She squints her eyes defiantly and fully sits on my lap. I groan, and her eyes light up. "You like this?" I nod as her ass pushes into me. She moans and I clench my fists. "I like it too."

"Tell me about your fantasy. What do Doug and I do to you?"

"It begins with me running through the field. A crescent moon hangs in the sky, and the breeze catches on my lace robe."

"That sounds beautiful."

"Shh..." Lily stops. "I won't continue if you won't let me finish."

"Oh, I'd never dream of it. I'll always let you finish Lady Lily."

"Good." She stands up and faces me. "Cuz I'm getting to my favorite part." I feign zipping my lips and her hands glide up my thighs. "As my heart races, I can hear them getting closer." Her fingers trail up my chest and stop to brace against my shoulders. "I stop running and look up at the moon."

Lily stares into my eyes. I lay my hands on her ass and she smirks, shaking her head. I frown and obey. "What happens to the beauty in the field?"

"Her Huntsman and Beast come for her, and they devour her. They take her till the sun comes up and make sure that she can't walk for a week."

"That sounds very tantalizing. Have you told Doug about this one?" I ask her. She shyly shakes her head. I grin. "You know I'm never going to see this boss monster the same way again."

"Nope." Her lips get close to mine. "You'll only ever see your succubus. The way her beautiful hair flows around her. The sheer white robe as it glitters in the moonlight. How she enthralls you as she dances in her grove of red lilies."

The music stops, and she stands in front of me. "If you could touch your succubus, what would you do to her?"

I stand up, getting as close as I can without touching her. "I'd worship her."

Her eyes gleam and she moans. "Please."

That word is all the permission I need. I pull her against me. Our lips meet and a jolt of electricity races between us. I bend my knees and she instinctively jumps into my arms. Her warmth presses against my stomach as I carry her to the wall.

I brace her against it, our passion intensifying. Her hands tighten around my shoulders as she stifles her moans against my lips. We briefly part, and I pull my cock out, lining it up against her opening. Holding her steady, I press forward.

Our passion intensifies. I can sense her desire. Know how she wants me to take her.

She can't relax. I'm not fully in. I stop thrusting and pinch her nipple, distracting her body. She cries out and tucks her head into my neck. Her warm breath pants out as I pull on it; just the way she needs. Her body surrenders to our lust.

She fully captures me deep inside. Her elation is muffled against my neck. She holds steady to me as I find my rhythm, pounding into her. Her sweet cries keep me going.

"JAMES."

Lily arches into me, and I take her breast into my mouth. I lose myself in her. Pressure builds inside of me; I burn in the wake of her heat.

"Please... James... Cum with me." Her moans pant out and she squeezes me.

My cock ravages her, wanting to give her what she needs. She sings to me, telling me she is right there. Her body tenses up. Her release is just out of reach. I let go of her nipple and adjust. Go where she needs me, how she needs it.

"Yes... Right there." She gasps at the sensation, still surprised every time we meet her unspoken wish.

My staff pumps into her, pulling her back to the edge. Her emerald eyes glow, and I ignore my burning calves to focus on her. Give her everything. Ecstasy rockets through us. Her breath catches, silencing her for just a moment.

I hold her gaze and lovingly demand. "Cum for me."

Lily melts into my arm as her body surrenders. Her bliss cries out. Her walls pulsate around me, begging me to join her. I joyously relent. Every grunt pumps my seed deep inside her, extending her orgasm. She hums her pleasure at being filled as I rock us against the wall, riding the last waves of our pleasure.

I hold her tight to me as we bathe in the aftermath of our bliss. I never want to let her go.

Chapter 24

You're Not a Coward

Doug

Wednesday, February 8th

Anxiety consumes me. My heart races and I can't concentrate on play-testing our game. I glance over at Lily once again, curled up on the couch. A book in hand, wrapped in a blanket. She has stolen my concentration so many times this last year. Those eyes, that hair, her hips... she drives me wild.

James elbows me, pulling me back to the game. I am surrounded by enemies and my character is swiftly dying. The animation plays out and I wait for the death screen. The controller stops vibrating, ending the scene. James smirks as I hand him the controller.

I can't keep her waiting any longer.

"Lily."

She doesn't move. Her eyes race along the page and I hesitate, not wanting to bother her as she enjoys her book. James elbows me again, his eyes stern. Ok, I get it.

"Lily..." I stand up and walk to her. Her eyes never falter, she is too engrossed to hear me. I lean over her and run my hand up her thigh. She finally notices my presence.

"Hi, sweetie."

"Are you ready for more?"

"Yes." Lily's eyes flash to the page, giving away her lie.

My lips flex knowingly. "How many pages?"

She turns the page. "One and a half."

"Ok, I'm gonna find you something to wear and leave it on your vanity chair. When you're done getting dressed, I'd like you to wait for me there." I kiss her on the forehead as she smiles.

I walk around the couch and nod to James as I make my way out of the room.

...

Standing in front of the bedroom door, I adjust my shirt once more and walk in. Lily sits at her vanity as she finishes braiding her hair. Her features shine back at me in the mirror as she wears the same dress from Christmas Eve.

"How do I look?" Her smile is captivating, and her body is enchanting.

I kiss her on the cheek. "You're stunning."

"Are you sure it's not too much?"

I chuckle at her roleplay, asking the same question she did that day. I gently shake my head. "Not at all." I offer her my hand and she stands. I pull her close to me and wrap my arm around her back.

"Did I tell you how much I like this color on you?" Lily's words pull me back to reality as her hands caress my chest.

"No, I don't believe you did. What else do you like?"

Lily bites her lips as she slides her hands behind me. "I love the way your ass looks in these pants."

"Oh, yeah?" I faintly touch her arm with my fingertips.

She nods and tilts her head to the side, humming sweetly.

"Turn around and face the mirror." I instruct her, trying to maintain focus. She slowly turns, dragging her body across mine as she does. Her head presses into my chest. I keep my attention fixated on her reflection. "Do you know what charmed me first about you?"

She lights up and rubs her hand over her braid. "My hair. You touch it every chance you get."

"Oh, your hair…" I gently wrap my hand around her braid and lift it off her breast. "It's the most infuriatingly sexiest thing about you."

Lily's brow furrows. "Was that supposed to be a compliment?"

"Yes, it's a compliment."

"Well, it was horrible. Try again."

I chuckle at the adorable sternness plastered on her face and lay her hair down, draping it over her breast. My fingertips graze her arm as they make their way up her neck to her cheek.

"Your laughter was the first thing to charm me." I stare at her body in the mirror as my fingertips caress her skin. "Your smile. Those eyes. You are enchanting Lily."

I glide my fingers down her body. "The way your body moves to hypnotize us. Your curiosity and optimism unlocked parts of me I didn't know I had. I have never felt the need to be so protective of anyone. But it is also vexing because you don't need protection."

I gaze into her emerald eyes. "You are the most alluring, fiery woman I have ever met." I grab her hips. "You used to come home cussing up a storm after dealing with idiots. It really got me going. Your ferocity, that temper, it made me want to take you right there."

My hand intertwines with hers, and I walk her to the lounge chair. "You are amazing... Accepting... Funny... Caring..." I touch her cheek as I kneel in front of her. "And so brilliantly incandescent."

Lily's smile is pure, and her eyes glisten in the room's glow. Pushing her skirt up slightly, I nestle my head between her thighs. The smell of peaches surrounds me so sweetly. Lily brushes my hair as I rub the side of her legs. My mind quiets as we sit in silence. Her skin is smooth under my touch and calming to my nerves.

I turn my head and rest my cheek on her thigh. "I've been wanting to do this again since Christmas."

"Do you like this?" Lily glides the back of her fingernails along my neck.

"Surprisingly, yes."

"Then why haven't you done it again?"

"Because I don't deserve this."

Her nails falter mid stroke. My heart races and my nerves flare. I squeeze her legs, holding myself still.

She's probably confused because I can never quite say what I mean.

I inhale deeply and take in her scent to calm me. "I'm a coward."

"You're not a coward."

I sit up and caress her cheek. "Not anymore." My finger brushes over her bottom lip as I gaze into her beautiful gem eyes. "I'm going to do things to you that will make your heart race." I lean in close to her lips. "Things I have never done with another before."

"I find that hard to believe."

I cup my hand around her cheek and rub my thumb over her lip. She closes her eyes and leans into my touch. No, I need to see those eyes. "Lily." She opens her eyes and beams at me as I say, "I love you."

Her eyes instantly gloss over. She gently wraps her arms around my neck. "I love you."

Emotions race through me as our lips meet. I've never felt so out of control. My need for her consumes me. I wrap my arm around her and we stand. Instinct takes over as I hungrily unzip her dress. Her moan matches my desire. She undoes my pants. Our lips part and the fire in my veins cools slightly.

Slow... You're supposed to be going slow.

Show her you love her.

As I seize control of my impulses, I bend down and kiss her neck. I pull at the hem of her dress and shimmy it off her body. Her curves tantalize me.

"Have I told you how much these hips have driven me crazy this last year?"

"No, never." She smirks as I grab them. I pull her close to me, kissing her stomach. She purrs for me. "I love it when you do this."

"I love doing it." I kiss her scar. "The way you moan." I kiss her lower and pull her in. "The way your body arches into me." She whimpers and I melt.

"Doug." She moans and I stand up. Her hands trail down my chest, unbuttoning my shirt, just like she did that Christmas night. She kisses my chest as she pushes my shirt off my shoulders. Lily gazes up at me with lust in her eyes.

"Turn around."

She bends in front of me, already knowing what I want. I follow the line of her thong to where it disappears between her cheeks. I glide my hands over the material and pull the small bit of fabric over her hips. Caressing her legs on the way down. She lifts her feet and I toss it to the side as she peers over her shoulder at me.

That seductive smile pushes me to my limits. I press my hips into hers as I curve over her. I slide my arm between her breasts and brace my hand under her neck.

"Do you remember what I said I was going to do to you?"

"Yes."

I tease my fingers over her hip. "Tell me."

"You said you were going to do things to me you've never done before."

"I'm going to give you everything you deserve." I straighten my back, pulling her with me. She moans as I caress her with my fingertips. I step back and twirl her to face me. Our kiss is gentle and sweet as I intertwine my hand in hers. I walk backward, taking us to the mattress. "Get in bed."

She crawls to the middle, getting comfortable as I undress. She loves watching me. I caress her legs as I move over her. My cock presses against her pelvis as I glide my hands over her breasts. She arches her back and moans that pure sweet sound.

I tease my tip between her folds, just the way she likes. She presses her lips together and whimpers. I kiss her neck and listen to her pleasure. As I get ready to enter her, I hold her glowing eyes captive.

"I'm going to make love to you."

Lily's eyes glisten as I slowly press into her. She cups her hand around my head. We rock together until she fully sheaths me. I groan as she arches her back and purrs. Her lips meet mine, and she gingerly kisses me. Our tongues softly caress as we enjoy the simple pleasure of our passion.

I buck into her and her moan vibrates against my lips. Her hands caress my back as I find my rhythm. Our lips part as she presses her hand into my back. Her moans are hypnotic as we enjoy the slow, deep strokes.

Her soft hands glide smoothly across my skin and fill me with pleasure I have never felt before. Tame pleasure. Her sensual purrs. Having her body pressed into me so soft and sweet, it's spellbinding.

I never want to let her go. I will never let her go. Whatever she asks of me, I will do. James and I will show her the world. Give her pleasures she has only dreamed about. More than just this. Everything.

Lily wraps a leg across my back and tucks the other around my thigh. "Doug." She gives me that look again. I melt. She is going to make me cum. "Right there... please... don't stop."

Lily closes her eyes as her moans escalate. She fights the urge to go faster, and I hold her tight. We passionately kiss as I push harder into each slow stroke. I can feel every rib of her wall as I soak in the bliss that she gives me.

Her wall clenches around me and she pushes up into each thrust, matching my slow force. I can't last for her any longer. Our lips part as her head arches back.

"Tell me."

"Lily... I love you."

She huffs out a scream as she orgasms, and it sends me over the edge. I cum with her.

CHAPTER 25

HEATHER'S WEDDING

LILY

SATURDAY, MARCH 4TH

A delicious spread of horderves and drinks greets us when we arrive in the wedding hall. Layla, Alex, and I make our way through the other guests to join Doug's family at a standing bar table. We eat and laugh, sharing in the collective merriment.

Paul and his boyfriend Dusty gush over the girls. Spilling lavish compliments over how beautiful they were standing at the altar. I smile, offer my agreement, and try not to roll my eyes at their boasting.

They both did a good job, of course, but do they have to go on and on about it?

You should be grateful. At least you got out of enduring a makeover yourself.

True.

Pauline's angelic voice raises from Paul. "Now the boys looked fabulous. Heather really knows how to pull colors together." She goes on with the others, gleaming and joking about how James and Doug made the cutest couple walking up the aisle.

The topics ebb and change course, flowing into those inevitable discussions that I try to avoid. As with all weddings, there is talk about babies and 'who's next'. Teasing, guessing, planning out the other couples' weddings.

When will Heather have a baby?

If Jane and Zach have been together the longest, why haven't they gotten married?

What about Matt? Is he still begging Susan for a kid?

I do my best to zone out.

They ramble on as I admire the décor. It sparks my inner designer to be in such a glamourous space. I recognize the clever repurposing. Many of the accents are decorations from the bridal shower, used in new ways. The floral arrangements are too flashy for my taste, but the color choices are spectacular.

Eucalyptus green, mauve, and lavender blend with a shimmer of white that dusts over the room. It is captivating.

"I wish I could become a grandmother," Denise says, drawing me back in from my distractions.

And here it is. The dreaded question.

"When are you going to give me grandbabies?" She asks.

I sigh and turn to Denise. But to my surprise, she isn't talking to me. I follow her gaze to a flustered Paul and Dusty.

I missed something, didn't I?

"Mom, I told you," Paul's shy tone tries to find a sternness he isn't quite capable of. "Not till after I get married. Then we'll need a surrogate mother."

"I'll do it!" Layla raises her hand enthusiastically. Alex and I glance at each other and roll our eyes.

"Want another one already, sis?" I taunt.

"Yes, I loved being pregnant." She beams.

"No. You loved the attention," Alex says under her breath.

"What was that, dear?"

"Nothing sweetie." Alex takes a sip of her drink to hide her cheeky smirk.

"Lily?" Dusty asks. "When are you having kids?"

I sigh and stare at the floor. This is the part I hate.

"Lily can't have kids," Denise says. My eyelashes flutter, shocked by the blunt statement. I'm silent, a bit in awe at the casualty of her tone. I didn't realize that she had come to terms with it. "She doesn't have any eggs."

"Yeah," Layla says. "She lost her eggs saving the life of a dying fairy. It's an epic tale of betrayal, curses, and even true love's kiss."

Dusty blinks rapidly. "Are you serious? I can't tell if you're being serious."

Layla and Paul snicker in amusement.

"It makes for a great fairy tale, doesn't it?" I say, easing the tension. Dusty relaxes. "The Tragic and Heroic Tale of Lily Callahan. It will make a great bedtime story for the kids one day."

"Yes, quite the bedtime story." Dusty takes a sip of his drink.

"Maybe Paul can read it to you one night." Layla teases.

"If he is a good boy, I might," Paul says, his eyes twinkle. Dusty's cheeks light up pink.

"So anyway, Dusty..." Alex says. I temper myself; I know that look. "When do you want to knock up my wife?"

Fred spits out his drink as Denise, Layla, and I choke on our delight.

"Yeah, sweetie..." Paul turns to Dusty and his bulging eyes. "When do you want to have a baby? Does this mean you're finally going to propose?"

"I guess I have to, now. We found us a baby momma." Dusty leans into Paul, kissing his forehead.

"Yeah!" Layla's enthusiasm spurs another round of laughter.

"You didn't answer her question, Dusty?" Denise taps her foot. The sound of her heel cracks against the stone floor. "Because I'd like to be a grandma, today you know."

I elbow Layla to get her attention. "Now's the time," I whisper, for her ears only. "Ask her."

"I could make that happen," Layla says as she and Alex step in front of Denise and Fred. "Mr. and Mrs. Beaufort, how would you like to become Eric's grandparents?"

Silence surrounds us as we wait for the reply.

Denise takes Layla's hand. "We would love to."

Layla hugs Denise as she tears up. Fred wraps an arm around his wife and grabs Alex to pull her into the circle.

Denise turns to me as they pull apart. "I'm grateful that you've come into our lives." She hugs me, and I'm surrounded by her sweet scent. "I know this is selfish of me, but I wish one day I could see you dressed in white too. Standing at an altar."

Fred hands Denise his handkerchief, and she dabs her eyes. My mouth lifts into the side of my cheek, giving her a moment to collect herself. "I want to get married, but I can't have this kind of wedding. I cannot marry in the eyes of your church."

"I'm sorry, that was cruel of me."

I tilt my head to the side curiously. "No, I think you misunderstand." All eyes are on me now as I explain. "I can get married. But only in the eyes of my religion. My handfasting ceremony will be small and surrounded by nature. You and Layla will help me pick out a dress."

Paul clears his throat loudly, and I smile at him. "And Pauline too." I point at him defiantly. "But I make no promises to makeovers or those over-the-top accessories."

"Oh, you'll change your mind when I turn you into the princess you are meant to be."

"I'll take that bet," Alex says, and we all laugh.

The cocktail hour is almost over. We continue talking, drinking, and polishing off the horderves as we wait for Mr. and Mrs. Elson to make their grand entrance.

...

James and Doug join us at the dinner table as the happy couple greets their guests.

"What did we miss?" Doug asks.

"Oh, not much..." Paul points to me. "Mom found out she's a grandma."

They turn to me, and I try not to giggle. James smirks and gazes at Paul and his boyfriend. "So, when are you guys expecting?"

The table breaks out into joyful giddiness.

Paul chokes out the words. "I don't know... Layla, when are you coming over?"

"You free next weekend?"

"Yes!" Denise bursts with excitement.

Paul curtly nods. "We are expecting nine months from next weekend."

"Oh, that's wonderful. Should we make something for the happy couple?" Doug offers, applying an adorable sarcastic grin.

"You won't have the time," Fred says. "You have to go ring shopping."

Doug and James' eyes widen, and their backs stiffen.

"No, they don't," I say.

"Yes, you must go this weekend," Denise says, ignoring me. "The wedding is practically planned, so you better hurry."

"It's ok, I don't like to wear jewelry."

"Paul," Fred says. "You better go with them. Since I'll be taking Dusty out, we need someone sensible to supervise. We don't need them to bring shame down upon our family name."

I lean toward Layla. "I'm being ignored, aren't I?"

"Shh..." Alex puts her finger to her mouth. "I'm enjoying the show."

"Speaking of names," Layla turns to me. "Which one would you put first?"

Everyone is silent, and I squint my eyes at her. "Oh, am I allowed to talk now?"

Layla brushes me off. "We heard you before. We just didn't care."

"I noticed."

"We heard you." Doug gestures between James and himself.

"If we want to buy you a ring, we will," James says.

"But I don't need one."

"Of course, you don't. That's the point." James says, and I raise my eyebrow.

"If we bought you a ring, are you telling us you wouldn't wear it?" Doug's eyes will me to defy him.

"I... um..." I pick up my drink and take a sip. Defeated by them, I turn to Denise. "What time are we coming over?"

I ignore the giggles and smug looks on James' and Doug's faces as more plans are made. This time, I'm actually happy with the direction this topic took us. For once, I am excited to join in.

Chapter 26

Here We Go Again

Doug

Thursday, May 4th

I follow the GPS instructions as we make our way through a maze of industrial buildings. I glance in the rearview mirror, taking in Lily's beauty.

James turns to her. "So exactly what is this surprise?"

"You'll see when we get there." Her defiant eyes glare at James.

"You do remember that it's your birthday and you're the one that is supposed to get the surprise, right?" I tease.

Her smile changes, and I am struck by how unique her expressions are. This one is unlike any other. It's hauntingly beautiful and devious. Her eerie silence raises goosebumps along my arm.

"Sir James," I say in my knightly accent. "Prepare yourself. I believe this is the part of the story where we are taken to the middle of nowhere, never to be heard from again."

"Yes, Sir Douglas. I have the same feeling I had when we first meet Lady Lily."

"Did you seriously think you were going to die when you met me?"

"No..." James lowers his voice. "Just on the way up to the castle, as we drove through an ice forest with gorgeous white beasts prowling the night."

She giggles and shakes her head. "If memory serves. You came with nothing but a spatula and dustmop."

James scoffs. "How dare ye! It is the Spatula of Smiting."

"And Dustmop of Doom, thank you very much."

"Don't you mean dooooom?" She mocks.

We chuckle as the GPS tells me to make another turn before announcing that we have arrived at our destination. The industrial buildings have suddenly come to an end. We make our way into a cottage-style townhome-business center.

"Follow this road around." Lily's hand pokes out between the seats, pointing to the unmarked path ahead. "It's the haunted abandoned building in the back, where no one will hear you scream."

"Oh," I say. "Thank you for being considerate. I don't want anyone to know I scream like an anime schoolgirl."

Her laughter rings out through the car. She grabs her ribs as she snorts. James and I fist bump.

"Still down eight, but you're finally catching up," James says, and Lily covers her face to tame her painfully joyous outburst.

I park in front of the last building at the end of the center, and the light in her eyes instantly peaks with excitement.

She is the first to leave the car and doesn't wait for us to follow her. James and I glance at each other.

Here we go again.

The walk to the front door is brief, giving me no time to admire the building. It appears to be nothing special. The landscaping is not up to Lily's standards. Though, knowing her, that won't take long to change.

Lily opens the door and steps to the wall. "You guys ready to start another adventure?"

"Yes!" James says, bouncing with eagerness.

"Nope." My voice overlaps James' as I shake my head.

The lights turn on and my eyes take a moment to adjust. A lobby stands before us, decked out in gray, black, and bronze décor. Two armored knight statutes flank the front desk. I am stunned. The lobby wall reads 'Shadow Knights Studio.'

James steps toward the statues. "You did this for us?"

"Yep." Lily's body shakes with excitement.

I set my eyes on her. "You bought us an office building?"

"No, don't be silly." Lily waves her wrist. "I bought the whole plaza."

"Oh, yes, of course," James says.

"How silly of us." I shake my head, more in awe than in jest.

Her head curtly nods. "Indeed."

Lily motions for us to look around. My eyes roam, taking in the details of the room. A shimmer of light hits the black and I inspect it. My mistake- it's not black after all. This is oil-rubbed bronze. Of course, she remembered my favorite metal effect. My joy lights up my face and courses through me.

James marvels over the stone statues, and I make my way to the wall. The logo has a matte finish and I run my hand over it. It's seamlessly flush with the wall.

"I can't wait to shove this in dad's face," I say, and Lily chuckles.

"Yes, well, take it easy on him. I wouldn't have been able to buy this place if it wasn't for him."

"Wait..." I turn to her as my shoulders tighten. "Are you saying my dad was involved in this?"

"Yes. A couple of days after Christmas, Fred met up with Mr. Dillon on the green. They got to talking and one thing led to another. They reached out, and Bam! I landed the deal of a lifetime." Lily gets antsy and motions behind us. "But enough about all the boring stuff. I want to show you around."

"Well, lead the way." James motions with his hands toward a set of doors behind the lobby desk.

My mind races as she leads us on a tour of the three-story building. I admire her passion, listening to her go on. She talks about pieces she is still waiting on, tells us about little details she wants to add, everything she wants to do to finish the place.

"We have a good start here..." Her voice floats away as she walks, finding her groove and gaining confidence in her professional business-talk tone. It draws me in, it's extremely attractive. I love watching her get lost in her work. "I'm confident that we can get you everything you need to have a proper studio."

She folds her hands proudly in front of her, satisfied. "The first floor will be the playroom and break area. I was thinking about a pool table. But realized then you'd never have a reason to come home."

"I doubt that very much," James says.

"I can think of a few reasons to come home." My voice deepens seductively for her, giving her the gaze that turns her to putty in my hands.

She blushes and quickly turns toward the stairs. Her hips sway defiantly as we make our way up. "The second floor will be the game design studio offices. The other designers will work on this floor once you are ready to expand."

And finally, the third floor.

"These two rooms will be your offices," she says as I turn to face them. "Layla is designing these rooms personally. So sorry in advance."

"When should we be expecting the bombardment of calls?" James asks.

"As soon as I tell her you've been here."

"How long has she been nagging you to show us the place?" I ask.

"Not long. Just two weeks." She looks at me. "Give or take a month."

I smile at her cheeky remark as James says, "I'm surprised she kept it a secret for that long."

"Me too!" She agrees.

"What's this door to?" I point to the door opposite our offices.

"That is the place where I will make you scream." She pretends to be menacing, but all I see is my sexy, cute little minx. James and I feign our fear, joining in the fun. "James, would you do the honors and open the door?"

James nods and holds the door open as we enter. Lily turns the lights on. I fall silent, and James freaks out.

"No, way! A sound studio! Are you shittin' me?" James gushes, running his eyes and hands over the equipment.

Lily's sweet features soak up every emotion James expresses. He drones on about the gear, the quality, and the specs. But I'm not listening. I can't take my eyes off the beauty before me. This is what she lives for. It doesn't matter to her that we could never come close to offering her such a grand and lavish gift.

I brush her hair behind her ear softly, her brilliant emerald eyes beam up at me. "How were you able to get a recording studio in here?"

"You can thank Layla for that. I told her it was a dream of yours and she worked her magic."

Lily gestures for me to join in the fun, and I join James in exploring. Our excitement is boundless.

The sound of glass being tapped on rings out, getting our attention. Lily now stands on the other side of the glass. She steps back, gliding to the middle of the room.

She bewitches us, unzipping her dress. It falls to the floor and reveals her naked body to us. I bite my lip. Loving that she wasn't wearing anything under it. She's becoming bolder.

"So..." Lily brushes her hair behind her, giving us the view we crave. "Do you guys want to test out the acoustics with me?"

Are You Ready to Visit
'The Rabbit Hole?'

Most valued reader, this club is for you.
I invite you to step into this place of wonder and desire,
to explore all of the pleasures it has to offer.

Exclusive interviews, insights,
and new connections with all of the characters you love.

Best of all... MORE BOOKS!

Starting with that exclusive chapter I promised.
Lily, James, & Doug's first visit to the den of sin.
Follow them (and their surprise guests)
along into a new adventure of passion and lust.
A night you'll never forget.

https://www.brittanycullen.com/herolily

What are you waiting for?
Let's go to 'The Rabbit Hole' together!